V

FOR VICTORY

Also by Lissa Evans

NOVELS

Spencer's List

Odd One Out

Their Finest Hour and a Half
(motion picture released as *Their Finest*)

Crooked Heart

Old Baggage

NOVELS FOR CHILDREN

Small Change for Stuart

Big Change for Stuart

Wed Wabbit

FOR VICTORY

A NOVEL

LISSA EVANS

HARPER
An Imprint of HarperCollins*Publishers*

This is a work of fiction. Names, characters, places, and incidents are products of the author's imagination or are used fictitiously and are not to be construed as real. Any resemblance to actual events, locales, organizations, or persons, living or dead, is entirely coincidental.

HarperCollins books may be purchased for educational, business, or sales promotional use. For information, please email the Special Markets Department at SPsales@harpercollins.com.

Originally published in Great Britain in 2020 by Doubleday, an imprint of Transworld Publishers.

FIRST U.S. EDITION

Extracts: p. 22, "The Fog" by William Henry Davies; p. 25, "Appeal" by Anne Brontë; p. 108, "The Song of Hiawatha" by Henry Wadsworth Longfellow; p. 275, "The Arrow and the Song" by Henry Wadsworth Longfellow.

Library of Congress Cataloging-in-Publication Data has been applied for.

ISBN 978-0-06-305983-2

21 22 23 24 25 LSC 10 9 8 7 6 5 4 3 2 1

For my friends Georgia Garrett and Bill Scott-Kerr

AUTUMN

1944

Where *T. Allerdyce, Textbooks & Stationery* should have been, there was nothing but a flight of stairs, silhouetted against a white sky. The air was full of grit, the rubble seeded with ruined books, their pages snapping back and forth in the cold wind. Noel flipped open a cover with his foot, and saw an illustration of the human digestive system, its cross-sectioned owner breezily eating an apple, apparently unconcerned that his innards were exposed to the world.

The whole street had gone, a roped-off crater showing where the V-2 had actually landed, the shops and houses marked only by the odd truncated wall or empty door frame. The staircases alone had survived, some still with remnants of carpet, some spoked with broken bannisters. Noel was tempted to climb the nearest, and see the destruction from a height, but half the treads were missing.

The V-2 rockets had been dropping out of the sky for a couple of months now, though 'dropping' implied that you could see them descend, whereas they fell at such speed that no warnings were possible; a crack and a boom, and then death. 'Like God clapping his hands,' Vee had suggested, fancifully. Each one knocked the roofs off a quarter of a square mile of houses, and flattened those at the centre; 'more like God stamping his foot,' Noel had said.

They'd been lucky so far this year, at home in Hampstead; nothing but the occasional Heinkel unloading H.E.s, and a single doodlebug which had landed in a pond on the Heath and hurled a flood of green water over the bank and down the road, marbling the tarmac with waterweed and sending a dead duck surfing through the chemist's door.

Noel let the book-cover fall. Last time he'd visited the shop, Mr Allerdyce had given him a cup of tea, and talked eloquently about his years as a teacher in Tonga. 'The young ladies there – how can I describe them? They have flesh as firm as a Michelangelo marble, but when they dance, every part of them vibrates . . .' Noel had thought about this image quite a few times over the succeeding months and had rather been looking forward to continuing the conversation.

There was a sudden movement in the rubble, and a rat emerged from behind an angled pipe, a packet of semolina in its teeth. It caught sight of Noel, and froze, and he hopped off the mound of bricks (best not to think of its grave-like contour) and walked away. Perhaps, he thought, Mr Allerdyce had been asleep when the bomb fell; asleep and dreaming of Tonga.

At the end of the road, a church had escaped the worst of the blast, though half the roof had fallen in, and the windows were empty. In the road beside it, glass crunched underfoot, a million splinters of indeterminate colour and occasional larger pieces, red and blue, a glimpse of a gesturing arm, a broken halo – and there, upright in the gutter, an unbroken rectangle of amber glass the size of Noel's palm, still edged with lead. He held it up to one eye and looked along the road, and the V-2 devastation was transformed into something much older, a sepia photograph from one of Mattie's books, Pompeii emerging from the ash. And between the excavated walls, a short, rounded figure, purposefully approaching. Noel slipped the glass into his pocket.

It was a lady ARP warden, two white stripes on the sleeve of her tunic, her boots filthy with beige dust, the legs of her slacks rolled several times above the ankle.

'Were you looking for something?' she asked, her tone brisk.

'I *was*,' said Noel. 'I had a list of books to buy at Mr Allerdyce's shop. Geography and History, mainly.'

'Oh dear. Well, you're out of luck, I'm afraid. You'd better cut along – half these walls are unsafe.'

'What happened to Mr Allerdyce? Is he still alive?'

'Yes,' she said, unexpectedly. 'He was in his basement, reading a book.'

'Which book?'

Her official expression eased and she almost smiled. 'I can't tell you, but it had a red cover – he was still clutching it when we got him out.' She looked back at the empty street, as if still unable to believe that anyone had survived. 'So where are you at school?'

'I'm not. I have tutors.'

'What – tutors in the plural?' She looked sceptical.

'Yes, actually.' There was a pause. 'It's not as grand as it sounds, they're just our lodgers. They teach me according to the areas of their expertise.'

'How old are you?'

'Fourteen. Nearly fifteen.'

'You look younger, but you sound older. So go on—' She glanced at her watch and then folded her arms, and shifted her weight more comfortably. She was quite young herself, with a pleasant, round face, and a frizz of brown hair beneath her beret. 'What subjects are you studying?'

'Well, Geography and History, obviously, though I'm tutoring myself in those at the moment, hence the text-books. English and Latin from Mr Jepson, who's a journalist. Mathematics and book-keeping from Mr Reddish – he's a cashier – sciences from Dr Parry-Jones, French from Miss Appleby – though, to be honest, I don't think she knows very much, only a few phrases like 'your eyes are very lovely' and 'how much is the lipstick?' – and cookery from Miss Zawadska, who's a canteen supervisor. She's also teaching me Polish.'

'You're pulling my leg.'

'*Dzien dobry. Mam na imię* Noel Bostock.'

She actually laughed this time. 'You're a tonic,' she said. She checked her watch again. 'Come and see something. It's quite educational.'

There was a cardboard sign reading 'DO NOT ENTER – DANGER!' strung across the door of the church, but she opened it anyway. Light spilled into a broad porch; there were hymn-books stacked on a bench and a print of a girlish-looking St Francis feeding doves. 'I think this part's Victorian,' said the warden, 'but the vicar says the main structure's far older. This was in the ceiling wreckage.' She pulled away a fold of canvas from something lying on the floor. 'It's called a roof boss,' she said. 'We think it's not seen daylight for centuries.' Noel crouched down. A wooden face the size of his own looked back at him, green vines pouring out of each side of the open mouth and encircling the head. He leaned back so that his shadow no longer fell across the carving, and the colours leaped out: the eyes pure white, a blue dot at the centre of each, the flared nostrils lined with red. It was as brilliant as if the brush had just been laid down – brighter, *newer*, than anything he'd seen for years, in this tired city where everything looked in need of a scrub or a lick of paint, or a wrecking-ball.

'What's going to happen to it?'

'Someone's coming from the University to take a look,' said the warden. 'There might be more in the rubble, the vicar thinks.'

'Will it go to a museum?'

'I suppose it might.'

'Which one? The V&A? I go there quite often.'

'Tell you what,' said the warden, taking a small notebook and a stub of pencil from her pocket and handing it to Noel, 'scribble your name and address down here and I'll drop you a card if I find out. Whatever happens, I hope they take it soon or it'll end up getting swiped – people will loot anything, you'd be amazed.' She pulled the canvas back across and Noel furtively patted his pocket to make sure he still had the glass.

Outside, the sky had darkened.

'Oh,' said Noel, tilting his head.

'What's the matter?' The warden turned from the door, and then heard it herself.

'Doodlebug.'

The faint clatter, like a stick dragged along an iron fence, was coming from the south-east.

'I thought we'd finished with those buggers,' she said. 'Pardon my Polish. Come along – there's a shelter on Cheshunt Road.'

Noel followed her, craning upwards as he walked. The ugly rattle grew louder and the V-1 came into view, far overhead, its silhouette as prosaic as a piece of drainpipe.

'It's going over,' said the warden, slowing her steps. 'Heading towards Finchley, I'd say, or Hampstead.'

A cold hand seemed to grip the back of Noel's neck. 'Hampstead's where I live.'

She gave him a quick, appraising glance. 'It'll probably go even further,' she said. 'It might end up missing London altogether.'

'All the same, I'd better get back to my aunt. Goodbye, and thank you for showing me the roof boss.' The last words were over his shoulder; he was already heading for the Tube, half running, a thread of panic reeling him in. Was Vee at home this afternoon? No, he remembered, she was at her Thursday knitting circle – in which case, was she anywhere near an adequate shelter? He could hear the V-1 grinding into the distance, the engine still running – a deadly clockwork toy, wound up fifty miles away and chugging to a random end somewhere in the suburbs.

And as he jogged past the rubble dunes, the same old

vision came sliding into his head, the final image of a recurring dream from which he regularly woke with a gasp: of himself sitting up in bed and looking out through a missing wall at a dawn sky, and realizing that the house had been bisected and that he was alone, poised on the edge of a vast, sandy crater.

'Hoi!'

He turned and saw the warden waving the notebook in which he'd written his address. She shouted something else – 'No', or 'I know!' – and beckoned, but he shook his head and hurried onwards.

'Biscuit, Mrs Overs?'

Vee peered into the tin and selected the last remaining custard cream. It disintegrated almost as soon as her teeth touched it, filling her mouth with crumbs and snowing a fine dust on to the half-knitted sock in her lap. She swallowed with difficulty, and washed the sludge down with tea.

'I've heard that Peek Freans have changed their recipes,' said Mrs Lunn, gingerly taking a digestive, 'they've reduced the amount of shortening. They can't get the lard any more.'

Mrs Claxton nodded. 'I've heard that they're using chicken fat instead of lard. How are your chickens, Mrs Overs?'

'Doing quite nicely, thank you,' said Vee. 'I'm thinking of getting another White Leghorn.'

'Laying regularly, are they?'

'Most of them, yes.'

'Of course, if they don't lay, then they're just an expense, aren't they? I expect you have to decide whether to hold on to those that don't lay.'

'That's right.'

'Or whether they'd be better off in the oven.'

Mrs Claxton waited for a moment, her bright little gaze poking Vee all over like a skewer. Vee smiled blandly. There were indeed two chickens over which the axe was currently hovering, but neither of them was going to end up on Mrs Claxton's table. One was earmarked for the elderly gas engineer on Frogmore Lane who nursed Vee's bathroom geyser from crisis to crisis, like a family doctor with a consumptive heiress, and the other for Noel's birthday. He liked a bit of roast chicken, though he'd mentioned he'd found a recipe for a wild-garlic-and-celery stuffing in the newspaper and she was going to have to put her foot down about that; she had the lodgers to consider. The card that she kept permanently in the newsagent's window mentioned 'good, plain cooking', as well as 'comfortable, spacious accommodation', and she didn't want someone leaving because Green Shutters smelled like a French back-alley. She'd already lost Mr Purbisson in the last month, though admittedly that was because of the V-2s rather than the food – he'd gone back to his sister in Gloucester, his nerves in shreds, which meant that Noel was now short of a Geography teacher, and the next time she interviewed a lodger she'd have to find out not only if they could meet the rent, but how much they knew about alluvial plains. Or perhaps she could persuade Mr Jepson to extend his range of subjects in return for a reduction in his bill. 'Or you could just go to a school,' she'd suggested to Noel, trying to make it sound light-hearted yet plausible, and he'd said, 'I'd rather clean Hitler's WC,' and had carried on making the sausage-meat fricassee that he always cooked on Thursdays. He'd followed it up with a steamed blackberry pudding that Miss Zawadska had announced was 'professional qvality', and Noel had flushed very slightly, which was the equivalent of an ordinary fourteen-year-old running round in circles punching the air.

'I saw your nephew up on the Heath yesterday,' said Mrs Lunn, who in between running the Methodist Soldiers' Comforts Knitting Circle and bringing up two daughters the size of carthorses had apparently learned to read minds. 'He was sitting on a bench with a book next to a young girl with plaits, and she was reading as well. From a different book,' she added, quickly, as if to absolve the scene of any indelicacy.

'She's the grand-daughter of one of my neighbours,' said Vee. 'Major Lumb.'

'Ooh, *Major*,' said Mrs Arnold, who liked a title.

'She goes to a boarding school, but they're on half-term and her parents are in Malta. Her father's an admiral.'

'Ooh, *Admiral*.'

Vee picked up her half-completed sock again, and the other women followed her lead, Mrs Lunn working at twice the speed of the rest, her face placid, her fingers a blur, as if there was an 'on' switch just below her elbows. Vee herself was an indifferent knitter, unable to maintain the correct tension, so that her balaclavas had necks as wide as the head, and face-holes that encircled the features like a snare; she couldn't imagine her efforts shortening the war by more than a second or two, and it certainly wasn't the quality of the conversation that brought her to the circle (Mrs Rice was already resuming her account of her daughter's wedding, an event that had taken place *eight years ago*). No, what kept her coming – and at least she was honest enough to admit it to herself – was the slight deference that she received from its members. In her role as Margery Overs, living in a very large house on the Heath, with distinguished neighbours, a lodger who worked at the BBC, and room for twelve chickens, she was somebody whose opinions were both sought and listened to. This was not something that had ever happened to her before. 'Oh, Mrs Overs, we missed you,' they said, when she'd skipped a week. 'Mrs Overs says that Alvar Liddell always has a mug of cocoa before he reads the news,' she'd heard Mrs Rice reporting, breathlessly.

By contrast, her actual neighbours in the Vale of Health were a snooty bunch who seemed to consider that she'd dragged down the whole tone of the road by opening a boarding house. Sometimes she was tempted to hang the washing out of the window, just to annoy them.

'And my sister-in-law,' continued Mrs Rice, 'that's the one who's married to my brother, not my husband's sister, who couldn't come because of her phlebitis – my sister-in-law—'

'Hark!' said Vee, lifting her head; the tiny, wicked noise was like a distant dentist's drill.

Mrs Rice paused with her mouth open and Mrs Arnold said, 'Oh no, oh *no* . . .' and the sound of the doodlebug grew from a far-off buzz to a nasty overhead roar, and then, abruptly, stopped.

Mrs Arnold got under the table first. They were in the verger's room at the chapel, a plywood lean-to about as substantial as a bed-sheet over a line, but the table was two-inch oak and there were suddenly seven of them beneath it, including Mrs Aldermayer, who couldn't normally stand up without two people helping. Mrs Lunn was saying the Lord's Prayer and Vee was counting in her head because Noel had told her that the average length of time between the engine cutting out and the flying bomb actually hitting the ground was twelve seconds, but she'd only got as far as 'eight Mesopotamia' when the bomb hit.

There was a tremendous bang, the windows went and something hit the tabletop with a smash.

Mrs Arnold screamed.

'Lampshade,' said Vee, as pale pink shards pattered to the floor.

'Well, if that's *all*,' said Mrs Rice, shakily. 'Where did that go down, do you think? Rosslyn Hill?'

'I'll go and find out, shall I?' said Vee, unfolding herself. As she picked her way through the glass she heard Mrs Arnold say, 'I wish I could be as calm as Mrs Overs,' and Mrs Rice replying, 'Well, she's been through it and out the other side, hasn't she?' and involuntarily, Vee raised a hand and stroked the scar that ran in a curve beneath her right cheekbone. It was true, in a way; she'd been under one bomb, and she knew, with inexplicable but absolute certainty, that she wouldn't be under another – she'd have bet a hundred pounds on it, if she'd had a hundred pounds. One of her lodgers, Mr Reddish, had sailed through the Great War without a scratch, and he'd told her that he'd known from the start that he wouldn't get touched, though he could never sleep afterwards for thinking of all the chums who'd gone west. Vee, too, often woke before dawn and watched the clock, though it wasn't bombs she was worrying about.

Outside, a plume of dust was lifting above the rooftops of Haverstock Hill and she could hear an ambulance bell. 'Bottom of Belsize Lane,' said someone. One old lady already had her broom out, pushing a pile of glass towards the gutter. 'It's the mess I can't stand,' she said, catching Vee's eye. 'I never liked mess, and now it's just filth and dust, morning till night. I can never get things straight.'

'They say it's Belsize Lane,' Vee reported back to the knitting circle, though half of them had already hurried away to check on their own windows. Vee stayed to help Mrs Lunn clear the floor and tack some muslin across the empty frames, and then she pushed the unfinished sock into her straw bag and set off back to the Vale of Health.

When you took the turning off East Heath Road, it was like walking back into the countryside – a muddy track leading downward through a belt of woodland; you half expected to smell manure and hear a tractor coughing into life, and then the track curved and the purplish bricks of 'Taormina' came into sight between the trees, and suddenly it was all fanlights and balustrades, and name-boards swinging from wrought-iron brackets. The choice of names always puzzled Vee: if you had so much money that you could afford to live here, why didn't you just up sticks and *move* to Braemar or Greenbanks or St Ives? Though given that half the houses were currently empty, the windows shuttered, the gardens a wilderness, perhaps the inhabitants had done exactly that.

Vee had just passed 'Llandudno' when she heard Noel call 'Mar!', and she turned to see him hurrying to catch up, limping slightly, as he sometimes did when he ran.

'There was a buzz bomb!' he said, his voice breaking mid-sentence, so that 'buzz' was shrill with tension, and 'bomb' a growl.

'I didn't think you'd be back yet,' said Vee. It hadn't occurred to her to worry about him, and she felt a rush of belated anxiety. 'You weren't anywhere near it, were you?'

'No. What about you?'

'Miles away,' she said. 'Barely heard it.' He was a terrible worrier, his shoulders up around his ears as he inspected her for possible damage. She patted his arm. 'What have you been doing? Your hands are black.'

'Oh.' He gave them a perfunctory wipe, his expression relaxing back to its usual blank watchfulness. 'I was looking at a mediaeval roof boss.'

'Were you?' She turned the phrase over in her head, but she couldn't face an explanation till she'd had a cup of tea. 'Did you get the books?'

'No. The shop's vanished.'

'Vanished?'

'It was hit by a V-2.' He paused, thinking. 'The interesting thing is that a whole row of houses was flattened, but the staircases survived, and I've been wondering if that has to do with the fact that they're right-angled triangles.'

'What?'

'The triangle is an inherently strong shape. Look at the Pyramids, still intact after thousands of years.'

'But no one ever bombed them.'

'But you can't imagine them collapsing if someone did. Would you prefer to spend a raid in a tower or a Pyramid?'

'A tower. Less cleaning up afterwards – think of the floor space in a Pyramid; it'd be sweep, sweep, sweep all day.'

He cracked a smile. 'Incidentally, I quite badly need the Bright's English History – Mr Jepson says it's essential for matriculation.'

'Does he? There's another year or two before you have to take that, isn't there?'

She pushed open the gate of their own house, and glanced up to see Miss Zawadska raising her blackouts. She worked nights at the BBC canteen and lived arsy-tarsy to the rest of them, eating Irish stew for breakfast and coming home to a supper of porridge.

'I bought some carrots,' said Vee. 'Though they look woody to me. Are you using up the rest of that liver?'

'Yes, in a hot-pot.'

'I've never seen a liver that thick before – when I asked if it came from a horse, the butcher pretended he couldn't hear me.'

'He should have said, "Neigh".'

She sniggered. 'What's for afters?'

'Apple charlotte.'

'Very nice.'

As usual, there was scarcely any difference between the

temperature outside and inside the house. There was generally enough coke for a fire in the drawing room and the kitchen, and Vee had found a cluster of stone hot-water bottles in the cellar, which meant that so far none of the lodgers had been found as a frozen corpse in the morning, but all of them wore coats in the house and Mr Reddish wore a deer-stalker hat, even during meals.

Vee filled the kettle and then started violently as a face appeared at the kitchen window.

'Is Noel in?' The voice was muffled, but imperious.

'It's your friend again!' called Vee, over her shoulder. 'I wish she'd come to the door instead of climbing over the fence, and if you're out there, can you . . .'

'Yes, I'll feed the chickens,' said Noel, already hurrying down the scullery passage, his heart beating almost as fast as when he'd heard the buzz bomb, though in a more pleasurable way. Genevieve Lumb was waiting for him outside the back door. She was wearing her blue school mac and a hair-slide in the shape of a bow, and her hair was in two short plaits, the ends fanning out like curtain tassels. Her eyelashes were dark and her eyes an unusual shade of brown; after considerable study Noel had identified them in an old paint chart as 'burnt umber'.

'Hello.'

'Hello.'

'I have something to tell you,' she said.

'What?'

'In a minute.' Genevieve's ambition was to write detective novels, and she liked to apply an element of suspense to her own conversations. 'Did you hear the doodlebug?'

'Yes.' At times, her presence seemed to rob Noel of the ability to speak in sentences. 'I did,' he added, inadequately.

'Three killed, apparently,' she said. 'I've heard that the V-1 blast is so bad that people can be blown to pieces and have to be identified by a piece of ear, or their foot. I don't think I have very distinctive feet, but my ears are quite unusual. What do you think?' She turned sideways and presented her left ear to Noel, and he leaned forward and examined its curlicues, the neatly rolled edge of the pinna, the velvety pinkness of the lobe.

'Well?'

'Yes, I'd definitely know your ear if I saw it again,' he said, a little huskily.

'And I'd certainly know *yours*,' said Genevieve. 'I don't mean that at all in a nasty way,' she added. 'It's just that they're very visible.'

Noel nodded glumly. 'What did you want to tell me?'

'I have to go back to school.' She pulled a face indicative of utter misery. 'Mummy's wired to say that London's too dangerous and she can't sleep until I'm back in Herefordshire. Will you write to me?'

'Yes. Hang on a minute—' He hurried over to the back wall, where a chicken was ineptly balanced, its head tilted, one silly eye contemplating the Heath beyond. Wary of the beak, he picked it up, disliking its prickly weightlessness, and tossed it back towards the summer house which he and Vee had converted into a coop.

'I was thinking,' said Genevieve, 'that in four years' time we can both go to Cambridge, and at twenty-one we can get married without my parents' permission, though

I'm afraid that I wouldn't want sexual relations until I was ready to have children. Perhaps not until I'm twenty-six or twenty-seven. Would you mind that?'

He shook his head dutifully, though merely hearing her enunciate the word 'sexual' meant that he had to turn away, crouching slightly, and pretend to look under a bush for eggs.

'Of course, you don't have any parents, do you?' asked Genevieve. 'So perhaps you could marry at sixteen if you wanted to. I meant to ask you why you call your aunt Ma.'

'It's "Mar" – M A R,' he said, 'short for Margery.' Except, of course, that her name wasn't really Margery, it was Vee, and she wasn't his aunt at all – just as his godmother Mattie, with whom he'd lived previously, hadn't actually been his godmother. He didn't have a family tree, he had a Venn diagram, in which none of the circles overlapped.

'Oh,' he exclaimed, 'look!' He pushed aside a swag of leaves; there were four eggs clustered in a shallow depression under the spotted laurel. Genevieve knelt beside him and reached into the hollow.

'This one's still warm,' she said, holding it to her own cheek and then his.

Vee was watching from the kitchen window. She'd been noticing lately that girls liked Noel – and not just girls; grown women went out of their way to talk to him, and she thought it was maybe because when he wasn't sounding like a junior member of the Brains Trust, he actually listened to people; he wasn't just waiting to tip in his own comments, like someone off-loading gravel. Or maybe it was because he had a way of making them laugh. It certainly wasn't his looks, God bless him.

The kettle was boiling, and Vee picked up the tea strainer and tipped the used leaves back into the pot. She couldn't remember the last time she'd had a good, strong cup of tea – or, for that matter, a slice of bread that had a bit of spring to it, or a bun with icing, or a whole handful of currants instead of a guilty couple from a hoarded packet. A hopeful belief had been sustaining her that when the war ended (and it couldn't be long now, the Allies snapping at the Siegfried Line) there'd be food in wagonloads again – but this idea had been squashed by Mr Jepson, who'd pointed out that Great Britain was up to her hair-roots in debt, and regretfully, in his opinion, there'd be rationing for at least another five years, so no end to the meanness, the blandness, the dismal substitutions and the counterfeits that fooled no one: sugar by the grain, sausages stuffed with bread . . .

She jumped again, as Noel knocked on the window. 'Eight,' he mouthed, holding up the egg basket.

'Good. Bring in a bucket of coke as well, will you?'

He nodded. The Lumb girl was lingering near the window, and before she could turn away, Vee hooked her eye and gave her a hard stare. She hadn't been mothering Noel for four years just so that some pert blonde piece could break his heart like a stick of charcoal. Genevieve Lumb stared back, faintly puzzled.

'I don't think your aunt likes me very much,' she said, joining Noel as he scattered fish-meal for the hens, 'though I'm not aware I've done anything to offend her.'

'Oh, you don't have to offend my aunt for her not to like you,' said Noel. 'There may be other reasons.'

'Such as what?'

He shook his head. Impossible to explain Vee's myriad antipathies, her constantly updated list of prejudices and judgements. 'Their name is legion,' he said. 'Though there are some we can discount – you're not a man with a yellow tie, and you don't have sideburns.'

Genevieve smiled, and Noel felt as if his heart were being slowly squeezed by one of her long-fingered hands. 'And you're not Welsh,' he added.

Dr Parry-Jones always gripped her cutlery very near the ends, manipulating the knife and fork with delicate precision. She had a similar approach to conversation, impassively pinning down and dissecting casual remarks, so that a phrase such as 'they say it's going to be foggy tomorrow' was left writhing under the scalpel. Vee had, in any case, only said it as a way of distracting the lodgers from the passage of the potato dish around the table – specifically from the sad, repeated *clink clink* of the spoon which indicated that there were only two each.

'It was someone in the haberdasher's that told me,' she said. 'I think they only said it "might be" foggy.'

'They said it "might be"?'

'Yes, I think so.'

Dr Parry-Jones continued to look at Vee enquiringly, as if awaiting more stringent clarification; she was a general practitioner, bombed out of her house but still cycling daily to her practice in Finchley, her age a mystery, her white hair strained into a French pleat, her crisply neat appearance a near-miracle in frayed, darned, second-hand London. She taught Noel Biology, Chemistry and accuracy; her steady gaze seemed to see and expect only the truth.

'Maybe I heard it wrong,' said Vee; the bowl of potatoes had reached her and there was only one left, which meant that someone (Mr Reddish) had taken three.

'There was definitely no mention of fog in the *Daily Telegraph* weather notes,' said Dr Parry-Jones, giving the conversational corpse a final prod.

Mr Reddish made the preliminary throat-clear that indicated that poetry was on the way.

'Do you need some salt, Mr Reddish?' suggested Vee, quickly, hoping to forestall him, but he was already in recital posture, chins lifted, one hand raised as if to ward off an attack. He worked in the accounts department of St Pancras Borough Council but spent his evenings performing in amateur entertainments. He had a very large head and had once, he claimed, been mistaken for President Roosevelt.

'"I saw the fog grow thick, which soon made blind my ken; it made tall men of boys, and *giants* of tall men."'

'Ooh, more poetry!' said Miss Appleby, with a giggle. 'I don't know how you remember—'

'"I clutched my throat,"' continued Mr Reddish, clutching his throat. '"I coughed. Nothing was in my head. Except two heavy eyes, like balls . . . of burning . . . LEAD."'

There was a tiny pause, while everyone waited to see if there was going to be another verse. 'Salt?' asked Vee again.

'I recall I was once lost in the fog with a young lady,' said Mr Reddish, abandoning his pose. 'What an experience that was!'

'I know that poetry shouldn't be treated as if it were factual,' said Noel, 'but I really don't see why the eyeballs are referred to as "burning" when fog's notoriously cold and clammy. In any case, lead actually only burns when it's powdered, in which case it's pyrophoric, and ignites spontaneously at room temperature.'

'Excellent, Noel,' murmured Dr Parry-Jones.

Mr Jepson looked up from his plate and, with a gesture that was habitual, gave his moustache a quick stroke. It was a sparse affair – more like an eyebrow than a moustache – but it caught the gaze because, unlike the hair on his head (brown threaded with grey), it was ginger. Vee suspected that he'd grown it in order to draw attention from his missing ear.

'The trouble is that "like balls of lead" wouldn't scan,' he said. 'It needs a couple of syllables in there for the rhythm of the writing. Perhaps "balls of *molten* lead" would have been an improvement.'

Noel shook his head. 'If they were molten, they'd no longer be balls and they'd simply dribble out of his eye sockets.'

'Well, how about "burnished"? No, I think maybe "burnished" only applies to bronze. I'll have to check that in Chambers.' Mr Jepson extracted a tiny notebook from his breast pocket, and made a tiny note with an equally tiny pencil. He wrote features for the *North London Press* and never had to ask Noel what on earth he was on about.

'By the way, the stew is excellent,' he said, picking up his cutlery again.

'Yes, very nice, Noel,' said Miss Zawadska, approvingly. 'And I taste pepper!'

'Someone told me a grocer in Tufnell Park had a delivery,' said Vee. 'I hurried over there and got the last packet!'

'And mushrooms,' said Miss Zawadska, continuing to address the culinary wunderkind and ignoring the woman who actually did all the queuing and shopping.

'I found a cluster of them just by the tumulus on the Heath,' said Noel. 'Obviously, I was extremely careful about identification. I have an illustrated guide.'

'Ooh,' said Miss Appleby, with a giggle, 'I hope they're not death caps!'

'No, we'd already be in the initial stages of irreversible kidney damage if that were the case,' said Noel. 'They're shaggy ink-caps, which are completely harmless unless taken with alcohol.'

Mr Jepson gave a hiss of amusement. 'Chance would be a fine thing.'

'Why?' asked Miss Appleby, suddenly sharp. 'What happens if you drink alcohol after eating them?'

'It results in violent vomiting.'

Miss Appleby stared at him, mouth open. The tip of her nose, which usually moved cheerily up and down whenever she talked or laughed, was ominously static, and her eyes – hare's eyes, slightly protuberant – were suddenly bulging with tears, and she pushed back her chair and ran from the room.

'Oh dear,' said Dr Parry-Jones, with no obvious emotion.

'Ah, the tender feelings of a young lady,' said Mr Reddish, sonorously. '"My eyes are tired of *weeping*, my heart is sick of *woe* . . ."'

'I wish the door would open, I'm desperate for the po,' finished Mr Jepson, *sotto voce*, to Noel. 'The song of the lodging-house bathroom.'

Noel laughed, and Vee rose, reluctantly. 'I suppose I'd better see what the matter is.'

When she'd started taking in paying guests, she'd thought that the worst of it would be the constant cleaning, the nasty surprises found clinging to sheets or round the bowl of the water closet, but far worse than those were the unwonted roles constantly thrust upon her by a houseful of strangers: she had to be confidante, captive audience, magistrate in inter-lodger feuding occasioned by repeated use of a toothpick during meals, and here she was again, missing her supper and following the sound of weeping up the stairs.

'Miss Appleby . . . ?'

Sheila Appleby was sitting on her bed. She had one of those delicate complexions that respond violently to emotion, and now looked as if she'd had a snowball rammed in her face.

'Whatever's the matter?' asked Vee, not really wanting to know. It would be a man, again.

'Auggie,' said Sheila.

'Is that the sailor?'

'Soldier.'

'The Canadian?'

'The American.' The latter word was broken by a sob

and extended across at least five syllables. The girl groped in her sleeve for a handkerchief. 'He's leaving tomorrow, Mrs Overs, his unit's going to Italy, though he's not supposed to have told me, so don't pass it on to anyone, and he's taking me to Rainbow Corner tonight and he says he has something for me and I keep thinking that it might be a ring . . .'

'Well, he can still propose to you if you don't drink alcohol, can't he?'

Sheila threw her an incredulous look. 'You don't understand what it's like there, it's not a *pub*, you don't sit in the corner with a glass of shandy - it's . . . it's . . . it's like a dream . . .' She waved her hands, trying to convey the fabulous extravagance of the American Servicemen's Club, as if Vee might somehow have missed all the gossip about the whisky cocktails in half-pint glasses, the plates of pink-and-white ice-cream, the hot doughnuts dusted with actual sugar, cigarettes full of tobacco instead of shredded string, the dustbins outside bursting with half-eaten steaks.

'I can't drink *lemonade*, like an old lady, he'd think I'd gone crazy. You just don't understand,' said Sheila again, and there was both dismissal and condescension in her tone, as if addressing a village crone who'd never been further than the duck-pond. She blew her nose and picked up her compact. 'Maybe if I just have the one, I'll get away with it . . .' she said.

Vee, tight-lipped, returned to the dining room, where Noel was stacking plates.

'I remember that I once took a young lady mushroom-picking,' said Mr Reddish, back on his favourite topic. 'It was very early morning, and the grass was thick with dew, and before we'd walked ten yards she gave a little scream and said that it was ruining her shoes, and that she wouldn't go a step further unless I gave her a piggy-back. Well, you won't believe me when I tell you that I carried her nearly a mile. I was sweating like a Trojan, up hill and down dale, and when we finally reached the field I set her down and she thanked me very nicely, I must say.' He leaned back with the air of someone who'd just held an audience spellbound; none of his stories had any point to them.

'My uncle died of a rupture after carrying a pig across a field,' said Miss Zawadska. 'Excuse me, I need to go to work. Could you save dessert for me?' She rose, and there was the usual reverent pause as everyone watched her move across the room – beauty incarnate, a nipped waist and a full bosom, a face like a cameo, hair the colour of heavy cream; 'the Madonna of the Vale', as Mr Reddish called her, his tone wavering between sentiment and senile lust. Vee followed her out with a tray of dishes, and caught up as Miss Zawadska paused beside the hall mirror and adjusted a hair-grip.

'You picked up your Red Cross letter from the hall table?' asked Vee.

'Thank you, yes.'

'Won't be too long now, maybe,' said Vee. 'Before he's back, I mean.'

Miss Zawadska's fiancé was a prisoner-of-war, captured just after D-Day; the photograph beside her bed was of someone as preposterously good-looking as herself.

'I am not impatient,' said Miss Zawadska.

'No?'

'He is safe now and we have our whole lives ahead.' She smiled placidly, and Vee shifted the tray to get past and glimpsed her own reflection in the mirror, looking like the 'before' illustration in an advertisement for nerve tonic. She had never in her adult life looked forward to the future; there had always been something up ahead to be dreaded or dodged. The end of the war might mean less chance of sudden death, but there'd also likely be more housing available and fewer lodgers, and there was barely enough money for the bills as it was. Noel, as usual, was unable to see any difficulties. 'I'm the sole beneficiary of Mattie's will, and you're my guardian. All we have to do is actually go to the solicitor and sign a few papers, and then you'd have access to the money.'

'But what if he asked me questions?'

'What sort of questions?'

'About Margery Overs.'

'He never met Margery Overs, so if I say that's who you are, and *you* say that's who you are, then why on earth would he think that you were someone else? She's hardly going to burst in and declare that you're an imposter.'

'Poor soul,' said Vee, automatically. She had met the real Margery Overs once, only hours before her death in a raid – had sat in her armchair and drunk her tea and now was unable to banish a vision of the large, nervous woman peering at her over the edge of a cloud, shocked and reproachful. 'It's having to swear. It's having to put my signature. It wouldn't just be me saying it any more, it'd be official, it'd be . . . you know . . .'

'Fraud,' said Noel, baldly.

'Yes.' Even the word was frightening. It made her nervous about giving out any personal information at all, however minor, in case she made a slip-up; the lodgers knew she was a widow, for instance, but not that she had a grown-up son, and when Mr Reddish had once enquired about Noel's parentage she'd shrieked, 'Oh, we don't talk about that,' even though the truth was that she had no idea, and neither had he, apart from the fact that he'd been born on the wrong side of the blanket.

The front door closed on Miss Zawadska, and Vee slid the dishes into the sink, and took the apple charlotte from the oven. Back in the dining room, they were talking about church roofs, the conversation all staves and corbels.

'I'd like to learn more about architecture,' said Noel. 'I think it would be rather interesting to be an architectural historian.'

'That's a real job, is it?' asked Vee.

'What do you mean?'

'Is it advertised? "Architectural historian wanted, usual rates apply"?'

'I don't know. Does it matter?'

'Of course it matters. What are you going to eat when you grow up? Bricks?'

She caught Dr Parry-Jones's eye and found herself reddening, again, and hoped it wasn't the change – she'd heard it could start at forty, and she was nearly forty-one now. 'We all have to earn a living,' she said.

'But we all also need to expand our minds,' said Dr Parry-Jones, with mild reproof.

So there we have it, thought Vee, sneaking a bit of extra crust on to Noel's plate – there we have it, the criteria for the next lodger: No pets, laundry extra, and knowledge of flying buttresses an advantage.

'The pudding's tip-top, Noel,' said Mr Reddish.

❧

Wardens' Post 9 was a Nissen hut, sunk into the corner of Deddington Square Gardens and covered with a skin of concrete and a foot of earth. It had been built in 1938 and was now as well camouflaged as a commando's hat, the top thick with brambles and wild raspberries. The sloping path that led to the entrance always made Winnie feel like Peter Rabbit entering his burrow.

'Hi ho!' she called before opening the door, just in case one of the other wardens was engaged in scratching his privates, or peeing into a bucket in the corner. In the event, only Addy was there, perusing the *Sporting Life* through half-moon spectacles. He had long silver hair, and the dreaming air of a Cambridge don, and had almost certainly been a burglar before the war.

'Hi ho, Shorty,' he responded, not looking up but marking something on the paper with a stub of pencil. 'Nothing doing?'

'No, all quiet.'

'You know what Smiler says: one of them rockets could be a mile above our heads as we speak, just waiting to smash us like a bleeding hammer.'

'Thanks, Addy.'

'You're welcome. Cup of tea? There's still a mouthful in the pot. Fenton's girl turned up and says he's seedy, won't be in tonight.'

'Smiler's coming in though, isn't he?' asked Winnie, pouring herself half a mug of treacle. 'And Basset?'

'Basset's swapped with Polesworth.'

'All right.' It wasn't much of a swap; Basset was worth ten of Polesworth, the latter a cerebral liability from the Classics department at King's, who pondered every decision (however trivial) as if it were a chess move. Four years before, during the night Blitz, there'd been twenty volunteer wardens and eleven full-timers at the post, but the long lull before the advent of the doodlebugs had pared down the roster, and now only Winnie, as Post Warden, and Smiler, as deputy, were on the council pay-roll, with a shifting band of part-timers helping out as the fancy took them. 'You can't hardly call us Air Raid Precautions Wardens no more,' as Smiler had remarked. 'We're Mopper-Uppers. You can't take no precautions against a thunderbolt.'

Addy laid down the paper and yawned; the small electric fire in the corner had built up a nice fug. 'You heard from that husband of yours, Shorty?' he asked.

'Yes. Got a letter on Monday.'

'What's he up to, then?'

'Oh, not much. The camp crosses out half of what he writes and the censor on this side cuts the rest.'

'Sends you his love?'

'None of your business.'

Addy smiled.

'I tell you what, though, I just had something quite

funny happen,' said Winnie, glad to change the subject. She took out her notebook and looked at the address that the boy had written in a neat italic script. 'I met a kid poking around St Aethelstan's, and I said I'd drop him a line when the chap from the University decides what to do with the Green Man carving. And when I looked at the address, I realized that it's somewhere I know – it's in Hampstead – and I don't only know the road, I know the actual house. It was owned by a suffragette called Miss Matilda Simpkin, and she ran a girls' club – my sister and I were both in it.'

'You got a sister?'

'A twin, actually.'

'Get away – I never knew that! Two Shorties!'

'She's four inches taller than me. The club was called the Amazons – we used to throw javelins and run around Hampstead Heath with feathers in our hair.'

Addy let out a silent whistle, and turned the page. 'Here,' he said. 'There's a runner in tomorrow's 4.30 called Feathered Friend – might be worth a punt. What do you say? It's got the usual number of legs.'

'All right, then. Sixpence each way.'

She was digging into her pocket for a coin when there was a knock at the door. A soldier was standing outside, pack on back, his head in beaky profile as he scanned the ruined terrace to the east of the square; he was very young and deeply tanned, the colour ending abruptly halfway up his forehead.

'I'm looking for the Shaws,' he said, his voice hoarse. 'Eileen and Horace Shaw. And the kids.'

'Sidney! It *is* Sidney, isn't it?'

He turned to face her. 'I know you,' he said. 'You was warden here before I left.'

He'd shot up, and broadened, in the years since she'd last seen him; all the Shaw boys were built like tanks, but beneath the sunburn, he looked exhausted.

'Where are they?' he said. 'I went to the house and no one answered and there's no bloody windows in the place – where have they gone? I bin travelling three weeks to get here and they're not bloody here.' He was close to tears, she realized.

'They didn't leave us an address,' said Winnie. 'I'm ever so sorry. There was a rocket bomb in Falcon Road a fortnight ago and it took the roofs off that side of the square. They've patched it up, but most people have left.'

'I bin in Egypt,' he said. 'I won a leave lottery, and now they're not even here and I've only got a week.'

'Can I get you a cup of tea?'

'No, I got no time.' He turned and walked back up the path, and she ran to catch him up.

'The Town Hall might have a record, but Mrs Aitcheson's still at number 19. Let's go and ask her,' she said. 'There's not much she doesn't know. Do you remember what the kids always called her?'

'Mrs Jungle Drums.'

'She hasn't changed.'

He nodded, too tired even to smile, and Winnie led the way.

Even before the war, the square had been shabby – a mere mile from Bloomsbury, but lacking both poets and stucco, with absentee landlords dragging their feet over repairs, and broken downpipes flaring green slime across the brickwork. It had always been full of people, though, three or four families sharing each front door; now it was three-quarters empty, boards across half the windows, and tarpaulins stretched over the exposed rafters.

Mrs Aitcheson had refused to move. She had been born in the square, married round the corner and widowed in the Great War, and was now living in her basement kitchen, her bed covered with a sheet of plywood during the day, her ear still glued to the ground.

'They've all gone to your mum's brother-in-law in Watford,' she said, instantly, to Sidney. 'The one who's a council officer with a motor-car. But have a bite before you go. Give us the news. How long since they've seen you?'

Sidney eased his pack to the floor, but didn't sit. 'Two and a half years,' he said, accepting a slice of bread-and-marge. 'But Victor's not been back in three.'

'Where's he?' asked Winnie.

'Ceylon, last we heard.'

'And the others?'

'Walter's in Greece, maybe. Frank's in Burma, they've not heard from him in a while.' He sunk a mug of tea in one long draught. 'I'm going. Thanks, Mrs Aitcheson.' He clumped away up the area steps, still eating his bread-and-marge. His father had cut a map of the world out of the *Daily Sketch* and kept it folded in his wallet, in case anyone asked about his boys.

'It's freezing in here, Mrs A,' said Winnie.

'I never feel it, dear. I wear my Arthur's great-coat and

I'm cosy as a kitten. Born hot-blooded, he always said.' She gave a chirrup of laughter. 'Mind you, Sidney's going to get a shock when he sees his sister. Eight months gone, no wedding ring, and I hear that the father's as black as the sole of your boot. Got tired of waiting for her fiancé to get back from his ship, I expect. How long since you've seen your hubby, dear?'

'Four years, ten months,' said Winnie.

'But you're a good girl – *you're* the faithful type, I can tell.'

Was that a compliment? It made Winnie feel like the baggier sort of fireside hound, resting its chin on the owner's leg. Glamorous, svelte women – women like her twin, Avril – were never labelled 'the faithful type'.

'Can I get you anything, Mrs Aitcheson?' she asked. 'Do you want me to put up the blackouts?'

'I heard we don't have to do that any more.'

'You heard right – just ordinary curtains. But I thought, maybe, for warmth.'

'Go on, then, dear. Did you hear about the barman at the Star and Garter? The one with the missing fingers?'

'Gibson? What about him?'

'He's been summonsed. They found a big pile of brand-new gentlemen's coats in the tap room that he said he was just minding for someone.'

'Well, maybe he was.' Winnie liked Gibson. He was a part-time fireman, and had the sort of cheerful face that it was good to see above a pile of smoking rubble; he'd lost the fingers to an incendiary in '41, and still turned out for the AFS, and, frankly, it would take more than a few swiped coats to lower her opinion of him. She let Mrs Aitcheson rattle poisonously on while she finished the blackouts.

Outside, twilight was dropping like a shutter and you could almost hear the crackle of the frost forming. She checked on the surface shelter in Bedale Road, and helped the steward to carry out the chemical toilet and tip the contents into a nearby crater, and then she returned to the Post, and briefed Smiler on the minimal events of the last twenty-four hours.

'Off you hop then, Shorty,' he said, lighting fags for them both. 'See you tomorrow evening, if we're not both dead.'

Her flat was half a mile away, past what remained of Falcon Road. Winnie flashed her torch across the ruins and a pair of cats stared back at her, their eyes like a switch-board signal, four green lights in a row. It still felt odd to be able to use an unshuttered bulb, or to see the glimmer of half-lit streetlamps. The night the rocket had landed, an American truck carrying a searchlight had arrived and bathed the whole area in brilliant white light, and an old man pulled from the wreckage had thought he'd reached heaven, and had asked for his long-dead wife. 'Typical of the Yanks,' Smiler had said, afterwards. 'They all think they're God.'

As she opened the front door, Winnie could hear dance music seeping from the ground-floor flat, the volume not quite loud enough to cover the sound of the baby crying. The post had been shuffled into neat piles on the hall table, and Winnie took her own bundle and started upstairs, passing Mr Veale halfway, as he left for his night shift at the Cossor Works. He nodded politely, but said nothing. It was not a friendly house – no one had been there long; no shared triumph or disaster had bonded them.

Inside her rooms, Winnie closed the curtains and switched on the light, and wrapped herself in a blanket crocheted by her grandmother. There was a letter postmarked Salisbury at the top of the pile; her father's firm had moved to Wiltshire at the start of the war and her mother sent her a weekly chronicle of provincial life which varied so little from letter to letter that Winnie played a type of Housey Housey when reading them, taking a sip of beer or eating a monkey-nut whenever she saw the words 'evacuee' or 'vicar' or 'soup'.

During Winnie's visits, her mother treated her like an invalid, speaking in hushed tones to callers ('the things she's *seen*') and draping a blanket over her daughter's legs whenever she sat down, but the funny thing was that none of her parents' friends or acquaintances seemed to have the slightest interest in what was happening in London. 'Yes, I heard on the news there'd been trouble,' they'd say, vaguely, before switching to the topic of the cheese ration or the sex-crazed land-girls who scandalized Chippenham on a Saturday night. It didn't help that the BBC's stock phrase was 'Rockets have fallen in the south of England', a deliberate obfuscation which sounded as if Jerry were idly scattering V-2s from Broadstairs to Worcester, with the capital just catching the odd one.

Winnie got the impression that the provinces thought London was clinging to the limelight, exaggerating its suffering, but perhaps the truth was that after five years, everyone was simply bored of bomb stories. Everyone was bored of everything, really; it had all been going on for far too long.

'Now, Winifred, you have to admit that you've definitely done your bit,' her mother had said, on her last visit. 'Why don't you come back here until Emlyn comes home? There's masses of things you can help with – the Savings Committee's always short of people, and I know that the Chippenham Players would *die* if you offered your services.'

'As what?'

'You're a trained actress!'

'I'm a trained warden. I even train *other* wardens.'

'Yes, but . . .' She could see her mother casting around for bait. 'They're going to be putting on *War and Peace*, and I'm almost certain they don't have a Natasha yet.'

Winnie had let out an incredulous hoot. 'Oh, Mummy, don't be ridiculous.'

'Why is that ridiculous?'

'Natasha's supposed to be sixteen and drop-dead beautiful – *and* she's the lead. Even when I was at drama school, I only ever played servants.' Three years of trudging across the stage with a broom ('Housemaid . . . Winifred Bridge'), of bobbing a curtsey, of answering a flimsy front door to willowy blondes, of attempting to wring character from the words 'Shall I collect the tea tray now, madam?' In everyday life, she might merely be classified as stocky, but the physical standards of the acting world were different; she'd realized quickly that lissom beauty was the norm and her own role was that of useful visual contrast, a bulky prop that might add ballast to a scene. In the end, she hadn't bothered to give the starched apron back to the college wardrobe department each time, but had just hung on to it for the next part. After graduating, she'd only had one professional job, touring the East Midlands in a thriller, playing an unnamed nurse ('Please don't tire him') while trebling as ASM, understudy and prompt, and then the war had started, and then she'd met Emlyn.

'I wouldn't stay even if the Chippenham Players cast me as Napoleon. Which might suit me, actually,' she'd said, and her mother had looked hurt.

'It's only that I want you to be safe. After all, it's nearly all over and it would be so awful if . . .'

'I got squashed by the last bomb of the war?'

'Don't say it, darling. You joke about the most awful things.'

'Sorry.'

She wondered what her mother would say if she could eavesdrop on Post 9, the air spiky with swear-words, no topic too delicate for a laugh, sudden death the casual punchline.

Under her mother's letter was one from her friend Elsie, a Wren stationed in Portsmouth, and having 'the most smashing time in my whole life, Winnie', and beneath that was a bundle held together by a paper band, the latter stamped with a Red Cross and signed by the censor. Winnie felt a familiar flattening of the spirits and then she broke the band, and three letters dropped on to the table. That made four from Emlyn in the last fortnight. She chose one at random, and slit the envelope.

Dearest Win, I have been thinking about our garden and I've realized something terrible – there is nowhere for us to sit! Of course, we could pick up a garden bench for a song, but I have been thinking along the lines of a little gazebo, nothing fancy, just a raised platform roofed with trellis, perhaps near the orchard, where we could sit and catch the last of the . . .

She stopped reading, the page drooping in her hand. There had been one letter from him last week and three the week before that, and she hadn't actually counted them all but if they averaged eight a month since May 1940, when Emlyn had been captured at Dunkirk, then that came to hundreds and hundreds and hundreds of letters, and the green rattan suitcase under her bed was packed tight with them and she was having to put the overspill in a sewing basket, and still they came. Winnie wrote to him once a week, trying to amuse with everyday gossip, and received in return these reams of domestic fantasy, microscopic in their detail – the motor-car the two of them would choose, the breed of dog they'd pick, the gramophone records they'd play, the proposed paint-colour in the imaginary porch of the house that they didn't own. *I think, on consideration, I'd prefer to concrete the drive rather than use gravel; the latter's very hard on tyres, although there's something rather swish about the noise, isn't there?*

She'd met him at one of her sister's awful parties; they'd both been very drunk, crushed together in a group on the narrow iron balcony outside Avril's Kensington flat, and when a warden in the street below had shouted that they were showing a light, Emlyn (who'd been an English teacher before joining up) had replied, 'It is the east and Juliet is the sun,' and Winnie (who had once played the Capulets' maid) had found herself supplying the next line, after which there wasn't much else they could do except finish the scene (to some applause), lock lips for the rest of the evening and then go to bed together. Winnie had married him a month later, and waved him off at the station a week after that, and she'd been so deeply in love that the train had seemed to drag half of her away along the tracks, and the awful truth was that now she could barely remember what Emlyn looked like. She had photographs, of course – it wasn't the outline of his features that she'd forgotten, but the play of his expressions: did he squint when he laughed, was there a line between his eyes when he frowned, did he show his teeth when smiling? She had no idea. Nor could she remember the timbre of his voice, or the sound of his yawn, or what he said when he sneezed, and because he wrote very little about the POW camp, even when she asked him to, she couldn't even visualize what he was seeing, or doing, so that there was nothing solid for her to hold on to, only those letters with their endless impersonal detail; she had fallen for Romeo and now found herself padlocked to the editor of *Modern Homes and Gardens*.

Sitting with the page in her hand, her future life planned down to the handles on her kitchen cupboards (lucite and chrome), Winnie felt the same coppery taste in her mouth, the same ominous visceral lurch as when she'd heard the doodlebug approach this afternoon.

At the Post, they'd had a sweepstake for the date of the German surrender. Smiler had picked out December '44, and Winnie had got June of next year. The terrible thing was that she half hoped she'd win.

❧

Vee hadn't expected Oxford Street to be so crowded. After spending a fortnight's meat budget on *The History of European Architecture* in Cullbright's ('Wouldn't you rather get a surprise for your birthday?' she'd asked Noel. 'No,' he'd said. 'I'd rather get precisely what I want.'), she crossed to Dickins and Jones at the top of Regent Street. Half the windows were still boarded up, but the place was heaving, and it took forty minutes of determined elbow-work to purchase a pair of flannel pyjamas and three vests for Noel and a pale-green crêpe blouse – marked down because of a water stain – for herself.

By the time she'd escaped it was edging towards twilight. It had snowed earlier in the week – just a sprinkling, but it hadn't melted and now the pavement was corrugated with ice. The book in its string bag banged against her knees as she walked; all the lodgers had chipped in to buy it, although 'all the lodgers' no longer included Miss Zawadska, who had transferred to BBC Drama at Evesham. So far, there had been no takers for her room; the card in the window of the Hampstead newsagent's was beginning to look rather dog-eared.

At the bus stop there was a long queue. An 88 had just drawn up, the platform already crammed, the conductress standing with one foot dangling over the edge and an arm curled round the pole. 'Room upstairs!' she shouted as people burrowed past her.

The line swayed forward. 'I can't get on there,' said an old chap with a stick, just in front of Vee. 'Want to go ahead of me?'

'No, I'll wait.'

The bus moved off again, edging into a stream of taxis.

'Be quicker to walk home,' said the old gent. 'If it wasn't for my leg, that's what I'd do.'

'War injury, is it?' asked Vee, scenting a talker, and wondering whether she was about to spend half an hour wincing at the news from Spion Kop.

'Turned me ankle dancing at the Palais.'

'Oh.' She gave him a bit of a smile. A car swerved and hooted as a green army lorry started to nose out of a side road opposite.

'*You* ever go dancing?' he asked, leaning against the lamp-post and straightening his injured leg. He had pink cheeks and thick white hair, cut very short, so that his head looked like a thistle.

'Me?' said Vee. 'No.'

'Why ever not? Youngster like you – we all need a bit of fun, don't we? Especially now.'

Vee shrugged awkwardly. A whole lifetime was wedged between the last time she'd danced and the present, though she could remember it clearly enough: she'd worn a tartan frock with a matching bow in her hair, and had accidentally kicked the girl next to her while attempting the Charleston.

'I met my wife dancing,' said the man. He tapped his red knitted scarf, like someone touching wood. 'She had the neatest pair of pins in Kentish Town. Still has.'

'That's nice,' said Vee. 'Nice thing to say.'

'She was dancing with another fellow and I went up to her and I said—' Brakes squealed and someone shouted. Vee turned her head and saw that the army lorry had pulled right out into the traffic and was swinging at speed into the wrong lane. She could see the white star on the door, she could see the driver, his face all mouth and eyes as he realized he was about to crash head-on into a taxi, and then the lorry jerked and seemed to glide sideways so that it was no longer heading for the taxi but directly towards herself. She had time to take a single step to the side. The lorry brushed gently past her coat and struck the bus stop with a muffled thud; muffled, because there was something soft between the front bumper and the pole. The soft thing folded over the bonnet, red scarf trailing.

Vee didn't faint, but the pavement bucked under her, and she had to rest a hand on the warm metal of the bonnet. Her mouth was full of saliva. She couldn't see the old man's face, just the back of his head, but the fingers of his right hand were splayed near hers – they were square-tipped, a little dirt under the nails; a gardener's hand. The thumb was trembling very slightly. She heard the steady hiss of an exhalation and the man's torso seemed to widen and flatten like dough spreading across a board. The thumb stopped twitching and someone behind her said, 'Oh God, oh God,' and Vee turned away and put a hand over her mouth. Sour liquid ran down her palm and on to the pavement.

She lost a moment or two, and then she was sitting on the kerb and a policeman was taking her name and address. 'Margery Overs,' she heard herself say (thank Heavens). 'And did you see how the accident occurred?' he asked, and if she'd been thinking straight, if she hadn't been feeling such a rag, she'd have said, 'No, I didn't, I'd turned away, I was looking in my handbag, I just heard a crash,' because that's what you did with the police, you kept your mouth shut, you never told them anything you didn't have to, but instead she nodded; instead, she said, 'I saw it all.'

'You'll have to go to the Wallace Street Station tomorrow and make a statement,' he said. 'Ask for Sergeant Bayliss.' After that, a lady from one of the shops, with a diamanté bow at her neck and purple lipstick, brought her a glass of water and offered to find a taxi, and handed over three shillings to the driver, so that Vee was borne in splendour back to the Vale of Health, which was just as well, because when she tried to get out of the cab, her legs were like rubber bands. The cabbie knocked on the door for her, and Mr Jepson came out and helped her along the path, as if she were a ninety-year-old.

'Do you have any brandy?' he asked, when she was sitting in the kitchen. 'Stupid question, I suppose.'

'I'd rather have tea.'

She watched him make it, not even protesting when he threw away the old tea-leaves and put three spoonfuls in the pot.

'Cigarette? Anything to eat?' he asked, as if he were

an usherette with a trayful of ices. She shook her head. 'Where's Noel?'

'In with Dr Parry-Jones. I think they're studying the circulatory system – I caught the word "aorta" as I passed the door. Do you want me to fetch him?'

'No, he'll only worry. I'll be all right in a minute.'

Mr Jepson gave his moustache a stroke. 'Where did it happen?' he asked.

'Near Bond Street. I'd come out of Dickins and – oh *dammit*, damn it all.' She stood, abruptly, knocking her chair back, and looking wildly around the kitchen, just in case the string bag that she had absolutely and certainly left in Oxford Street had somehow miraculously flown back home. And then she sat down again and burst into tears, something she hadn't done in a long while, and certainly never in front of a lodger.

Mr Jepson reached into a pocket and gave her a folded handkerchief, and then he poured the tea as she wiped her eyes.

'Sorry,' she said, taking a gloriously strong mouthful. 'All these bombs we've had and I've never seen a dead person before. Except in a coffin.' She thought of her father's oddly healthy appearance as he lay in his box in the front parlour; she thought of her husband, looking as if he'd never been alive. 'And the poor old chap was talking about his wife to me, before it happened. He was saying lovely things about her, how he first met her at a dance in Kentish Town, and now she'll just be finding out, I suppose . . .' Her lips trembled and she pressed her fingers to them. 'Could I have that cigarette after all?'

It struck her, as she coughed her way through the first fag she'd had in years, that Jepson wasn't looking as uncomfortable as you might expect for a man whose landlady had just wept noisily and unexpectedly in front of him.

'You do this, don't you?' she asked, with sudden realization. 'For the newspaper. You talk to people after they've seen horrible things.'

'I do on occasion, yes.'

He hesitated, and then pulled out a chair opposite her and sat as he always did, a little on the slant, so that she couldn't see the crumpled depression where his left ear had been.

She had never asked him about it; she touched a hand to her own ear. 'The Great War, was it?'

'Yes. They tried to sew it back on, but it didn't take. Still, I wasn't exactly Valentino to begin with, so . . .' He gave a twitch of a smile. He still had the slender build of so many of those grinning lads who'd marched off to war carrying packs nearly as large as themselves. He had, too, the careful, raw, guarded air of those who'd returned – a generation dropped and then carelessly mended, the pieces not quite aligning. Bits missing.

'Were you already married then?' she asked.

He looked startled. 'No. No, I met Della afterwards.' The conversation seemed suddenly to stall, and Jepson's face lost all expression, his fingers picking at themselves, his pale eyes focussed on someone who wasn't in the kitchen. *You'd think* he *was the one who'd lost a spouse*, thought Vee, and then realized that she was mixing him up with a previous lodger whose wife had gone to her aunt in Cheadle, to escape the bombs, and that Jepson had never before even mentioned a wife, and that she had undoubtedly just put her foot in it.

'Well . . .' she said, awkwardly.

'And what about you, Mrs Overs?' asked Jepson, with an obvious effort, and still looking as if he'd accidentally swallowed a lead weight. 'Where did you meet your husband?'

And now it was her turn to stall, since it was exactly the sort of question she always worried about, but never planned for. She heard herself give a false and breathy laugh – 'Ooh, that was a long time ago, wasn't it!' – and then Noel came in, thank God, and she didn't have to decide which particular lie to tell. Though it wasn't until she was giving Noel a dry summary of the accident – one that omitted her own near-miss – that she remembered tomorrow's appointment, and felt her heart trip over itself.

'Oh, I've come across Sergeant Bayliss,' said Jepson. 'He's not a bad sort.'

'What will I have to say to him?'

'Simply what you saw. He'll talk to all the witnesses, and then get a draughtsman to draw up a diagram of the scene so that they can use it in court.'

'In court?'

'It'll be a coroner's case – road traffic accidents always are.'

'But I won't have to be in court, will I?'

'Well, it's . . . it's . . .' She could see him framing the word 'likely' and then clocking her expression and changing the shape of his mouth. 'Possible,' he said.

Court. *Court.*

'So I'd have to stand up in the box and swear my name

on the Bible and—' She could feel rather than see Noel's warning look, and she took a breath, and tried to look like someone so consistently law-abiding that she'd only ever read about such things.

'If there was a white star on the door, it must have been an American lorry,' said Noel, taking the egg-box and a dish of pallid sausages out of the larder. 'And that'll be why he was driving on the wrong side of the road. Would that be manslaughter, Mr Jepson?'

'I doubt it will get that far. I've been at the court for a couple of similar incidents, and the American army look after their own.'

'What do you mean?' asked Vee, tea cup halfway to her mouth.

'It's quite likely that the driver in question will be sent out on manoeuvres, or some such, and won't turn up on the day, so that everything has to be postponed, or shelved altogether.'

'Oh. Oh, I see.' That was a bit better, then. Jepson went off somewhere and Vee sat and drank her tea, and watched Noel cracking eggs.

'Toad in the hole, is it?'

He nodded, intent on his work.

'How was your lesson with the doctor?'

'Quite interesting. Until William Harvey, the general belief was that blood moved up and down the body like a tide. That was Galen's theory – he was a Roman – and for sixteen hundred years that belief persisted, until one experiment changed everything.'

There was an abrupt rumble somewhere to the west of

the house. The floor vibrated for a second or two and from the larder came the clink of jars.

'Kilburn,' said Noel. 'Or maybe Willesden.'

'I did something stupid,' said Vee. 'I bought you that book you wanted for your birthday and then, in all the fuss, I went and left it in the street.'

Noel shrugged. 'It doesn't matter. I'll get it out of the library.'

She smiled faintly. 'You're a good boy.'

He looked up at her, rather startled, and she felt suddenly close to tears again, and this time it wasn't the fate of the old chap that was setting her off, but the nearness of her own death, because if she died now, she'd never know what would happen to Noel, and it would be like walking out of a cinema halfway through the feature, just as the plot was starting to unwind. Whatever the afterlife might be like – and a thousand chapel Sundays had still left her with no clear impression beyond general radiance and a preponderance of thrones – Vee was absolutely certain that it didn't offer a balcony view of the world below.

Noel was still looking concerned. 'Would you like me to come to the police station with you tomorrow?'

'No, thank you.'

'Are you sure?'

'Yes, I'm sure.'

'I don't mean that I'd come into the interview with you, just that I'd be there as company. Besides, I've never been to a police station, so I'd be interested in observing the procedures, and seeing how they compare to those in detective novels.'

'No.' Vee could just imagine him correcting the desk sergeant on an abstruse legal point while some drunk staggered about taking a swing at people. 'You stay here and get on with your school-work. If I have to see the coroner, you can come with me then.'

Noel cracked another egg, and examined it carefully. 'Dr Parry-Jones is going to show me how to inject a yolk-vein with vegetable dye.'

Vee closed her eyes. What were you supposed to say to that kind of remark? I mean, what was actually the right word?

'Good,' she said.

Her interview with Sergeant Bayliss was a surprisingly benign affair – almost pleasant, in fact; she was treated like a guest and given a glass of water while the sergeant asked straightforward questions and carefully transcribed her answers, and for the first time – ever – she had an inkling of why some people seemed to trust the police force. Even when he told her that she would definitely be required at the inquest, she managed not to wring her hands or let out a bleat of anguish, but instead said, 'Yes, Sergeant, I quite understand,' just like a normal person, and the weather outside – a sudden thaw, a blast of sunlight – seemed to reflect her mood. This feeling of self-congratulation lasted for at least an hour, until she returned home to find that a pipe had burst and there was water cascading down the staircase and saturating the long rug in the hall.

'It's Turkish, I think,' said Noel, pressing a foot on it and watching the liquid pool around his shoe; as a very little boy, he had traced the grids and lozenges of the pattern on to greaseproof paper. 'Mattie brought it back from Serbia.'

'And how in the world are we supposed to dry it? *How?*'

It took five of them to carry it into the cellar and drape it over two chairs. Within days, it was green with mould.

'How much would that carpet have cost?' asked Vee, still fretting over it as she sat with Noel in the kitchen on the evening of his birthday, darning while he worked at his books, a green scarf wound twice round his neck. A tenor on the wireless was wailing about the Mountains of Mourne.

'Mattie said she swapped a pair of wellingtons for it. Or maybe that was the one in the drawing room.' Noel paused over a page of Latin grammar, trying to pin down the memory. More than four years had passed since his godmother's death, and it was only in dreams, now, that he could hear the exact tone and emphasis of her voice, its buoyant swoop; what remained with him was that sense of being borne along, of seeing the world from a height, at a gallop, the horizon wide and blue.

'She wouldn't have minded about the rug,' he said. '*Tout passe, tout lasse, tout casse.*'

'And what's that mean?'

'Everything passes, everything becomes wearisome, everything breaks.'

'Cheery,' said Vee, her teeth clamped on the needle, as she turned one of his sweaters inside out. 'How's your scarf? I wasn't sure about the shade.'

'I like it. It reminds me of verdigris.'

In lieu of the lost book, she'd knitted him a present to

add to the modest pile at the breakfast table – a bar of Empire Military Chocolate from Miss Appleby (now seeing an Australian), a ring-bound notebook with a brace of sharpened pencils from Mr Jepson, and a worn copy of *Palgrave's Golden Treasury* from Mr Reddish.

Dr Parry-Jones had ordered a rat in formaldehyde for Noel to dissect at her surgery, a prospect that appeared to please him.

'Oh, there was something else,' said Vee. 'I forgot – that card on top of the dresser.'

Noel stood up and reached for it, and she realized that he'd grown. More trousers to buy.

'It came yesterday,' she said. 'Postmarked Hereford. Go on, open it.'

Noel recognized Genevieve Lumb's neat but forceful handwriting. Even the thought that she had licked the envelope was quite physically stirring.

'I'll read it later,' he said.

Avril didn't issue invitations to lunch. She didn't ask the recipient, or even beg; she *summoned.* Almost everything about her twin irritated Winnie, and this imperiousness was the annoying start to the inevitably infuriating encounter that followed, but on the other hand, the lunches were invariably expensive and delicious – Winnie would often mentally re-consume them while drifting off to sleep at night – and when weighed against Avril's presence, the scales hung almost level.

'So I've booked Canuto's for Tuesday at one,' announced Avril on the telephone.

'But how do you know I'm not on duty then?'

'Are you?'

'Well, no, as it happens. But what if I had been?'

'Couldn't you have got out of it? It's not as if you're busy at the moment, and I've got something tremendously important to tell you.'

'Of course I'm busy.'

'Well, we're all *busy*, Winnie – I'm rushed off my tiny feet – but I still don't pretend to imagine I'm so vital to the war effort that the Allies will lose if I take an hour off to go and eat roast plover followed by an ice-cream.'

'*Ice-cream?*'

'Yes, the dairy ban's been lifted and they're allowed to make it again now, didn't you know?'

'But it's snowing outside.'

'Apparently, Americans eat it all year round, whatever the weather, and Canuto's is always full of them – I only managed to get a table because of Clive. So I'll see you there, shall I?'

There was a pause.

'What flavour ice-cream?' asked Winnie.

'Custard vanilla, I think.'

Winnie arrived early; she was led downstairs by an elderly waiter and seated at a corner table next to a peeling mural of the Grand Canal. At night, Canuto's was a club, occupying the whole of the basement, but by day, a red velvet curtain was drawn across half of the room. In front of it, a pianist in a dinner jacket was giving a lacklustre account of 'Berkeley Square'.

Despite Avril's comment, there were no Americans among the diners. At the next table two Senior Ministry types, grey complected, with receding hairlines and tortoiseshell glasses, were discussing the Appian Way and eating devilled kidneys; both looked like Avril's husband, Clive – as did most of the men in the room, though none of them actually were, since Clive was currently abroad, doing something for the Foreign Office. He was a very nice man, diffident and slightly bewildered, like a staid dog who'd been taken for an unexpectedly vigorous and sustained walk. The couple had met in the basement air-raid shelter of the Ministry of Information, where Avril was employed in the publications department. 'I fell for his intellect,' she always said, not mentioning the houses in Belgravia, Norfolk and the Loire. There was no need to ask what Clive had fallen for; heads snapped round whenever Avril stalked past. They did so again now, as she tip-tapped down the stairs ahead of the waiter.

'Darling Winnie!' she called, from across the room, and the other diners simply stopped with forks halfway to their mouths. She was striking rather than beautiful – seemingly drawn with a stronger pen than everyone else. She had also, since the last time Winnie had seen her, dyed her hair red.

'What do you think?' she said, sitting down. 'Clive came back from his last trip with a packet of henna rolled in his underpants. Obviously, we mustn't speculate about where he went, but I do hope they hold another conference in North Africa.'

One of the diners on the next table was trying to fish his spoon out of his soup.

'Hello, Avril,' said Winnie, used to this ruthless annexing of attention. 'I don't really like it, to be honest. It makes you look very pale.'

'Renaissance, Clive said. Titian's *La Bella*.' She took a compact out of her bag and inspected herself for a moment or two. 'I think I should be wearing a darker shade of lipstick, though – more the colour of yours, perhaps.'

'I'm not wearing lipstick, Avril.'

'Really?'

'They're just chapped. And don't say, "It suits you."'

Avril leaned across the table and patted her hand.

'Dear old Twinnie, cross as ever. You're looking a little bit tired, if you don't mind my saying.'

'That's because I was on shift last night.' She had slept on a camp bed at the Post, and been woken at half three by an explosion so loud that she'd assumed a bomb had landed in the next street. Scrambling outside, she'd found that all was quiet, a full moon prinking the frost so that the ruined houses looked like cliffs of quartz, and then, as she'd stood listening, her breath fogging the view, there'd been another blast, this one preceded by a noise like a rifle crack, and followed by a flood of orange light above the rooftops to the east. She'd set out in that direction, and had met Doreen Hurst from Post 8 coming towards her, a torch in each hand and a hat with ear-flaps under her helmet.

'Nothing,' Doreen had said. 'Not in our sector. I don't know where they fell.'

Miles away, it had turned out – one in Stoke Newington and one in Southwark, the first landing harmlessly in a park, the second squarely on a block of municipal flats, killing twenty-two and injuring scores. There was a scientific explanation for the way the noise seemed to leap across the city, but the effect was to make the rockets feel ubiquitous, constant, inescapable. Winnie had heard yet another on her way to the restaurant – a thud that had shivered the pavement and sent every shop-window trembling so that reflections had scurried across the glass.

'So what's this important news?' she asked. She wondered if Avril was expecting, though it seemed unlikely from the look of her, a green leather belt cinched tightly around the waist of her charcoal dress. Winnie herself had missed a monthly just after Emlyn had gone off to fight, and though it had come to nothing, she sometimes speculated on what would have happened if she'd actually been pregnant. Presumably she and the child would have gone to live with her parents for the duration, and she would never have discovered that she was capable of using a broom to dislodge an incendiary from a roof gutter while leaning over a parapet with someone holding her feet – nor would she have learned how to mend a stirrup pump, or win at Shove Ha'penny, or instruct a hall-ful of middle-aged men on 'The Duties of the Incident Officer', or to carefully collect in a bloodied canvas bucket the shreds and wedges of what had recently been a person.

'Let's order first,' said Avril. 'It's on me, obviously.'

'Thanks.' Winnie, currently bringing home two pounds five shillings a week, had long ago swallowed her pride on that score.

Disappointingly, there was no plover, so she settled for ravioli followed by fried whitebait, her stomach giving an audible groan of anticipation.

'Go on, then,' she said. 'What is it?'

Avril pursed her lips, enjoying the moment. 'I've written a book,' she said.

Winnie had to adjust her expression, from one of cynical expectation to one of genuine surprise. So many of Avril's triumphs were not only irritating and apparently unmerited, but seemed framed specifically in order to annoy – 'Mr Carson told me confidentially that the reason that I was so bad at secretarial work was that I was too clever and that was why he was going to promote me' – but this was a concrete achievement.

'A book? You never told me you were writing one!'

'I don't tell you everything.'

'Oh yes, you do, usually in the most tremendous detail.'

'Nonsense.'

'Then how do I know about Clive's birthmark? It's not anything I would ever have *asked* you, but you told me anyway and now I can't look at him without thinking about it.'

'I think it's probably better to tell people too many things than sit like a total clam-shell, refusing to give any details of your private life at all.'

'Are you saying that's what I do?'

'Yes, absolutely. And if you bottle things up, they end up fermenting inside you.'

'I don't bottle things up. I just don't tell *you*.'

Winnie's voice was shrill enough to turn the heads of the diners at the next table. She took a hasty sip of wine. Every conversation with Avril was like this – a series of skirmishes interspersed with the odd, fragile truce. Their relationship now was almost indistinguishable from the one they'd had at ten, an unfriendly rivalry in which the balance of power was always Avril's, though over the years, surreptitious kicks and deliberate sneaking had been replaced, on Avril's side, with kindly condescension, and on Winnie's with utter recalcitrance.

She could see her ravioli approaching. 'So, go on, tell me about this book,' she said, gripping her cutlery.

Avril lit a cigarette. 'Do you remember the pamphlet I wrote about women at work?'

'The one you interviewed me for?' It was quite a pleasant memory: Avril sitting listening to her, making notes, refraining from criticism or contradiction, asking questions and then actually allowing Winnie to answer them rather than vaulting in with her own replies. The written account (succinct and surprisingly accurate) had appeared between that of a policewoman and a member of a barrage-balloon crew. 'Aren't you going to eat?' she asked, her mouth full of pasta. 'This is delicious.'

'In just a minute.'

'So did the MoI ask you to do a longer version?'

'It's not actually a Ministry publication. It's a novel.'

'A novel? What's the title?'

'*Tin Helmet*.'

'A *war* novel?'

'Yes. Of sorts. I was at a party last year and a man from Hatchards started saying that there were plenty of good first-hand accounts of the Blitz, but thin pickings fictionally. Have you read Greene's *Ministry of Fear*?'

'No.'

'Oh, it's all spies and spivs. Very good on the raids, but nothing with any soul or depth. So I thought, *Why not give it a go?* After all, when my short story was published in *Isis*, the editor said the prose was both luminous and excoriating.'

Avril seemed to be smoking with tremendous concentration, knocking off the ash with such assiduousness that a plug of smouldering tobacco fell on to the table. Winnie automatically doused it with a splash of wine.

'You've made a hole now,' she said, peering at the mess. 'Someone will have to bleach and then darn that.'

'The book's about a female air-raid warden,' said Avril. 'Now don't get hold of the wrong end of the stick,' she added, as Winnie's head jerked up. 'It's a novel, it's not about you.'

'It's not about me, but it's about a female air-raid warden? How many other female air-raid wardens do you know?'

'It's a novel, Winnie. The character is fictional.'

'So you keep saying, but you seem awfully nervous about something.'

'Well, I was worried that I'd get exactly this reaction,' said Avril, lighting another cigarette. Her soup was beginning to congeal. 'Obviously, I drew on your notes, and on what you've told me over the years. I wouldn't want to be inaccurate.'

'Are you going to let me read it?'

'Yes, of course.'

'Aside from anything else, I'd like to double-check all the facts.'

'Actually, Clive's friend Arnold has already done that. He's the ARP regional commander for Westminster.'

'Oh.'

'He even helped to find me a publisher.' She was reaching down into her bag as she spoke.

'You've found a publisher?'

Avril straightened up. 'Here we are!' she said, brightly, holding up a small black book. 'It's out just after Christmas.'

Winnie stared at her twin. It was unprecedented for Avril to have delayed the announcement of such thrilling news; when Clive had proposed by moonlight, she'd sent Winnie a telegram *that evening.*

'This is your very own copy, Twinnie,' said Avril, avoiding her eye. 'Do take it.'

It was a typical wartime edition, meanly bound and lacking a dust jacket. Winnie looked at the red lettering on the spine. 'Avril Bridge?'

'We decided that Clive's surname is too distinctive. Some of the plot is quite near the knuckle.'

Winnie opened the cover and read the brief synopsis.

Belinda Holdsworth, raised in a comfortable London home, has, in her twenty-one years, encountered little to disturb or enlighten her. Her route from naivety to a bitter understanding of the facts of love and war is the subject of this tense and important novel.

'Tense and important,' she repeated, unwillingly impressed. 'Is that a quote from someone?'

'No,' said Avril, 'I wrote that, but I'm getting some awfully good reviews as well. *Lilliput* magazine says that I'm the first fresh fictional voice of the war, and *New Thought* says that my prose feels like an inoculation of truth.'

'Blimey.' Winnie started to leaf through the book. 'Do you know what the phrase "inoculation of truth" reminds me of?'

'No, what?'

Winnie straightened her shoulders and tuned her voice to a foghorn. ' "Say not the needle is the most proper pen for women." '

'I beg your pardon?'

'Don't you remember? It was one of Miss Simpkin's quotes when we were in the Amazons. Together with "Abused patience turns to fury." '

'I'd forgotten,' said Avril. 'Don't read the book now, though – let's not waste time when we could be talking. How's Emlyn?'

'Oh, he's—' Winnie frowned and turned back a page. 'Binnie,' she said, staring at the top paragraph. '*Binnie?*'

'It's short for Belinda.'

' "Binnie, for God's sake, come back to bed." '

'No, don't read it out loud.'

' "A flare lit the room through the uncurtained window and an illusive surge of green light, unsounding, sentient, filled the space." '

'Please don't.' Avril reached for the book, but Winnie leaned away from her, still reading, her tone incredulous.

'"Roderick's profile had an ancient blankness, as of a frieze in a torch-lit passageway. Binnie turned, silently, knelt on the mattress and slid her cushioned form alongside his. 'If we died now there'd be no more pretence,' she said. She imagined their two bodies fused by violence into one melded, bloodied being, ensexed eternally."'

Winnie caught the eye of the couple at the next table, both listening avidly. 'Are you enjoying it?' she asked. 'It's about me.' The man turned pink.

'Twinnie—'

Winnie put the book on her lap, and resumed eating, very fast.

'Twinnie, it's absolutely not about you.'

'Except we've got exactly the same name, almost.'

'That's just a coincidence. Her lover's the only one who calls her that.'

'She's fat.'

'She's not.'

'So "cushioned" means "thin", does it?'

'No, it means "voluptuous". And she's having an affair with a married man, which I'm sure you're not.'

'How do you know?'

'Well—'

'You *don't* know, because, as you pointed out, I don't tell you anything, and thank God I don't. Do you want that soup, because I'm not staying for the second course?'

Without receiving an answer, she swapped the bowl with her plate, and started spooning up the lukewarm contents.

'The thing is,' she said, between mouthfuls, 'whatever you say, everyone will think it's about me.'

'Twinnie—'

'Don't call me that, please. I must have asked you about fifty times not to. And this isn't actually very nice soup. I'm glad I'm not paying for it.' She dropped the spoon with a clatter and stood up, the book in one hand and a certain amount of *consommé de bœuf* on her sweater. Avril looked up at her with amused wariness, as if observing a drunk on the Tube.

'I wanted to tell you that Clive's going to host a little New Year's Eve party to celebrate the publication,' she said. 'I do hope you'll come, and I also hope you'll read it, and find out that there's really nothing to get so annoyed about.'

Winnie's snort made even the pianist falter. Resisting the urge to lean across the table and slap her sister, she walked away, the feeling of justified outrage propelling her up the stairs and out of the restaurant, and then bathetically back into it again, since she'd forgotten her coat and hat.

A wind like an Alaskan river was sweeping along the road and she leaned into it, re-running the conversation in a vehement mutter and this time trouncing Avril with a series of crisp responses that left her twin both defeated and apologetic. 'I've been so dreadfully thoughtless,' said Avril, tears in her eyes. 'At last – something we can agree on!' rapped out Winnie, rather like Gertrude Lawrence in *Private Lives*. 'Yes, Avril has the cruellest *mouth*,' she added, cleverly, turning her head to see the reaction of the other diners and instead meeting the alarmed eye of a small boy pushing a pram.

'Hello,' she said, attempting to rearrange her expression

into something more friendly. 'I hope your baby's wrapped up warm.' He broke into a wordless sprint and passed her at speed; the pram was full of coal.

'Oh, damn,' she said, recalling the dreary agenda for the meeting she would be having with the sector fire-chief, later in the afternoon. The inadequate night supervision of the local emergency coal dump was the second item, preceded by a discussion on what to do about the static water tanks in the district – they were all frozen solid and local children *would* keep breaking through the wire and sliding on them. And then there was next month's shift schedule to draw up, and a letter to write to the council about shelter sanitation, and she could feel her adult-self reassembling, the pieces bolting together, armour covering the raging, skinless goblin she became when she was with Avril. 'Just laugh at her,' Winnie's friend Elsie had once urged. 'Laugh right in her silly mush, tell her you don't care what she thinks of you.'

'But I do care,' Winnie had said. 'That's the trouble.'

It wasn't until she was standing on the Tube platform, skimming through *Tin Helmet* on the look-out for egregious mistakes, that she suddenly remembered her encounter in the ruins of Falcon Road with the pleasingly odd boy who had turned out to live in Miss Simpkin's house – she owed him a letter about that church carving, now that she came to think of it.

Of course, *there* was someone who had never cared about the opinions of others: Winnie pictured Miss Simpkin in the middle of Hampstead Heath, eye-glasses askew as she demonstrated the basics of ju-jitsu, utterly unruffled by the stares of passing strollers. Yes, that was the way to do it. Bold. Lofty. Unafraid.

❧

A man was selling bunches of holly in the street outside St Pancras Coroner's Court, and berries were scattered across the pitted ice. Vee was unpleasantly reminded of the previous week, when she had slipped on the pavement outside the grocer's and dropped the tiny jar of maraschino cherries for which she'd just paid six shillings (*six shillings!*); the glass-strewn contents had looked like the obscene aftermath of an explosion. She'd been planning to save the cherries for the Christmas dinner table, to go with the pink blancmange that Noel had decided on for dessert, but now he'd just have to make do with evaporated milk.

'That holly was sixpence a bunch,' said Noel, as they followed the usher downstairs. 'It's a pity that the tree in our garden is male.'

'I beg your pardon?'

'Only the female trees bear fruit. Hollies are dioecious, you see.'

'You'll need to wait through here,' said the usher, indicating a door. He had pince-nez and the pursed expression of someone who's just chipped a tooth. 'Obviously, the boy can't go into the courtroom with you.'

'He's just here to keep me company,' said Vee. 'Ooh, it's *warm*,' she said, opening the door.

'It's next to the boiler-house. The conveniences are through there and to the left, should you need them.'

With the door closed, it was as balmy as July. Vee sat on one of the long benches against the wall and took off her gloves.

'How are you feeling?' asked Noel.

'I'd be better if you didn't keep asking me.'

'Do you want a cigarette?'

'What?'

'I brought some with me, in case you needed to stay calm.'

'You didn't!'

He grinned, and slid a packet of Woodbines out of his coat pocket.

'I'm all right for the time being,' she said. 'Anyway, they might make me cough in court.'

'I had a talk with Mr Jepson, and he said most likely all that will happen is that your statement will be read out, and you'll be asked if it's correct. The coroner or the counsel for the relatives may ask a supplementary question or two, but that should be it.'

'Good.'

'It won't be like being up in front of the magistrate.'

'*Shhhh.*'

'There's no one else in here.'

'Even still.'

'I just mean that any questions will simply be to elicit information. You're not in any personal trouble.'

'I know that. I know. It's just . . . just . . .' And she was back in the St Albans magistrates' court, the oddly greenish light filtering through window-glass so ancient that the view of the rooftops seemed to ripple. During her four visits there – three for non-payment of rates and one for alleged shop-theft – Vee had attempted to keep her gaze fixed on the wooden roses in the panelling just above the bench, so that she wouldn't have to see the expressions of contempt. One old goat – a retired surgeon – had called her 'a very tiresome woman', and a lady magistrate with a car and a chauffeur waiting outside, and a hairstyle that looked like a zinc cauliflower, had suggested that Vee 'simply didn't *try* to make an honest living', which was unfair and only partially true, given that she had actually been working in Woolworths at the time she was supposed to have swiped a scarf from their silks counter. She'd avoided a sentence for that one only because the hearing had come directly after lunch and one of the magistrates had audibly fallen asleep during the shop-walker's statement, before waking with a grunt of 'yes, please' while holding out an invisible wine glass to an imaginary waiter. There'd been laughter from the public gallery and the case had been brought to a hasty close; Vee had got off with a warning, lucky for her.

'And of course,' said Noel, 'there's the essential difference that this time all you have to do is tell the truth.'

She gave him a look.

'I'm not being facetious. Honestly. Honestly, Mar.' He sounded genuinely contrite.

'You just read your book,' she said, and he took out something with diagrams in it.

Of course, she'd been Vera Sedge back then, and not Mrs Overs, a respectable Hampstead landlady in a good coat – 'good' being a relative term, of course, for something bought second-hand in 1936, but she'd recently re-lined the worn collar with stiffened navy-blue velvet cut from an old evening bag she'd found in a cupboard, and had used the rest of the bag to make a new hat-band. When she'd inspected herself in the hall mirror before leaving, she'd been satisfied by the general impression. You'd trust that coat.

She leaned her head against the wall, wishing she'd brought her knitting, and the next thing she knew, the usher was calling her name and she'd risen in a fluster, dropping a glove.

'No need to get up,' he said. 'There's been a delay. The principal witness still hasn't arrived.'

'Oh, hasn't he?' As she sat down again, she glanced at Noel and saw him discreetly cross his fingers. 'Would that be the lorry driver?' she asked.

'Yes, the American soldier. Sir Bentley's *very* annoyed.' The usher spoke with a certain satisfaction, as if there'd been a sweepstake as to the exact degree of the coroner's annoyance, and he personally had put a half-crown on 'very'. 'This is far from the first time that this has occurred,' he added. 'Sir Bentley put in an official complaint only last week, but clearly to no avail.'

'Oh dear.' Vee tried to look disapproving. 'So do I need to stay?'

The usher lifted his watch from his waistcoat pocket and checked the time.

'Sir Bentley has said he will wait until eleven before postponing, so that's another twenty minutes.'

'Where does that leave me?' called a man sitting at the

other end of the room, who must have turned up while Vee was dozing. 'I'm a witness in the McCromarty case.'

'I'm afraid I can't tell you,' said the usher, 'though clearly it won't begin on time.'

'I've got to get back to work.'

'Could you telephone your employer?'

'No.'

'Why not?'

'Because I don't have one. Got my own window-cleaning business.'

'I'll endeavour to keep you informed,' said the usher, actually sliding out of the room during the final word of the sentence.

'*Endeavour*,' repeated the man, derisively, folding his arms. He was fifty or sixty, suited and newly shaven for the court, his skin as mottled as if he used a scouring pad instead of soap. 'This is a lark, I don't think.'

'At least it's warm,' said Vee. 'This weather must be terrible on your hands, in your line of work.'

'It is, yes.' He sounded gratified. 'I used to put paraffin oil on them every night, but you can't get it now. Mac – that's what we used to call McCromarty – he swore by goose grease, not that you can get that neither.'

'Was he a friend of yours, then?'

'I knew him. I can't say he was a friend.'

'Enemy?' suggested Noel.

'*Enemy?* No, we was in the same trade, we worked the same patch, didn't we, so he had his houses and I had mine.'

'Rivals, then.'

'Yeah. Rivals. But friendly.'

'So what happened to him?' asked Noel.

'Well, that's the question, isn't it? What happened to him?' The man folded his arms and leaned back, weighty with knowledge. 'That . . . is . . . the . . . question,' he repeated, nodding a few times.

'And what's the answer?' asked Noel, who still didn't know how to play along with these little manly games.

'Go on, do tell us,' said Vee, encouragingly.

The man turned slightly, so that he was definitely addressing Vee rather than Noel.

'Well, I clean at four, six, eight, fourteen and twenty Wintergreen Terrace every other Wednesday, though it should be every week now, there's that much filth in the air. We have a joke about it – there's either no windows, or you can't see through the ones you've got. Anyhow, Mac does the other side of the street on the same day, and then my next call is Myddleton Square and he goes on to Fairleigh Crescent. So on this particular day, I finished ahead of him, and I'd only walked a hundred yards when there was a bang and a whoosh and I was face-down in a hole.'

'A rocket?' asked Vee.

He nodded. 'It landed smack in the centre of the road just at the end of Wintergreen Terrace. Water-main burst, all the roofs off, but no one dead. They *thought*.'

'McCromarty was underneath it,' said Noel.

'Oh, so you know the whole story, do you?' said the man. 'Then you carry on and finish it, sonny.'

'Sorry, it was just a fictive prediction,' said Noel, stiffly.

'He doesn't mean it,' said Vee, as if apologizing for the village idiot. Noel opened his book again.

'So go on,' said Vee. 'I'm on the edge of my seat. Why's it come to court?'

'Well, that's the nub, isn't it?' he said, slightly mollified. 'They didn't find no definite bits of him so they can't prove he's dead. And if they can't prove it, then his wife's not a widow and she can't get the insurance, or the pension, so what they do is weigh up all the evidence, such as who saw him last – which was me – and where he was headed, which was Fairleigh Crescent. It's called the balance of probabilities. Of course, there's another side to it – they want to stop people skipping off.'

'Skipping off?' repeated Vee.

'Hearing a bomb and taking the opportunity of doing a flit. Say McCromarty didn't get on with his old lady, and had a young lady somewhere else, or say he owed money, or he done something he shouldn't have and the police was after him – he might think, *This is my chance. If I disappear now, everyone will think I've copped it.* And then he might call himself another name and start again in another town. There's all sorts of fiddles they have to look out for.'

Vee didn't trust her own voice; instead she cranked her features into a facsimile of innocent interest. Beside her, Noel seemed to have turned to stone.

In the momentary silence, they all heard the noise of fast and heavy footsteps approaching, and a blare of overlapping voices.

'—and he said he couldn't do that because he did not have a snow shovel, and I said—'

'Is it that door, or is it the one on the left?'

'—that cannot be called snow, that is powdered sugar, and what you need, sir, is a *spoon*.'

'Americans,' muttered Noel, as the door opened.

A huge figure in a great-coat entered first, head almost scraping the lintel, felt cap rammed on dark hair, big features in a flushed face, and he was followed, like a perfect punchline, by a short, neat, colourless man in officer's uniform.

'Wrong door,' said the second. He disappeared again, and the first raised his hand apologetically and said, 'Please excuse us for the disturbance!' at the sort of volume that you might expect from someone hailing a taxi during a violent rainstorm, and as he turned to go again, Vee realized, with absolute certainty, that he was the man she'd seen through the windscreen of the lorry. The door closed.

She swayed slightly, as if caught by a gust of wind, and she felt Noel put a hand on her forearm. 'You'll be fine,' he said.

It was another forty minutes before Vee was called into court, though it felt like a week, and by that time, her mouth was so dry that when she confirmed in front of the coroner that her name was Margery Olive Overs (so help her God), every word was accompanied by little creaks and snaps, as if her lips were made of leather.

For the first time, she learned the dead man's name: Frederick Embleton. He'd been seventy-two, a retired plumber, and his wife was in the courtroom with a grown-up daughter on either side of her. The old lady was dry-eyed, as upright as a pea-stick, and the daughters were hunched and weeping; Vee could hear their occasional shuddering breaths under the voice of Sergeant Bayliss, who was reading out her own statement in a steady monotone.

'"I heard a shout and I looked over and saw the lorry turn left out of the side road opposite but instead of going into the nearest lane, it went right across the road and then turned, so it was going the wrong way, against the traffic. A taxi was coming straight towards it. The lorry braked and then seemed to skid. It went off diagonally and pinned the gentleman between the front bumper and the bus stop."'

One of the daughters gave a sob, and Vee looked away, trying to dispel the awful image of Mr Embleton's last moments. The courtroom was nearly empty: a single reporter in the back row, and a stenographer working at a desk to one side. The two Americans were sitting as far away from Embleton's family as they possibly could, the driver of the lorry looking down at his enormous boots, and the officer staring directly at Vee. She felt another jolt of nerves.

The coroner was making a series of notes; for a minute or two there was no noise except the soft scrape of his pen, and then he looked up at Vee. She knew the type: a homely potato-face and a gaze like a paring-knife.

'So, Mrs Overs, would you say you had a clear view of the accident?'

'Yes, quite clear.'

'Could you speak up a little, so that our stenographer can hear?'

'Sorry. Yes, it was clear.'

'And how near to the deceased were you?'

'I was next to him.'

'Could I remind you to speak up, Mrs Overs?'

'Yes, sorry. I was right next to him – I was talking to him just before it happened. If I hadn't stepped away, I would have been hit myself.'

'And are you certain of the sequence of events in your statement: first the lorry made the complete turn into the wrong lane, then it braked, and then it skidded?'

Was she certain? She'd related the memory so many times that it now had all the lustre and detail of a scene in a film, whereas at the time it had simply been a sliding blur.

'I think so,' she said, suddenly less confident.

'You think so?'

'Yes.'

'I see.'

He made another note. 'And Sergeant Bayliss, can you assure me that efforts were made to find the taxi driver in question?'

'Yes, Your Honour. We made enquiries at all the West End ranks, and left a wall poster appealing for information at the nearest cabmen's shelters, but no one came forward.'

'It's a great pity. A crowded street, and we have only a single witness. Quite an indictment of public spirit, I'd say.'

Yes, thought Vee, *because who wouldn't want to spend a freezing December morning dragging themselves halfway across London in order to be treated like a criminal, for no pay?*

'Very well, so be it. Thank you, Mrs Overs – no, don't leave quite yet. Captain Van Steen?'

The coroner looked over at the American officer, who stood up and straightened his jacket before walking in a leisurely fashion towards the witness box.

'Captain Van Steen is counsel for Corporal O'Mahoney, the driver of the lorry,' said the coroner, to Vee. 'He wishes to ask you one or two questions, on behalf of the Army of the United States of America. Captain Van Steen, in this country, we address the witness from the counsel's stand.'

'I'm sorry, Your Honour.' The captain turned, but not before he'd got so close to Vee that she'd caught a whiff of his shaving soap. He had pale blue eyes and hair so blond and close-cut that it was almost invisible. He returned to his seat and stood in front of it, hands clasped across his stomach, just above his belt.

'Mrs Overs, I imagine that it must have been a very frightening experience for you?' His voice was unexpectedly soft, and his accent was strange to her, neither Gene Kelly nor Gary Cooper. *Ah ee-magine. Ver' fratt-nin.*

'Yes,' she said.

'And it must all have happened very fast?' *Ver' fay-ust.*

'Yes.'

'And it was a very cold day, I understand, and the road was very icy?'

'Yes, it was.'

The coroner made an impatient gesture. 'Captain Van Steen, *could* I request that you confine yourself to questions to which we don't already know the answer? As I'm sure you're aware, we are already running nearly an hour behind time, due to your late arrival, inadvertent though the delay may have been.'

'I'm sorry, Your Honour, I was just trying to set the scene.'

'Consider it set.'

'Yes, Your Honour.' The pale blue eyes moved back to Vee again, but the brisk exchange had had an oddly calming effect on her; the American's knuckles had been rapped, but hers were unscathed. She almost wished that Noel had been allowed in, so that he could see how well she was conducting herself.

'Could you tell me then, Mrs Overs, precisely what you were doing when you heard a shout.'

'I was talking to the gentleman.'

'To the deceased?'

'Yes.'

'Talking about what? Can you recall?'

'Well, we were talking about . . . about his wife, as a matter of fact. He was telling me that he'd hurt his ankle out dancing at the Palais, and that he'd first met Mrs Embleton at a dance in Kentish Town. It was a nice conversation – a happy one.'

She dared to glance at the family. Now all three women were crying.

'So you were occupied in discussing this when you heard the shout.'

'Yes, but then I looked up straight away and I saw a . . .' She hesitated, trying to remember what the Yanks called lorries – they had a different word for them. Wagons, was it?

'*Vee*,' said Captain Van Steen, clearly and firmly.

The world seemed to stop, but momentum flung her

onwards so that she lurched towards the front of the witness box and stuck out a hand. It clapped against the wood with a hollow boom.

'It's Mrs Overs,' she said, her voice a startled gabble. 'Mrs Margery Olive Overs.'

Van Steen's head was cocked, his expression that of someone who'd just heard a dog miaowing. Out of the corner of her eye, Vee could see the coroner lean forward.

'Are you feeling unwell, Mrs Overs?'

Unwell? She felt as if she were just about to drop dead. She looked from one man to the other. What was *going on*? Was it a trap of some kind? How did the American know her real name? Was she about to be arrested for impersonation?

'I'm all right,' she said from a mouth full of sand.

'You were telling us,' continued Captain Van Steen, 'that you saw a vehicle.'

Vee-hicle.

He pronounced the word with the emphasis all on the first syllable.

VEE-hicle.

Oh, for heaven's sake, thought Vee, revelation dawning. She heard herself make a noise like the starting wheeze of a set of bagpipes, half relief, half hysterical laughter at the absurdity of her mistake, and she brought up a hand to her lips to choke it off.

'Mrs Overs, do you need a glass of water, or a brief adjournment?' asked the coroner. 'I do hope not,' he added, pointedly. Vee shook her head, though the courtroom seemed to be gently rotating, with the Embletons and the

Americans bobbing up and down, as if on a merry-go-round.

'It was a lorry,' she said, between her fingers. 'A . . . a . . . *wagon*.'

'Could I remind you to speak clearly, Mrs Overs.'

'Do you mean a truck?' asked the captain.

'Yes, an army truck. And it turned and skidded.'

The captain seemed to stiffen.

'It turned. And it skidded.' He repeated the words slowly, as if they had tremendous significance.

'Yes, and it braked. It braked as well as skidded, it did both, I saw it do both.' Words seemed to be spraying out of her mouth, almost at random.

'And *before* it skidded, had the truck completed the turn, or was it still in the process of turning?'

'Captain Van Steen, we have already been through this sequence of events,' said the coroner.

The American ducked his head, deferentially. 'I beg your pardon, sir, but I believe this sequence is the crux of the matter, it being the only point on which the driver and the witness differ. And if the witness is not entirely certain about it, and I submit that it appears to be the case that she is *not* entirely certain, then I'm sure you'll understand the need to go through it one more time.'

'Oh, very well, then. Mrs Overs, could I ask you to concentrate extremely hard on what Captain Van Steen is about to ask you?'

She nodded, aware that the eyes of everyone in the court were fixed upon her. Even the lorry driver was looking up now. He had the wide, loose, black-eyed face of a mastiff.

'So Mrs Overs,' said the captain. 'What exactly happened after you saw the VEE-hicle begin to turn?' And there it was again, that misplaced syllable flying across the room and knocking her off course so that her answer was a hopeless fumble of contradictions in which the lorry either skidded, turned or braked before either braking, turning or skidding, and even as her mouth moved, she was doubting her own words. It was like recounting a fever dream, the images splintering and dissolving. Had she even been in Oxford Street in the first place?

'Thank you, Mrs Overs,' said the captain, interrupting her.

'. . . I *think*,' she heard herself add, in a final flourish of self-doubt.

'Thank you,' he repeated, sounding genuinely grateful.

'You may step down, Mrs Overs,' said the coroner, not sounding grateful at all.

The usher gestured her to the exit, and as Vee passed the three Embletons, the old lady gave her a pale nod, a tiny flexion of the features that was perhaps an attempt at a smile, and Vee didn't know what to do with her own face – whether to offer sympathy or apology – so she mouthed, 'I'm sorry,' which covered both.

Noel clapped his book shut when he saw her.

'What's wrong?' he asked.

She kept walking towards the outer door, and he hurried to catch up with her. The hall outside was patterned with wet footprints, and she could see a thin, icy snowfall rattling against the lobby window, like rice at a cheap wedding.

'I think I made a fool of myself,' she said, putting on her gloves. 'Not for the first time.'

'Did you tell the truth?'

'I tried,' she said. 'But it's not nearly as easy as you'd think – one of the Yanks was badgering me about what I'd seen, he was going on and on, and then for a second I thought he said . . . well, I'll tell you all about it on the way to the bus stop. Knowing you, you'll think it's funny.'

Noel opened the door, and snow blew into his face. 'I'm just going outside and may be some time,' he said, cryptically, pulling up his green scarf to cover his nose and mouth, and she followed him into the street, ducking a little as the cold wind hit her. He was almost tall enough to shield her from the weather and she shouted the vee-hicle story over his shoulder as they walked towards Kingsway, and sensed, rather than heard, his laughter.

'The Americans will be pleased, anyway,' he said.

'Why?'

'Because I expect the driver's story was that he'd started to turn correctly before accidentally skidding across both lanes, and since you're the only witness to say otherwise . . .'

'You mean that he'll end up getting away with it because of me?'

'Probably.'

She didn't quite know how she felt about that. 'I suppose, either way, it wasn't deliberate,' she said.

'But it was careless. If I waved a kitchen knife without

looking and accidentally killed Mr Reddish, would that be my fault? And should I be punished for it?'

'If you did it when he was halfway through a poem, I'd give you a prize.'

Well, she had done her utmost, she thought – though it seemed that her utmost had been, as ever, inadequate. And then she checked her stride, her whole body suddenly suffused with a glorious slackness, an unknotting that was almost spiritual ('Burst Satan's bonds, oh God of might!') because the ordeal was over now. Other people might eulogize about love at first sight or joy in the morning but, personally, she didn't know of any feeling more wonderful than that of sheer relief – the trap avoided, the snare broken. She'd got away with it again. Even though this time, of course, she hadn't actually done anything wrong.

The cataclysm occurred three days later, on a viciously cold and sunny afternoon.

Noel had spent the morning at Dr Parry-Jones's surgery in Finchley, dissecting the embalmed rat that she'd ordered for his birthday. It had actually been rather less interesting than he'd anticipated, but then the same applied to most of Dr Parry-Jones's lessons. She taught him the sciences one fact at a time – cementing a straight and unvarying pathway, along which they progressed at a steady pace. There was thoroughness to her method, but no excitement or spontaneity; it made him ache for the way that Mattie had unfolded knowledge like a vivid map, showing him a dozen routes to every destination. Nevertheless, he found occasional, comfortable echoes of his godmother in the doctor's presence: the large, blunt-nailed hands with their shiny knuckles, the coiled and plaited white hair, the knee-creaks, the deliberation it took to rise from a chair.

Noel and the rat had been placed in a small, windowless room – a makeshift pharmacy adjoining the consulting room, and containing a spirit stove, a pestle and mortar, a set of scales and a padlocked cupboard. While Dr Parry-Jones had been seeing patients, Noel had worked from the diagrams in a brittle-leafed textbook. He had measured the length of the gut (two feet, seven and a quarter inches from mouth to anus) and dissected the heart, flushing out the dark sludge to reveal the neatness of the four chambers. He had also sketched the lungs, weighed the liver and failed totally to find the spleen. The rat's eyes had been partially open, its expression one of understandable disbelief.

Far more interesting than rodent viscera had been the odd snatches of speech seeping under the door. He'd tried not to be prurient – had actually stuffed his fingers in his ears a couple of times – but despite this, the hoarse weeping of one woman had cut through: '. . . he *promised* he'd be careful, he promised, he promised. Oh God, what will I ever tell my husband . . . ?' Dr Parry-Jones's answer had not been audible.

'Your initial cut has a distinct slant,' she said afterwards, inspecting the hollow carcass. 'I wonder if you suffer from astigmatism. When did you last see an optician?'

'I can't remember,' said Noel, who had never seen one.

Mattie had trusted her own judgement in all matters political, educational and medical, and Vee rigorously avoided talking to anyone at all in authority, just in case they wrongfooted her with a trick question such as 'What is your name?'

'I've noticed that you've recently had a growth spurt, which can accentuate minor ocular irregularities. But apart from that' – the doctor peered at the cluster of organs laid out like a Lilliputian butcher's display – 'you've done quite well. Where is the spleen?'

'I must have vented it,' said Noel. There was no change of expression on the doctor's face beyond a slight crease of puzzlement. 'I don't know,' he amended, rather feebly.

'Perhaps you should think about studying medicine,' said Dr Parry-Jones as he helped her to clear up, swabbing the marble counter-top with disinfectant. 'You have both the brain and the stomach for it.' Noel mentally filed the suggestion next to 'architectural historian'.

On the way back to Hampstead, the combination of Jeyes Fluid and formaldehyde meant that he had the front seat of the bus to himself. The morning frost had held hard, though a strip had melted along the very tops of the hedges, and the sight of this prompted Noel to ring the bell two stops early, and alight at Winnington Road. The official entrance to the nine-hole Hampstead golf course was halfway down it, but Noel took his usual route, walking brazenly along the side passage of a house called The Cedars, and squeezing between a fence post and a tree. He emerged into a crystalline world, every twig and bramble feathery with hoar frost, the grass of the fairway squeaking underfoot. A single golfer was visible in the far distance, teeing up on the third.

Noel kept to the sunlit parts of the course, his gaze on the ground. Almost immediately he spotted a ball at the edge of the rough, its skull-cap of ice newly melted. It was greenish-grey, old but intact, and he pocketed it and carried on looking, kneeling to grope around the familiar hollows at the base of a beech, and to prise the ice from a half-thawed rivulet. He'd found another two by the time he'd reached the solitary golfer.

'Available for purchase,' said Noel, holding out a ball.

'Is it, indeed?' The man looked at it speculatively. 'How much?'

'Six shillings.'

'Oh, don't be ridiculous.'

Noel nodded and turned away.

'No, no, wait a moment.'

The man was already groping for his wallet. He was wearing a Russian fur hat, dewed with condensation, and a leather coat, a muffler at the neck. 'Do you just have the one?'

'Three, altogether.'

'I'll give you ten bob for them.'

'No, the total for three is eighteen shillings.'

'Don't be cute. I'm bargaining.'

'And I'm selling golf balls at six shillings apiece. You're welcome to buy them elsewhere.'

'Yes, very amusing, you know quite well that they're not available.' The man took off a glove and picked out two notes and a handful of coins. 'I've been jewed, no doubt. Why aren't you at school?' he asked, stowing the balls in his golf bag.

'Why aren't you at work?' countered Noel, walking rapidly away, the money crackling in his pocket. Vee would be tickled pink.

He arrived home to find a lorry parked outside the house – an American Army truck, grey-green, the cab empty, the engine still ticking. A tarpaulin was stretched and roped over a large and irregular load, and across the tailgate someone had painted a life-sized reclining blonde woman in a very short skirt, her stocking tops fully visible. The words 'IDLIN' IVY' were written beneath her.

The driver was sitting in the kitchen.

'Oh, Noel!' said Vee, turning as he came in through the scullery door. 'This is Corporal O'Mahoney.' She looked strange, her mouth relaxed, almost as if she'd just been laughing, her face flushed. It was a moment before Noel could pull his gaze away from her, and look instead at the baggy Hercules on the other side of the table.

'Hey there!' said the American, holding up a hand as if he were a traffic policeman, and then, in the same breath, continuing with an anecdote, his speech rapid and slightly hoarse: '—so that's when they heard footsteps outside the storeroom and then the major opened the door and there's Lonnie standing on a chair, holding the two-pound can of corned beef, and he snaps a salute with the same hand, and knocks himself out cold!'

Vee gasped, her expression that of a child at a pantomime.

'Call me Mario,' said the American, reaching over to Noel, hand outstretched. He was forty or thereabouts, with a large nose that someone had hit at some point, curly dark hair and eyes the colour of prunes. 'Good to meet you. This lady says you're in charge of the cookhouse.'

'Look what Corporal O'Mahoney brought us,' said Vee.

'Mario,' corrected the corporal.

'*Mario*,' repeated Vee. She swept a hand towards what looked like a shrine on the dresser – a carton of cigarettes topped by a bunch of bananas and flanked by two tins of golden syrup. '*And* this,' added Vee, gesturing towards a brown paper bag on the table. 'You'll never guess what's in it. Dried cherries! Take one!'

The cherry looked like something you'd prise off the sole of a shoe, and tasted like manna. Noel took two more.

'Good?' asked Mario.

Noel nodded.

'Those cherries were picked, dried and sent across the ocean by my own mother, who is afraid that I will starve to death unless she can personally cook for me three times a day. In fact, it would come as no surprise to me if she volunteered and I found her serving my oatmeal tomorrow morning, and forcing me to take a third scoop. "The army's letting my little Mario fade away!" ' he added, in a voice like Chico Marx, checking his watch as he did so. 'Heck, I'd better head off.' He stood up and banged his head on the lampshade, just as Miss Appleby entered the room. She performed a little skip of surprise and Mario gave a shrill whistle – 'How many good-lookers can one house contain?' – winked at Noel, said, 'So long, see you Thursday' to Vee, and left the room. The kitchen seemed suddenly dimmer and shabbier, the silence as noticeable as if somebody had just switched off a fairground ride. There was a long pause. Noel heard the gate slam shut.

'I just came in to say that there's a mouse in my room,' said Miss Appleby, still blushing. 'It's dead,' she added.

'I'll come and clear it up,' said Vee.

'Thanks.' Miss Appleby left again.

'Thursday?' asked Noel.

'Sorry?' Vee was examining the syrup tins.

'Did he say he was coming back on Thursday?'

'He says he wants to take me out, just to say thank you.'

'It's the Methodist Christmas Party on Thursday.'

'Oh, I forgot.'

'I spent three evenings last week writing the prize quiz, after you asked me to.'

'It went right out of my mind.'

'Anyway, what does he want to thank you for?'

'Well . . .' Vee opened a cupboard and started to rearrange the contents with unconvincing concentration. 'It was something about the coroner's ruling,' she said, her back to Noel.

'What was the ruling?'

'Oh, it was . . . let me think . . .'

'Accidental death?'

'Yes.'

'So he got off. Because of your evidence.'

Vee turned to face him, suddenly indignant. 'I did my best. I went there and I got a grilling. I could have told them it was all a blur in my memory, but I didn't, so don't go shaming me, Noel Bostock. I wasn't the one driving the lorry.'

'But *he* was. And now you're going out with him to celebrate.'

'It's not a celebration, it's a . . .'

She looked around the kitchen as if an alternative word might be written on the wall.

'Celebration,' said Noel, flatly.

'I'm not arguing with you,' said Vee. 'I don't have your knack with words. The corporal told me he was very sorry about what happened, and that he'd written a letter to Mrs Embleton, but if he'd been charged and gone to prison, how would that have made anything better? I didn't mean to help him, but when it comes to it, I'm not sorry I did.'

'And how did he find out where we lived?'

'He spoke to the stenographer. And he knows the area, he said. He likes walking.'

'You mean he likes walking when he's not driving a gigantic lorry on the wrong side of the road?'

Vee pinched her lips and buried the tins of syrup right at the back of the cupboard, well out of Mr Reddish's eye-line, should he choose to open the door. The lingering taste of the whole astonishing visit – the wild largesse, the exoticism of an American sitting at her table, the funny stories, the hole punched into her grey routine, the giddy lightness, as if the kitchen had been filled with laughing gas – had all dissipated.

'I sold some golf balls,' said Noel.

'Is that so?' Vee shut the cupboard and, without looking at him, took the cigarettes and hid them in the scullery, under a folded oil-cloth. When she returned, the kitchen was empty, but there was a small pile of money at the centre of the table.

'Thank you!' she called along the passage.

There was no reply.

❧

The small child in the living room of Flat 3, Easton House, had gradually manoeuvred her way around the cluttered space until she had a clear view of Jepson's missing ear. He was busy taking down her father's story in shorthand, but he could almost feel the intensity of her gaze.

'After that I just walked,' said Private Birrell. 'Bumped into an American unit – well, they looked like Americans, but they talked funny and I thought for a moment they were Germans in disguise, but it turned out they were all from Wisconsin. Sort of up-and-down accent, like Norwegians. They gave me a lift to . . . where was it? Ancona? Feels like half a year ago, and it was only last week. Ancona, I think, and then – I can see you, little Shirley Birrell, come out of there.' He held out his arms to his daughter, but she stayed behind the drying rack, bending her knees so that she was concealed behind a hanging night-dress.

'She doesn't know me yet,' he said. 'She couldn't even walk when I last saw her. And of course, I've never seen *him* at all.' He nodded towards the high-chair where his wife was feeding the boy mashed carrots. 'I only came home on a forty-eight-hour pass, didn't I, Lena? That was just before we were sent to Tunis. The next letter I got from her was months later, when I was in the camp – *You'll never guess what's happened, Tom . . .*' He winked at his wife.

'Now stop it,' she said, flustered, trying not to laugh. 'And I hope Mr Jepson won't print that bit in his paper. Come on, Shirley, let's get your hair brushed.' She hitched the baby on to her hip, and led the child out of the room. The door shut, but the walls were like cardboard, Shirley's voice as clear as a choirboy's.

'That man's got no ear.'

'Shhh, don't be rude.'

Birrell looked embarrassed. 'Sorry. You got kids?'

'No.'

'Hark at me, voice of experience, I've only had 'em myself for about ten minutes, all told. I got called up in 1940, twenty years old, fancy free, met Lena first home leave, blinked twice and I've got a family. I don't regret it, I'm not saying I regret it, but look at this place.' He glanced around the room – the muddle of cheap furniture, a pile of ironing on the table, a makeshift play-pen for the baby in one corner, one wall missing half its plaster.

'Oil bomb in the next street,' said Birrell, nodding at the wall. 'Still waiting for the landlord to do something. No hot water. This isn't a place to bring up kids, but half the borough's smashed up now, so where are we going to live? They'll have to build, won't they? Someone was saying they'll need a million new houses, and they'll have to do them properly – inside lavs, and modern heating and somewhere outside for the kids to play. We haven't spent half a decade being shot at just to come back and roll over and put up with the same old bollocks.' He grinned, tiredly. 'Maybe you shouldn't print that either. But there'll need to be a big shake-up when this is all over, won't there?'

'Oh, yes,' said Jepson. 'I think this government's going to get a hell of a shock.'

He was interviewing returned soldiers nearly every week, now; the paper thought it gave a bit of lift to the front page ('Home Again for Holloway Man'). Some had been liberated from prisoner-of-war camps by the Allied advance or had chanced an escape in the chaos of the German retreat; some were merely on leave, having crossed continents to get home; all of them, however convoluted or lengthy their journeys, had seemed shocked by the dismal grind of London life, the V-2s still slamming down, the queues for fuel, the frozen rubble. They were impatient for the end and scenting change; tin medals weren't going to be enough this time round.

Mrs Birrell came back in. 'Can I get you another cup of tea?'

'No, thanks,' said Jepson, checking his watch. 'I'm off somewhere shortly. Just a couple more questions?'

She settled on the arm of her husband's chair and Birrell rested a hand on her hip, an easy, tender gesture. Their faces were alike, in expression if not feature – they shared a straightforwardness, an air of unselfconscious decency; one would hope, thought Jepson, that they stood a good chance of happiness. Since the end, just a year ago, of his own, terrible marriage he found himself studying other couples, like someone conning an aircraft recognition chart – spotting those tics and phrases that signalled contempt or boredom or fear, and when he saw those, he wanted to take one or other of the pair aside, and say, 'Finish it now. Don't do what I did, and let it drag on for a couple of decades.' But then, would he himself have listened? For a long time, he'd thought that those odd moments of shining joy were worth all the rest. It was only since Della had left, abruptly and irrevocably, that he'd seen the whole truth of it, as if those decades were a crumpled sheet of newsprint he'd smoothed out and made legible again.

'So do you know where you're being sent next?' he asked.

Private Birrell shrugged. 'I'm in no hurry,' he said. 'They'll tell me when they want me. With any luck, I'll get to Berlin just in time to spit in Hitler's bunker.'

'With any luck, you won't get further than Dover,' added his wife. 'You've done your bit.'

Jepson typed up the piece at the office, entitled it 'The Son He'd Never Met' and gave it to the sub, who eschewed poetry and who would almost certainly change the heading to 'Home Again for Caledonian Road Man'.

'Fancy a pint?' called Longford, from his desk in the corner, where he was sorting glumly through a sheaf of letters. Ninety per cent would be about the inadequacy of the council repairs department.

'No, I've said I'll go to the Hampstead Methodist Christmas Party.'

'Really?' Longford looked aghast. 'Never took you for the religious type.'

'You probably never took me for the tombola type either, but that's what I'm in charge of.'

Mrs Overs had beckoned him aside the day before, just after breakfast; she'd been biting her lip with anxiety and he'd prepared himself for a rent increase, or another plumbing disaster. What she'd wanted, though, was a favour. 'I'd be ever so grateful, Mr Jepson, I couldn't think of anyone else to ask, Miss Appleby's off seeing her Australian again, and Noel's – well, to be honest, he's in a bit of a huff with me at the moment. You'd only need to be on the stall between seven and eight, and if you could just tell Mrs Claxton – she's the one in charge, you can't miss her, Monty with a permanent wave – if you could just tell her that I'm feeling a bit off colour.'

'Oh, I'm sorry about that.'

She'd darted him a look to see if he was serious. 'Well, obviously, I'm not really. I've had a . . . well, an unexpected invitation.' If she'd had a different sort of face, she'd have dimpled; instead, a smile – a rather lovely one – had briefly surfaced and then disappeared again. 'But I don't want you to feel you have to tell an untruth.'

'Oh, I've told a few white lies in my time,' he'd said.

The prizes for the tombola ranged from a fruitcake to a tin of pre-war talcum powder, speckled with rust. Each had a numbered ticket attached, and for sixpence, you could buy the chance to dip into a drum and pull out a matching ticket. 'The thing is, Mr Jepson,' said Mrs Claxton, in confidential tones, 'we have a little *system*. If certain of the prizes were to go early on, then no one would buy any more tickets, so what we do is set aside some of the duplicate numbers – say for the fruitcake, or the tin of pears in cream – and only pop them into the drum later in the evening.' Her expression bland, she slid a couple of tickets across the table towards him.

Jepson thought fleetingly of the article he could squeeze from this ('Fraud Allegation Shatters Methodist Merriment') and nodded understandingly, tucking the duplicates into his jacket pocket. The stall was situated at the back of the Drill Hall, between another selling knitted goods and a long table on which helpers were setting out sandwiches. An attempt had been made to decorate the room, faded crêpe-paper streamers pinned between the rafters, and a small holly bush in a tub in one corner, the decorations cut from tinfoil.

The place was dreadfully familiar to him from his four years of Home Guard parades, those interminable evenings of shuffle and stamp, of repetitious tasks and tedious duties, of winter rain on the windows and the pervasive smell of damp serge, of stifling summer nights when all one wanted to do was sit on a hillside with a beer.

Early in the war there had seemed some point to it – during the night Blitz, Jepson and other veterans from his platoon had been deployed on the crew of an anti-aircraft gun, thunderously loosing twenty-eight-pounders against the bombers – but during the years that had followed, as the threat of invasion receded, thrice-weekly attendance at the Drill Hall had become yet another petty home-front penance to be endured, and none of them had been sorry when the Guard was officially stood down in the autumn.

Jepson had reported for the *North London Press* on the final mass parade – seven thousand men selected from all over the country, boots shining, music playing, the King taking the salute. There had been one final absurd twist when the Irish Guard's band had played the march-past at a fearful lick, too rapid for some of the older members, who had nevertheless managed to keep up, turning variously grey or pink, according to the condition of their hearts. Some of the watchers had laughed, and Jepson had had to turn away, pierced by the derision; they were laughing at men who, night after night, year after year, had come home after long shifts and then wearily changed into khaki before setting out again, unpaid, unlauded. And he remembered Della, pressing a hand to her smiling mouth after seeing him in his Home Guard uniform for the first time. 'Sorry,' she'd said, 'I know you can't help your ear, but that helmet does look silly, all tipped to one side.' It was painful, now, to think that he had smiled back.

'We'll be opening the hall doors very shortly,' said Mrs Claxton, 'and once they've eaten all the buffet – and they *will*, Mr Jepson, it'll be like the Gadarene swine – we'll begin the entertainment. We have quite a full programme.' She gestured towards the blackboard propped on an easel beside the stage; an elderly minister was chalking 'QUIZ' at the bottom of a long list, and Jepson spotted the name 'Reddish' halfway down, next to the ominous word 'Recitation'.

'I'm sorry, though,' continued Mrs Claxton, 'that Mrs Overs is unwell. Was it sudden? Her nephew didn't mention anything about it when he arrived earlier.'

'A bilious attack, I believe,' said Jepson, looking around

for Noel, and spotting him sitting on his own in the middle of the rows of empty chairs, studying what looked like a letter. It had arrived that morning. Noel, sorting the post into piles for the lodgers, had been surprised to find one envelope addressed to himself. It contained a single sheet of notepaper, and amidst the neatly written lines, the word 'Simpkin' had drawn his eye as if picked out in gold leaf.

> *. . . and I promised to let you know what happened to the Green Man carving found in the church ruins. It's been taken to the Victoria and Albert Museum, but the expert wasn't able to tell me whether it would be on display or not, as most of the portable contents have been taken out of London for safety. Incidentally, your postal address rang a very happy bell with me – when I was younger than you, I belonged to a club for girls called the Amazons, run by an extraordinary woman called Miss Matilda Simpkin, who lived in Green Shutters (she called it 'The Mousehole') and who had been a suffragette. I think I remember hearing that she died a few years ago, but I'm sure some of the local residents will still remember her. I once broke a pane in your next-door neighbour's greenhouse with a badly aimed javelin!*
>
> *Yours sincerely,*
>
> *Winnie Crowther*

And his godmother Mattie was back in his head, whole and vivid, her voice as clear as if she were shouting through the letter-box, and he was once again at the warm centre of a world in which his every speech and action provoked enthusiasm and comment: 'Yes, well remembered, young Noel, it is indeed called a *pilum*, and I think that with your sureness of grip as well as your grasp of Latin vocabulary, you would have made a very fine Roman legionary. Incidentally, I was in the bath and I suddenly realized that it's possible to sing the words of *Lars Porsena of Clusium* to the tune of 'My Old Man Said Follow the Van'. Shall we give it a go?'

That sensation of warmth had dwindled during the day, snuffed out finally by Vee's question in the hall that evening, as he'd pulled on his balaclava:

'Where are you off to?'

He'd looked at her, incredulously. 'The Drill Hall. The *Methodist Party*.'

'Oh, yes, sorry, I keep forgetting.'

She was wearing lipstick, and a dress that he didn't recognize, and in response to his stare she checked her appearance in the hall mirror, though the glass was so old that every reflection looked fickle, freckled. She dabbed at her mouth.

'Do I look all right?' she asked, half to herself. 'This is that brand-new lipstick you found dropped on the Heath last year. *Rose Blush*.'

It looked orange to Noel. 'So where's the corporal taking you?'

'I don't know, he didn't say.'

'And are you going in the lorry?'

She didn't answer that one. Noel tucked the bundle of quiz questions into the pocket which already contained the letter. 'Have a nice time, anyway,' he said, stiffly.

'Thank you.' She reached out a hand to pat his shoulder, and then changed its trajectory and picked a piece of lint from his scarf. 'I hope you haven't made the questions too difficult. Mrs Claxton keeps on saying to me that she's praying that the team from the local council wins.'

'Why?'

'Because the bomb-hole in the road outside the chapel's been there since last July, and the gulley next to it's still half blocked with rubble so that when it rains it all overflows into the chapel porch, and you don't want the clerk of works drawing up his repairs list and thinking, "Oh yes, the Methodists. I hope they're enjoying their prize of two bottles of home-made wine and a side of bacon sent by Mr Orchard's niece in Canada." '

'I see.' Noel pulled on his mittens. 'Do you think Mrs Claxton's comments to you are in the nature of a hint?'

'A hint? What sort of hint?'

'Is she hoping that your quiz-collating nephew might find a way of ensuring that the council team wins?'

'No, of course not!' said Vee, sounding, and possibly even feeling, a little shocked. There was a pause. 'Could you?'

'I suppose, theoretically, I could rearrange the question order so that the council team get fewer on, say, chemistry and more on the subject of popular entertainment. Or I could give them "rivers of England" as a Geography sub-category, while the lay preachers get "rivers of the African sub-continent". And so on. It would be quite easy.'

'Oh.'

Their eyes met in the old, complicit connection; fleetingly, they were the Vee and Noel of the grey suburbs, breath not quite steady, pulses running a touch fast, the world a little sharper and brighter than usual as they rattled their fake charity box, ears strained for the policeman's footstep.

'No,' said Vee, reluctantly. 'No, we shouldn't. It's not as if it's for anything really important, is it?'

Noel shook his head. The disappointment was slight but palpable.

Ten minutes after the Drill Hall doors had been opened, not only was there nothing left of the buffet, but the empty plates looked as if they'd been licked. Noel had tried the strawberry jelly and found that it tasted slightly of glue, but its sheer novelty was such that small children had carried pieces away in their cupped hands, unsure as to whether it was food or a plaything. The meat-paste sandwiches had tasted of nothing at all, but one elderly man had taken five, folded each like a small book, and inserted them into his trouser pockets.

'If everyone has finished eating,' called a large woman from the stage, 'could you be seated for the entertainment?'

At the tombola stall, Noel was eyeing the prizes to see whether it was worth venturing a shilling or two. The large tin of pears in cream was calling to him. He knew exactly what he would be cooking for the savoury part of the Christmas Day menu, but the pudding was still lacking in pizzazz. 'I'll take three tickets, please.'

Mr Jepson seemed strangely reluctant to sell them to him. 'Three? Are you sure?'

Noel fished another sixpence from his pocket. 'Four, then.'

'No, I mean, are you sure you want them now? Wouldn't you rather wait until the interval?'

'Why?'

'Oh, just to . . . to even things out.' Jepson seemed to be attempting to convey something important, using only his eyebrows.

'Hurry *up*,' said the woman behind Noel in the queue. 'I want a good seat.'

'How about if I take one now,' said Noel, carefully, 'and another couple later?'

'Yes, good idea.'

'Well, aren't you the lucky one?' said the woman, as Noel unfolded his ticket.

As he took his place in the audience, he scrutinized the tin of scented talcum powder (*French Lavender*) that he'd won. As far as he could ascertain, it had never been opened; if he sanded off the rust spots, it might make a good present for Vee.

The trouble with being given flowers, thought Vee, was that now she'd have to carry them around all evening. And it wasn't just a buttonhole, it was a whacking great bunch of pink-and-blue silk gardenias. She had kept it on her lap during the Tube journey, and then clutched in one hand as they'd exited at Leicester Square, emerging into jostling darkness, absorbed into a near-invisible crowd that swayed and heaved like a turning tide, almost lifting Vee off her feet. She'd gripped the corporal's sleeve as he steamed through, and by the time they'd reached a pub he knew of, along the Strand and down a flight of steps by the river, the bouquet looked as if summer had come and gone.

'What can I get you to drink?' he asked.

'Just a lemonade, please.'

The place was packed, but she was able to watch her companion's progress all the way to the bar, his head bobbing above the others' like a buoy. Most of the customers were GIs – they were so *clean*-looking, thought Vee, and so smart, their uniforms might have been made to measure, smooth fabric stretched across well-fed bodies, everything gleaming, even their skin, even their teeth. The few visible Tommies looked used-up by comparison, grey and juiceless, uneasily jingling the change in the pockets of their sagging khaki, trying to stop their girls' gaze from wandering over to the Yanks.

Vee edged one buttock on to a window seat, taking a moment's respite. As she'd waited, nervously, for the corporal to ring the doorbell, she'd wondered what would be expected of her over the evening ahead – would she be required to talk or to listen? Most men, in her experience, were either tongue-tied, so that conversation had to be pushed along like a stalled motor-car, or wedded to one particular subject to which they returned at every single opportunity, so that the main problem was not that of thinking of topics, but of remaining awake so as to make the right kind of appreciative noises during a round-by-round account of a boxing-match that had taken place in 1923. Corporal O'Mahoney ('Call me Mario'), however, had not only talked non-stop from the moment he'd arrived, a stream of stories and jokes, but had peppered his speech with questions, so that she'd had to stay on the alert – *no, 'Hampstead' had nothing to do with 'Ham' so far as she knew; yes, she'd often seen squirrels on the Heath; no, she had never killed and roasted one* – and then the train had stopped in the tunnel just before Camden Town and the lights had first flickered and then failed and Mario had immediately started telling a ghost story about a haunted garment factory where mysterious weeping was heard and a sewing-machine whirred in the darkness, and his deep rasp of a voice was so compelling that when the lights in the carriage suddenly came back on, everyone was leaning forward with slackened jaws, and there was an actual groan of annoyance when the carriage jolted into the station. 'Tell you the end on the way home!' Mario had shouted towards the exiting crowd, and there'd been grins and waves.

'Can't you tell me the end now?' Vee had asked, as the train doors closed again.

'Haven't thought of it yet.'

'You were making it up?'

'Every word. You ever see a ghost?'

'No. Have you?'

'Only a couple.' And he'd headed off on a tale about a box of doughnuts and a set of footsteps in the snow, and Vee had realized that her nervousness had dissipated because she didn't have to *do* anything, it appeared, only hold on to her hat and enjoy the ride.

He came back from the bar with a lemonade, a gin and French, two beers and a whisky.

'I'm not much of a drinker,' said Vee, when she realized that the gin was for her.

'Why's that?' He'd already downed the whisky.

'It was the way I was brought up, I suppose. Methodist.'

'That like a Baptist?'

'Like a Baptist but . . . without the baptizing.'

'And they think drinking liquor's a sin?'

'No, not a sin, exactly. Frowned upon.' Regarded, even by those Methodists who hadn't actually signed the pledge, as an activity dangerously close to enjoyment.

'*I'm* not frowning,' said Mario, pushing up his cap so she could see his forehead, broad and pock-marked. 'You see me frowning? If you take a sip, I won't even peek.'

She wet her lips, just to be polite. It wasn't as unpleasant as she remembered.

'I'm a Catholic,' he said. She nodded. When he'd paid for the Tube tickets she'd seen a picture of Jesus Christ in his wallet, one of those illustrations in which the Saviour was exposing His pierced heart with an oddly simpering expression. The corporal took the wallet out again now, paused momentarily over the painting, and then thumbed through and took out a couple of photographs. One showed a crowd of people standing in front of a shop, smiling at the camera.

'This is our bakery, it's called Bernardi's – Bernardi was my grandfather's name – but they call it Fat Pat's because you put on ten pounds just looking in the window, and that's my ma and pa' – he hovered his forefinger above the photo – 'those are my brothers, Michael, Pat junior, Iggy, Paul, Francesco, and their wives, and my sister, Carmen.'

Great cheerful slabs of men with the same large features as Mario, and buxom, shining women.

'And this is my godson's First Communion – those are cousins, mostly.' A scrubbed small boy stood in a room full of yet more people with Mario's chin.

'Goodness – how many of you are there?'

'A million. Maybe two.' He grinned, drained one of his beers and reached for the second. 'You got a big family?'

'No.' Only a mother and a grown son that she never saw; she felt the usual twist of the heart at the thought of Donald, that rosy, roaring baby who had patted her face and gurgled and grown into a young man who'd had no further need for her, who had brushed her off like lint from a coat. 'Just my nephew,' she added. Who wasn't really her nephew, of course. She took another tiny sip of gin as the pub door opened yet again, admitting a ribbon of cold air and at least a dozen sailors. The noise level rose, so that she could hardly catch what Mario was talking about. Behind her, two girls were having a shouted conversation about someone called Dolly, while over Mario's shoulder she could see a fair-haired GI nibbling the neck of a brunette, while the latter placidly checked her lipstick in a compact mirror.

'You even been there?' asked Mario.

Vee realized that she hadn't heard a single word of the previous sentence. She shook her head, since that was probably the correct answer; she'd never been *anywhere.*

'Nothing but stones, miles of little stones,' said Mario. 'In the US, we'd call it a driveway!' She could tell from his expression that this was a punchline, and she gave an unconvincing neigh of laughter, just as the brunette snapped her compact closed. The girl's gaze flicked in her direction and lingered critically for long enough to allow Vee to feel like the oldest woman in the world.

'Hey,' said Mario, 'how about we go for a walk?'

'A walk?' She sounded like a dolt, repeating the word, but who went for a walk after dark in December, with the wind snapping at your ankles like scissors?

'Just a little stroll somewhere quiet,' he added, and she felt a premonitory lurch of the stomach. The infectious looseness of American morals had been the subject of many dark discussions at the knitting circle, especially the ability of GIs to turn Nice Girls Who Ought To Know Better into Little More Than Street-Walkers at the wave of a pair of nylons. Also notable, apparently, was their willingness to extend appreciation of the female form to those who would normally consider themselves exempt. Mrs Ogden had had her thigh stroked in the blackout while queuing for a bus, and had shone her torch into the face of the perpetrator, to discover that he was approximately the same age as her grandson. He had appeared completely unabashed, saying 'Good evening, ma'am' with exquisite politeness before offering to carry her shopping.

'Are you drinking this?' asked Mario, indicating her gin. Vee shook her head. 'What it is,' he said, leaning his huge head in towards her, his voice dropping to a low rumble, 'is that I have to ask you something.' Almost absent-mindedly, he downed the gin.

'Oh,' said Vee. 'Can't you ask it here?'

'It's kind of private,' he said.

'Right. Only it's perishing out, I can't think how I'll ever keep warm.' Which sounded, she realized instantly, exactly like a phrase from a lurid newspaper article about good-time girls; she might as well have snapped her garter and named her price. Fortunately, the corporal was lighting a cigarette, and didn't see her wince.

'All right, then,' she said, buttoning up her coat. 'Just a quick one.' God *almighty*, and now she sounded like Max Miller. 'I mean, a walk – I mean, a quick walk – that's what I meant.'

'You OK?' he asked, squinting through the smoke at her.

'Yes, I'm very well,' she said primly, and followed him out into the polar wind.

Noel amused himself during the entertainment by composing caustic imaginary reviews. *Mr Harry Wallford, of Wallford's Plumbing Supplies, performing under the stage name 'Happy Hal', made a number of jokes that would have been commendably topical were it still 1939. The exception was one about the recent bomb plot to kill Hitler, the final line of which – 'It blew his trousers off!' – resulted in audience consternation and the hurried removal of a small child from the hall.* Happy Hal had been preceded on stage by a trio of singers, The Treble Clef (. . . *they're all tone deaf*) and followed by the Dorita Juveniles, the protégées of Mrs Claxton's daughter, Dorita, who ran a Saturday ballet school (. . . *I think we can safely say that the dying swan has never before felt quite as definitively dead*). After that came Junior Master of Dexterity, Nigel Dunville, whose card tricks were performed with a minuscule pack that had clearly come from a pre-war cracker (. . . *is it the Jack of diamonds, the ace of spades or an indecent photograph of Mata Hari? No one beyond the front row could possibly know* . . .), and then Mr Reddish came on stage, cloaked in a maroon rug that Noel had last seen in the lumber room at home, and wearing a tie knotted round his head into which he'd stuck a couple of feathers. From the wings came a dull, repeated thud which was either Redskin war drums or Nigel Dunville hitting an upturned bucket with a sink mop.

Mr Reddish lifted his eyes towards an imaginary horizon, and matched his delivery to the low, steady rhythm.

'By the shore of Gitche Gumee,
By the shining Big-Sea-Water,
At the doorway of his wigwam,
In the pleasant Summer morning,
Hiawatha stood and—'

The floor shuddered and there was a noise like a quarry blast: a cracker-snap of explosive preceding the long, distant roar of falling rock. A woman yelped. Chairs toppled as people rose. 'East, that was,' said the man in front of Noel. Someone opened a door and the rumble rose briefly in volume and then slid gradually away, to be replaced by the noise of a bus changing gear as it tackled the long rise of Pond Street. People began to sit down again. 'Miles away,' muttered a man, dismissively. 'I'd say that was Islington.' Attention shifted back towards the stage, where Mr Reddish was still reciting, one hand cupped to an ear, his features bunched in an attempt to convey delicate wonderment:

'Something in the hazy distance,
Coming nearer, nearer, nearer,
Was it Shingebis the diver?
Or the heron, the Shuh-shuh-gah?
Or the white goose, Waw-be-wawa . . . ?'

'Excuse me,' whispered Noel, exiting the row and walking rather hurriedly towards the door that led to the cloakrooms. In the corridor beyond, he found a coat cupboard, and he stuck his head inside and pressed his face to the heavy folds of a duffel coat until he'd stopped laughing. He could hear applause from the hall, and a piano playing the opening bars of 'We'll Gather Lilacs', and he turned the other way and opened the kitchen door to find Mr Jepson sitting alone with a book and a cigarette.

'You've caught me AWOL,' said Jepson, looking rather guilty. 'I'll be back on the tombola at the interval.'

'What are you reading?'

'*Great Expectations*.'

'Which bit?'

'I've just reached the death of Magwitch.'

'You had a child once,' said Noel, in hushed tones, as if whispering to a dying convict, 'whom you loved and lost. She lived and found powerful friends. She is living now. She is a lady and very beautiful.'

'And I love her!' said Jepson. 'Well remembered.' He stroked his moustache, which he seemed to do in lieu of smiling. 'I really ought to read something more modern – there's interesting stuff being published – but it's always the old friends that call to me from the bookshelf. Any news about where that rocket landed?'

'Someone mentioned Islington,' said Noel. 'I was talking to the librarian at Hampstead during the week and she said that nobody wants to read anything at the moment except Trollope and Mrs Gaskell. Incidentally, I put my Latin under your door – I picked a piece from the *Evening Standard* about fuel. I had to absolutely cudgel my brains to come up with a translation for "gas fire".'

'What did you decide upon?'

'*Aer calidus ignis*. "Hot vapour fire".'

'That sounds a decent attempt. I'll look at it when we get back. *Aer calidus ignis* . . .' he repeated, fingering his moustache.

He'd been a lodger at Green Shutters since the beginning of the year, arriving with a canvas rucksack and a heavy cold. Noel had been initially doubtful.

'Mr Jepson's very . . . enervated,' he'd said to Vee, after his first lesson.

'Which means?'

'Spiritless.'

'Spiritless? He went to a university,' said Vee, exasperated. 'He knows Latin. He writes for a living. What do you want, party hats? The last person who answered the advertisement spelled "lodging" with a "j" – is that who you'd want teaching you English? Is it the ear that's worrying you?'

'No, it's not that.'

'Well, what is it? You've never complained about Dr Parry-Jones being enervated, and I don't see her dancing any jigs.'

It had been clear that this was one of those times when it really wasn't worth pursuing a discussion with Vee, and Noel had taken his doubts away again, and examined them in private. Perhaps 'enervated' had been the wrong word; 'extinguished' might have been more accurate. Jepson was present but unlit, so that in the dining room he was more furniture than inhabitant, talked around and over, but never *to*. But in lessons there were glimmers – he had seized Noel's first essay and pushed the words around the page like backgammon counters, showing him how to introduce a subject, how to make a neat and satisfying ending, how to prune and rearrange the content. 'If I have any talent at all, it's for editing,' he'd said, and out of that tiny wisp of self-praise had grown their first real conversation – on the subject of dull openings to novels – and after that it had been easier, and Jepson had gradually become a visible member of the household, though never a very audible one, unless you could get him on his own.

He was, too, a surprisingly rigorous marker. Both he and Dr Parry-Jones appended detailed notes to Noel's written work, and set him masses of prep. Mr Reddish, on the other hand, was content to lie on his bed listening to *Appointment With Fear* on the wireless, while Noel worked his way, largely unsupervised, through *Mathematics for Matriculation* and *Fullday's Manual of Book-Keeping*, while Miss Appleby had lately abandoned all pretence of teaching him any French, and instead used him as a sort of confessional booth for her love life. She had broken off her engagement to the Anzac after seeing an informational film about Australian spiders, and was now walking out with an asthmatic tax inspector. 'Would you call that a step up from a soldier, or a step down?' she'd asked. 'He has lovely hair, though of course he's not as muscular as Douglas was.'

From the drill-hall kitchen, they heard a prolonged rattle of applause, followed by footsteps along the corridor. Mrs Claxton entered the room and Jepson closed his copy of *Great Expectations*, his expression stoic.

'Do you want me back on duty?' he asked.

'No, no' – she was opening cupboards, looking for something – 'I think Cathy Jackson is giving an encore, and then the Merry Whistler – that's the Reverend Bagshott – is doing requests before the interval. I'm searching for something large enough for one of the Dorita Juveniles to vomit into. I do hope it wasn't the paste sandwiches, otherwise there'll be mayhem – ah, here.' She took a china basin from a cupboard behind Mr Jepson's head and turned to go. The noise of sliding crockery came from the shelf she'd just removed it from, and she shot out a hand towards the cupboard door. Mr Jepson made an equally abrupt movement in response and, for a frozen moment, Noel stared at the peculiar tableau that had formed in front of him: Mrs Claxton with one hand outstretched, and Mr Jepson hunched over the table, his arms wrapped protectively around his head.

'Oh dear,' said Mrs Claxton, in a low voice. 'I'm so sorry.' Quietly and rapidly, she rearranged the contents of the cupboard, and then took the basin and left.

'Are you all right?' asked Noel. It seemed a stupid

question. When there was no reply, he touched his tutor's sleeve, and Mr Jepson straightened, stiffly, his features a flattened mask of humiliation so that he looked suddenly years older, and hideous.

'Can I get you anything?' asked Noel.

'No, thank you.' Jepson stood without looking at him. 'I think I'd better leave now. Please give my apologies to Mrs Claxton.' And he was already scuttling out of the kitchen door, head down.

'I'll man the tombola!' Noel called after him. 'Don't worry.'

From the hall came scattered applause and then the first whistled phrase of 'Danny Boy', the rising notes as plangent as an evening blackbird. Noel stood, uncertainly. Two minutes ago, he'd been discussing gas fires, and now, inexplicably, the evening was fractured, unrecognizable; a single blow had punched it out of shape.

Jepson had left his book on the table, and also the matches and cigarettes, and Noel took a Mellow Kensitas out of the packet and attempted to light it, coughing gouts of acrid smoke across the kitchen and eventually retching into the sink. He crushed it out and sat down again, opened *Great Expectations* near the end and was at once back at home. The book had been his childhood frame of reference: the local fishmonger sounded like Joe Gargery; his godmother's solicitor looked like Wemmick; the booming of thunder over the Heath was the noise of the guns from the prison hulks. And now he accompanied the adult Pip to Satis House (in Noel's imagination, a cross between Green Shutters and the Natural History

Museum) and together they climbed the cobwebbed stairs. Miss Havisham had just gone up in flames when the scrape of chairs in the hall heralded the interval.

A dense smell of river mud hung over the embankment, stirred by more delicate currents of petrol and sewerage. Vee breathed through her mouth as she hurried to keep up with the corporal's long stride.

'Can you swim?' asked Mario, breaking off from an anecdote about his short-sighted neighbour, who'd once adopted a skunk, thinking that it was a cat.

'No,' said Vee. 'Can you?'

'Had to learn in the summer in one of the ponds up by your house – did it by numbers, a hundred guys in short pants and an instructor with a bullhorn. '*Scoop with your arms, kick with your legs. One, two, three, SWIM!!!!*'

The final word was so loud that there was an answering shout from one of the passing barges; there was a line of them in both directions, their blueish bow-lights stroking the choppy surface. Mario finished his cigarette and flicked it over the parapet.

'So,' he said, halting. 'I have to ask you something.'

'Oh, yes?' Vee had been walking a careful hand's breadth away from him, but he'd made no attempt even to take her arm, and now that they were standing facing each other, there was at least a foot of icy air whistling between them. She found herself thinking that if he gave her a squeeze, at least she'd be warm. His head was a giant silhouette, with the moon balanced on his right ear. He leaned down towards her and the moon disappeared.

'Couldn't say this in front of other people,' he said, 'but I can get you a turkey.'

'Beg your pardon?'

'A turkey. I drove a truckload for Thanksgiving, I know a farm where I can get one.'

'Oh!'

'Would you like that? Isn't that what the English have on Christmas Day?'

'Yes. That's right.'

'Don't know when I can get it – it'll all depend what deliveries I'm making – but when I get it, it's yours.'

He straightened up again, and the moon jumped back into place. 'Thank you very much,' said Vee, formally.

There was a series of hoots from the river, where a large ship was nosing under Blackfriars Bridge. It sounded, to Vee, like sarcastic laughter.

'OK, you want to go to a mushroom bar?' asked Mario. 'That's what they're calling them – they spring up in the night, some of them even have a band. There's one around here somewhere.' And they were off again, Vee taking four steps for every two of his so that by the time they got back to the Strand she had a stitch, and had to stop and lean against a lamp-post, like an inebriate, while Mario consulted a passing American sailor for directions.

'Just up that side alley on the right,' he said, returning to the circle of dim light in which she was standing. 'You need me to carry you?'

'*Carry* me? No, of course not. It's just you're a fast walker.'

'I'm a fast dancer as well.' He performed a little hop and

a twirl, ridiculous but oddly graceful for someone so large, and she couldn't help but smile. 'You like dancing?' he asked.

'I used to,' said Vee. 'I think I've forgotten how.' She could hear the music, now – the agonized squeal of a trumpet.

'No one forgets,' said Mario. 'It's like . . . what do you say over here? Laying an egg?'

'Riding a bicycle. Everyone there will be half my age.'

'Except for me, and who cares, anyhow? Aw . . . come on.' He held out a hand like a shovel and Vee took it. It was so easy, she thought, as he led her towards the music; *he* was so easy – a printed postcard, when every other man she'd ever known was a sealed letter filled with blank pages or mystifying codes. And perhaps you didn't always have to worry about every damned thing, every second of the day; perhaps sometimes you could just dance.

It was after midnight when she arrived home. She let herself in through the back door, and groped along the scullery passage, hesitating when she saw a wavering light on the wall ahead.

'Hello?' she called softly.

'It's me,' said Noel. He was sitting at the kitchen table, wearing an old blue dressing-gown over his clothes, a brick of a book open in front of him, and a candle burning. Vee had a sudden memory of coming home late after a dance in St Albans, twenty-odd years before, and her mother bearing much the same rather pursed expression.

'You didn't have to stay up,' she said.

'I wasn't tired. How did you get back?'

'A friend of Mario's gave us a lift.' A US Army motor-car, holding at least eight people, a jolting, draughty and hilarious journey, everyone singing, a toothy ATS girl screaming whenever the driver braked.

'I didn't hear a vehicle,' said Noel, sounding like a policeman.

'The driver wouldn't come down the lane – he said the ruts would tear the bottom out. The corporal walked me back.' He had taken her arm on the muddy track, and saved her from a couple of spills – not that she was tiddly, it was just that after two hours of dancing she felt as if her feet had been savagely broken and then carelessly re-set – and when they'd got to Green Shutters Mario had said, 'Keep a look-out for that turkey!' and then plunged off into the darkness of the Heath, apparently intent on walking to Camden guided only by moonlight and a failing torch with a bulb like a glow-worm.

'I see,' said Noel, marking his place and closing the book. 'The council won the quiz, by the way, even though I was scrupulously fair in every possible respect. And Mrs Claxton gave me the left-over prizes from the tombola.'

'Oh, well, that's all right, then.' Vee found herself yawning, hugely. 'I'd better get off to bed, plenty to do tomorrow. Same goes for you, young man. Nighty night.'

Noel listened to her footsteps along the hall. She seemed to be limping with both feet. He'd stayed up partly to check that she arrived home safely and partly to tell her about some of the more amusing events at the Drill Hall, but it seemed that she'd already been sufficiently amused this evening. She hadn't even noticed the tin of pears and cream or the fruitcake.

'It's very odd that nobody won the best prizes,' he'd said to Mrs Claxton, during the tidy-up. 'Could the matching tickets have inadvertently been left out?'

'Why don't you take them home, dear,' said Mrs Claxton, apparently failing to hear the question. 'You've been a great help. Your aunt must be very proud of you. And do thank Mr Jepson, when he's feeling better.'

Their eyes met briefly.

'My husband never turned a hair during the raids,' said Mrs Claxton, 'but if someone lights a match in the dark, he's straight under the table. It takes him back to the trenches, you see – snipers. And the *language* afterwards . . . he's ashamed, though he can't help himself. I should think it's the same thing with your Mr Jepson – some nasty event in the past must have set him off.'

She folded the tablecloth with sober precision, her smooth, bright manner momentarily dented. 'I hope this is the last war,' she said. 'I hope you youngsters manage it better than we did. I hope you find better things to do than kill one another.'

'"And they shall beat their swords into plough-shares,"' said Noel, by way of agreement, clattering the last chair on to a stack. It was one of the few Bible verses of which Mattie had approved.

On her way to Post 9 on Christmas Eve, on a morning so cold that the water in her kettle had frozen overnight, Winnie saw a black-and-white cat hanging around the ruins of Falcon Road – on the look-out for rodents, presumably, given that any residents had long since left. The only visible human being was a familiar bearded figure carrying a bucket and wearing a brown mohair hat that he claimed had been given to him by an Afghan tribesman. Rather than, say, swiped from a second-hand clothes shop on the Caledonian Road.

'What?' he shouted, catching sight of Winnie. 'I am doing nothing wrong. Nothing. This is PERSECUTION.'

'Looting,' said Winnie. 'Article 2:4 of the Special Wartime Measures Act. "The removal by a private individual of household objects from the site of a dwelling destroyed or partially destroyed by enemy action." What's in the bucket today?'

'One or two things that caught my EYE.'

He was perhaps in his seventies, a tartan shawl knotted across his stained coat, his jaw constantly moving as if chewing tobacco, his speech peculiarly uncontrolled, so that every phrase started slowly and accelerated into a gabbled shout. Winnie only knew him as Jim. It was possible, she thought, that he also only knew himself as Jim.

She peered into the bucket. Two-thirds of a china shepherdess lay supine across a few lumps of coal and a smashed clock.

'So you going to arrest me?' His eyes flickered, as if Winnie were a train going past.

'*I'm* not, but you know quite well if the police see you,

you'll be straight down the station and in front of the beak.'

'I'd plead my case, I'll tell them who's boss, I've done it BEFORE.'

'I bet you have. If you come to the Post, I'll make you a cup of tea, if you like.'

'No, no, you won't try to trick me that way.' He coughed; the noise was like mud being shovelled.

'Your chest sounds bad, Jim.'

'Blame the Boche for that, THE BOCHE. Dirty way to fight.'

'You should get in the warm.'

'That's what that bugger on Falcon Road said to me, he said, "Why are you standing in the COLD?"'

'Which bugger's that, Jim?'

'The one who's living there.'

'Living where?'

He flapped a vague arm and then stumped off, eyes scanning the ground like a beachcomber.

Winnie turned to go, and then hesitated. At the Post, they kept lists of the occupants of each address in the sector, but Falcon Road had been deserted for weeks, half the street obliterated and the remaining houses roofless and windowless, three storeys of Edwardian solidity reduced to crenellated bungalows. She glanced back at the empty road, and immediately saw the cat again. It was sitting on a gatepost; not hunting, but waiting, and it stood as she approached, and pushed its face into her cautiously outstretched hand.

'Why are you here?' she asked. No gate hung from the

gatepost, and the house beyond was just a façade, the ground-floor window framing a tree in the back garden, but the front path had been partially cleared, the plaster and broken slates pushed to one side, so that one could easily reach the gap in the wall that led to the basement steps. Which had also been cleared.

'It was very neat,' she said to Basset, later, warming her hands on a mug of cocoa. That had been her first impression, when no one had answered her shouted greeting and she had first knocked, and then tried the door. Whoever was living there had arranged the remaining furniture into a snug, the items clustered around the kitchen fireplace, in which the ashes were still warm. A bowl and a plate had been washed, and beside them on the table, a shining teaspoon sat in a clean cup, though when, out of curiosity, she went over to the sink and tried the tap, there was no water, only a hollow thudding from the pipe. Three blankets had been folded and placed on the sofa. A duffel bag hung over a chair.

'A Mrs Fergus and her daughter used to live in that flat,' she said. 'I checked. They left before the V-2s.'

'I remember them,' said Basset.

'What did they look like?'

'Irish.'

'It's pretty obvious that it wouldn't take much to bring down the rest of the house,' said Winnie. 'Who'd choose to live there now?'

'Someone who didn't want to pay rent.'

'It's a man, according to Jim.'

'Any description?'

'His exact words were "that bugger on Falcon Road".'

'Narrows it down,' said Basset. He carried on cleaning his nails with a used matchstick, applying the same concentration and thoroughness that he brought to every task. He was a volunteer in his fifties, a lathe worker in a tool factory, laconic, pallid and sporting a set of poorly fitting false teeth which gave him mouth ulcers, the only thing she'd ever heard him complain about. He arrived on time for every shift at the Post, never swore, never panicked and barely showed anxiety, even at the height of the night Blitz, when it had been merry hell from dusk to dawn. He was the sort of person who ought to get a medal after the war but who probably wouldn't, and he was absolutely nothing like any of the characters in Avril's book, which Winnie had finished the previous evening. And for 'finished' one could substitute the phrase 'thrown across the room'. What was especially galling was that Avril had managed to get all the detail right – the parameters of an incident, the timings, the procedures, the almost unbearable slowness with which Heavy Rescue dug in search of casualties, the exhaustion, the dirt, the chaos of an ever-changing landscape. It was the people and emotions that were all wrong, and the idea that the Wardens' Post was a cauldron of simmering lust in which every glance could be pantingly misinterpreted, and then acted upon later that evening under the *raw pale moon that thrust through the panes, thrust again, yes, and again!* Death, in Avril's novel, was inevitably followed by sex, whereas in Winnie's experience, what one yearned for most after dealing with a corpse was a bath or a beer. And no one in *Tin Helmet* ever discussed the sort of topics that were regularly chewed over at Post 9, such as what you could put in a gas meter instead of threepences, or how much Churchill actually drank; they never told terrible jokes, they never did the crossword or compared chilblains – no, it was all sliding obliquities so that you had to re-read every half-page to work out what they were actually talking about.

'Biscuit?' asked Basset, reaching for the tin.

'It's empty, I'm afraid.'

'I'll bring some in. The missus got a tin from the lady she used to clean for.'

'Nice.'

'Soft-soaping her. Wants Min to go back after the war.'

'Will she?'

He shook his head. 'She says she'll stay on, helping at the day-nursery, if they'll have her, loves it there. What about you, Chief?'

'After the war?'

'Yup.'

Winnie shook her head. 'I've no idea.' Her own job was utterly finite; the armistice would come, and then no one would need air-raid wardens any more. The whole intricate jigsaw of Civil Defence – the ARP, the Heavy and Light Rescue, the Fire Service, the WVS tea-vans that turned up at incidents as if conjured like Cinderella's coach – all these pieces would be shaken apart, and she herself, after five years of steadily increasing responsibility – a woman in charge of men – would suddenly be in charge of nothing at all. It was like being in rep: a role learned, played and discarded.

'The thing is,' she'd written to Emlyn recently, 'I'm now so used to putting on a boilersuit that I can't imagine having to wear a skirt to work, and where, in any case, will I find an employer who lists "ability to run across uneven ground while carrying two full buckets" under "qualifications needed"?'

He hadn't yet answered – in fact, it was almost a fortnight since she'd received his last letter, which had consisted of a full-page rumination on the subject of orchards – should they grow damsons or plums on their hypothetical half-acre? Perhaps they should stick to apples, in which case would she prefer Worcester Pearmain or Blenheim Orange, though he'd heard the latter only flourished in sandy soil? He'd ended with a sketch of a fretwork planter he'd once seen at Kew, and the usual 'all my love, Emlyn'. The letter had gone under the bed with all the others.

'Right,' she said, finishing her cocoa. 'I need to get over to Myddleton Square and see if anyone's turned up to repair the shelter roof yet. If I'm not back by lunch-time, have a merry Christmas, won't you, Basset? And best wishes to Min.'

'Thanks, Chief. Where are you spending yours?'

'With my parents. I'm getting the train tonight.' And returning on Boxing Day, if she could possibly manage it, with the excuse that her friend Elsie would be turning up on leave from Portsmouth at some point. And then there was Avril's party on New Year's Eve; the invitation had arrived, with 'Please come, dearest Winnie. It won't be a proper celebration without you' handwritten on the back, while the front bore a rather clever line-drawing of her sister's striking profile above the typed words 'This slender volume will shock many; it will, however, impress a great many more – *New Statesman.*' Winnie had inked a moustache on the picture, before propping it on the shelf above her gas fire.

On the way to Myddleton Square, she called again at the basement flat on Falcon Road, and again there was no answer. The cat, though, was still waiting outside.

Noel's most vivid memory of past Christmases was of a moment simultaneously marvellous and catastrophic.

'Now be rather careful while opening this,' his godmother had said. He'd been six or seven years old, seated on the wicker armchair with the brown velvet cushions, and Mattie had placed something very heavy and smooth and round on his lap, the whole wrapped in white tissue paper and tied with a green ribbon. He had pulled on one end of the ribbon, and the paper had whispered away to reveal a glass sphere, enclosing a tiny pine wood, and at its centre a cottage with a puff of smoke emerging from the chimney. Standing in the doorway, carrying a basket and about to step on to the path that wound through the trees, was a small girl in a red cloak. And in the leafy shadows hid a wolf.

'If you carefully tip it up, just see what happens,' Mattie had said, and he had tipped it and snow had fallen from nowhere, drifting like ash, a silent, delicate blizzard. He had never forgotten the wonder of it. And when the last flake had settled, he had tipped it again and somehow misjudged the weight, so that the globe had rolled over his hand and off the edge of the chair. The precise noise of it hitting the floor had never left him.

'It was an *accident* and not in any way your fault,' Mattie had said, consoling him with one of her enveloping hugs. 'We should have opened it at the table, and I will make it my life's purpose to hunt for another,' though she hadn't ever been able to find one exactly like it. But over the years there had been other astonishing presents – his own pair of binoculars in a leather case, a box of magic tricks, some of which had taken him weeks to master ('Bravo! I shall henceforth call you the Great Noelini!'), an enormous illustrated atlas, with whales spouting in the South Atlantic, and Japan shaking cherry blossom across the Tsugaru Strait. One year there had been a tree so large that there was still a long, scraped mark on the drawing-room ceiling.

His narrow, rationed Christmases with Vee had been unremarkable by comparison, the gifts inevitably home-produced, the disasters limited to occasional power cuts and roast fowl of varying toughness. This year, Noel had modest hopes for the main course; he had found a recipe in a library book about the history of food preservation, and since the evening of the 23rd, the chicken had been steeping in brine, to which he'd added the peel from the single lemon allocated to Vee after a Sicilian shipment had resulted in a two-hour queue at the greengrocer's. By the time he went to bed on Christmas Eve, he had already prepared the parsley and sausage-meat stuffing. The potatoes were washed, the carrots scrubbed and the ring of pink blancmange had set satisfactorily and was under a cover in the larder. Before switching off the light, he re-read the Christmas card he'd received from Genevieve Lumb, which she had signed with five 'X's. He remained a little troubled by the message, which mentioned that she was spending Christmas 'with my cousins, Andrew, Lloyd and Alistair. Alistair has just won the South of England under-16s long-jump trophy, although, as you know, I don't much care about sports.'

He woke abruptly, jaw clenched, from a vile and familiar dream of destruction. It was still dark. The alarm clock was ticking reassuringly, its luminous hands at twenty past four, but he could also hear what sounded like the tail end of an explosion, a low growl that, as he listened, resolved into the sulky mutter of a motor-car engine, and then stopped altogether. A door squealed, a door slammed; in the sudden silence he fell asleep again. He awoke a second time to see yellowish light oozing around the edge of the curtains, and he parted the folds to see a film of ice on the inside of the glass, and unbroken fog without. It was ten to eight. Time to take the chicken out of the brine.

The first sign that the day was to prove unprecedentedly memorable came at the top of the stairs. Noel could hear someone snoring, and the snore grew louder as he descended, rising to a climax as he approached the drawing-room door, which was slightly ajar. Peering round, he saw Corporal O'Mahoney wrapped in a great-coat and lying on the ottoman, his stockinged feet projecting over the end, like planking on a builder's van. A pair of muddy boots lay on Mattie's favourite rug. Fastidiously, Noel removed them and then dropped each boot from waist height on to the stone floor beside the window seat. There was no break in the easy rhythm of the snoring.

The kitchen was empty, but someone had made tea and the pot was still warm. He poured himself a cup and stared broodingly out through the kitchen window. If, as he suspected, the American had come for Christmas lunch, then the small chicken would be utterly inadequate and Vee would just have to open the tin of corned beef she'd been saving since August. And the corporal needn't think he'd be getting any of the white meat.

The fog was slowly shifting, no longer uniformly opaque; the bulky rectangle of the coal bunker emerged gradually from the soup and a flake of soot wandered past the window. The fruitcake, thought Noel. If he sliced the tombola fruitcake and served it with the blancmange and the tinned pears, there would, at least, be more than enough pudding for them all. Another flake of soot followed the first, and then a whole flurry of them, each minutely curled and fronded, almost feather-like. Or not just feather-*like*, he realized, with surprise; actual feathers.

He found Vee just outside the back door, muffled in coat and balaclava, plucking a turkey.

'Happy Christmas,' she said. 'Look what arrived this morning.'

The turkey's head jerked back and forth, ridiculously

small by comparison with its body, the wattle like a pendulum.

'What are we supposed to do with that?' asked Noel.

'*Do* with it?' Vee glanced up, a tiny feather glued to the end of her nose. 'Roast it, of course. How long since you've had a Christmas turkey?'

'But that'll take all day. And we have the chicken.'

'And now we've got a turkey as well. Can't we joint it? Mario drove nearly all the way to Norwich last night – he said he'd fetch us one, but I didn't tell you because I didn't know for sure if he'd manage it.'

'But if I'd known, we needn't have killed Fleur.'

'Who? Oh, the white one. But she hadn't laid since September – you knew there was no point in keeping her. I've asked the corporal to lunch – after all, there's going to be plenty.' Her hand was moving automatically as she spoke, the dark feathers hanging in the air around her.

Noel turned away. He was not sentimental about the hens; on the other hand, Fleur (he had been reading *The Forsyte Saga* when she'd arrived) had seemed more characterful than the rest of the flock and his choice of cooking method had been, in a small way, a tribute to that.

'You've not got a coat on,' said Vee. 'You'll catch your death.'

'Have you fed the hens?' he asked. He could hear them crooning impatiently, the wiry scrape of their feet.

'Not yet.'

Still coatless, he aimed through the fog towards the coop, and shovelled some fish meal through the flap on the side. 'No,' he said, in response to the commotion inside, 'you can't come out yet. Later, maybe.' There was a hint of brightness overhead.

'Have a look in the larder!' called Vee. 'You'll never believe it. And your present's on the dresser.'

When, ten minutes later, she brought in the turkey, now reduced to pimpled nakedness, Noel was already halfway through the first chapter of *The History of European Architecture.*

'Thank you,' he said, a little stiffly.

'There wasn't another one in Cullbright's, but Mr Jepson found a copy in a shop in Wood Green,' she said. 'Are you pleased?'

'Yes. And did you like yours?' He had wrapped the talcum powder and left it outside her bedroom door.

'I did, it's a treat.' She waved a wrist in his direction, and the smell of lavender cut through that of raw meat. 'So, if you've stopped being cross, can we get this in the oven?'

'I'm not cross.'

'Did you see what else he brought? Did you see the little bags with tea in them? I cut the end off one, and there was nearly a spoon and a half in it, so I'm going to open them all and put the tea in the caddy – the only trouble is that it's so fine it'll go straight through the strainer, it's like dust. I might see if I can cut up a stocking and use that instead. And the ham! Did you see the sliced ham? And the great big oranges!'

He had never heard her so animated. 'They're grapefruit,' he said.

'Are they?'

'They're grown in California and picked by itinerant

workers from the Oklahoma dustbowl, as chronicled by John Steinbeck. People in the USA have them for breakfast.'

'What do they taste like?'

'I don't actually know,' said Noel, with reluctant curiosity.

'We could have an American breakfast,' said Vee. 'That'd be a Christmas surprise for everybody, wouldn't it?'

The corporal slept on. Only Dr Parry-Jones really enjoyed the grapefruit, and Vee had to remove the sugar bowl from the table after Mr Reddish had lunged for a third spoonful.

'I'm assuming it's not ripe,' he said. 'I once had to help a young lady in the street – she'd eaten a very sour lime and had developed the most terrible muscle shudders, and I had to give her my arm to the nearest Tube station.'

'Muscle shudders?' repeated Dr Parry-Jones, arrested in the act of raising a tea cup to her mouth. 'Spasms, you mean? Or was it fasciculation? Though I can think of no link between unripe fruit and either of those.'

'Perhaps she'd been dipping it in gin,' suggested Miss Appleby.

'Again, I can think of no clear link,' said the doctor. 'Muscle *weakness* and inebriation, yes, but the symptoms that Mr Reddish is describing don't fall into this category.'

'She was a delicate little thing,' said Mr Reddish, nostalgically. 'When we arrived at the entrance to Goodge Street, she said, "Thank you, sir, you're very kind," and skipped away towards the escalators like a damsel-fly.' He flicked his fingers in an impression of gauzy delicacy and

Noel had to bite his cheeks and glance towards Mr Jepson, who'd always been a useful collaborator at these moments, able to balance a poker face against a gleam in the eye. But Mr Jepson was concentrating on his grapefruit. Since the evening of the Methodist Entertainment, he had moved around the house as if on a different track to Noel, smiling as he passed, still in the vicinity but no longer heading the same way. And during their Tuesday Latin lesson, Noel had turned the page on an unseen translation and had found himself picking his way through a Pliny passage extolling the fortitude of Vespasian's forces: 'When the men fought they were as brave as wild-cats and as unbending as the pines that grow upon the Palatine Hill. Though spears fell like snow they did not flinch.' He had hurried on, but embarrassment had crackled in the air and Mr Jepson's face had lost all its humour and alertness so that he'd resembled a ventriloquist's dummy, cheeks painted red, the expression stiff and unnatural. All the ease of their usual conversation had disappeared, and for once, Noel had been glad when the lesson had ended and he'd been able to leave the room. Thinking about it afterwards, he'd found himself torn between sympathy and irritation; he'd seen it before, this tendency of adults to let a single flawed moment ruin everything, and he wished he could say something bald and straightforward: 'Mr Jepson, despite my youth, I have been present at the worst minutes of several other people, by which measure the incident in the kitchen at the Drill Hall pales into insignificance, and I can assure you that I have no intention of ever referring to it again, nor do I think the less of you because of it, whatever its cause. Can we now carry on making puns about Suetonius?'

Without Mr Jepson to bounce off, the breakfast-table conversation seemed to Noel to have a dreadful flatness, emphatically lacking seasonal cheer. Mr Reddish had heard on the morning news that the Germans were continuing an extensive counterattack on the Western Front. He had also heard that the Tube strike had been extended over Boxing Day, that three rockets had fallen in South London on Christmas Eve, and that Ming the Panda had died at London Zoo. Mr Reddish and Dr Parry-Jones agreed that the Tube strikers were not only unpatriotic but almost certainly communist. Miss Appleby said that she'd once been to see Ming when accompanied by a sailor she'd been walking out with who was himself now dead. Mr Reddish remarked that many people who had been alive at the start of the war were now dead. Miss Appleby started to cry and said that the war had only taken the best, and Dr Parry-Jones said that, as a matter of fact, she'd known of several ne'er-do-wells who'd died as a result of enemy action, and that death was the great leveller, winnowing saints and sinners alike. Mr Reddish recited '*Death Be Not Proud*', Vee cleared the dishes, and breakfast was over.

'You're not with us for Christmas lunch, are you, Mr Jepson?' said Vee. He seemed to be lingering, a small parcel in his hand.

'No. I'm walking to Finchley to see my old editor – he lives alone and is in rather poor health, so I thought . . .' He held out the parcel to Noel and aimed a smile at a corner of the kitchen. 'A little gift for you, not sure whether you've read it already, it's light but tremendously gripping.'

It was a slim volume entitled *Rogue Male*, and Noel was padlocked to the pages for the entire morning, unfastening himself periodically to baste the turkey. Each time he looked up there was more light spilling in through the kitchen windows, and by the time Major Quive-Smith had come to a deserved and satisfying end in a Dorset lane, the sky was a cold, clear blue, and Corporal O'Mahoney was awake.

∞

Mr Reddish raised his glass. 'Here's to the Greek government in their continuing fight against the rebels.'

'The Greek government!' said everyone, not quite in unison. The corporal's final contribution to the meal, brought into the house in a kit bag, had been a box of chocolates ('for the kid'), two bottles of Californian white wine, a bottle of Portuguese sherry and a hip-flask full of whisky. All the usual toasts – Peace, the King, Health and Happiness, Our Mothers – had already been made, and Mr Reddish was now working his way through the current news.

'I believe that ELAS is regarded as a liberation force, rather than a rebel group,' said Noel, who was drinking lemon squash.

'ELAS poor Yorick,' said Mr Reddish, holding up a drumstick. 'Where be your gibes now? Your gambols? Your songs?'

'More turkey, anyone?' asked Vee, reaching out to the

plate and knocking her glass of sherry over the remains of the sausage stuffing. 'Damn.'

'Here's to the Russians consolidating their hold on Budapest.'

'Where *is* that?' asked Vee. 'I think my mother went to Bude once.'

'Hungary,' said Noel.

'I have no great desire to travel,' said Dr Parry-Jones, her diction unnaturally precise, 'but I sometimes wish I could have visited the Antipodes. I have read that a male kangaroo can leap over a twelve-foot fence.'

'I saw one in the zoo the same day that I saw Ming the Panda,' said Miss Appleby. 'It had a tiny little baby kangaroo in its pouch.'

'London Zoo doesn't have kangaroos,' said Noel. 'I imagine that what you saw was a wallaby.'

'That's what it was doing,' said Miss Appleby, with a shriek, bouncing her fingers across the table. 'It was going *wallaby wallaby wallaby* all over the place.'

Noel stood and started to clear the dishes.

'Where's our genial transatlantic visitor got to?' asked Mr Reddish, twisting round to look at the kitchen door, his face still shining with the lingering joy of the corporal's first remark to him – 'Say, did anyone ever tell you that you look like President Roosevelt?'

By way of reply, the clank of pipes heralded the flushing of the bathroom lavatory, and it was followed shortly afterwards by the sound of Leviathan descending the stairs. 'Never been in a place this size before,' he said, his voice preceding him by several yards. 'You have servants?'

'Just me,' muttered Noel.

'More turkey?' asked Vee, for at least the fifth time. She had a very high colour – in fact, everyone in the room looked rather pink and dishevelled, as if they'd just finished dancing round a maypole, the maypole in question being Corporal Mario O'Mahoney.

'Surely there must be many houses as large as this in the United States of America,' said Dr Parry-Jones.

'I'm from the city,' said Mario. 'I grew up in an apartment. No one where I come from has a house like this – I had to hire a guide to find the bathroom.'

Everyone laughed with a vigour that suggested they were in the presence of Oscar Wilde.

'When I was a little girl,' said Dr Parry-Jones – a phrase that Noel had never before heard her use – 'I went to a Christmas party in a house this size, and we played Sardines. I have never forgotten it.'

'Sardines? Is that like Blackjack?' asked the corporal, without apparent facetiousness.

'What is Blackjack?' enquired Dr Parry-Jones.

'It's a card game favoured by professional gamblers,' said Noel. 'An American variant of Pontoon or Vingt-et-Un.'

'No, no, Sardines is quite different. What happens is that a chosen person finds a place of concealment . . .'

Noel picked a scrap of chicken from his plate and let it melt on his tongue. The brine recipe had been a triumph, but everyone except himself had eaten turkey. And now never again would Fleur mistake his shoelaces for a worm.

'Surely that's just Hide and Seek,' said Miss Appleby.

'No, in Hide and Seek one person searches while

everyone else hides, whereas Sardines is completely the opposite,' said Dr Parry-Jones, firmly. 'Eventually, only one person is still looking while all the others are packed together in the hiding-place *like sardines*.'

'Hey, kid, want to see something else disappear?' asked the corporal, holding a cork in one palm. He tossed it in the air, bounced it off one elbow, caught it in his gigantic mouth and swallowed, and then plucked another cork from behind one of Noel's ears. There were gasps and applause and Noel went into the larder to look at the blancmange, taking *The History of European Architecture* with him.

'Oh, there you are,' said Vee, a few minutes later. 'We're going to play Sardines.'

'Why?' asked Noel.

'Oh, go *on*,' she said, giving his arm a pat. 'Just some Christmas fun. Mario's hiding first. I know it's silly but . . . it means we don't have to sit and listen to Mr Reddish talking about young ladies, doesn't it?'

'Everyone's drunk.'

'Everyone's enjoying themselves, for once in their lives. I'm sure I saw the doctor smile – unless it was wind. Won't you join in?'

'All right. As soon as I finish this page.' When she left, he turned the blancmange round again, and took another spoonful. He waited until he could no longer hear footsteps criss-crossing overhead, and then he exited the larder. He walked past the wreckage of the Christmas dinner, into the hall and up the stairs, pausing at the top. He knew precisely where the others were hiding; every creak and scuff in this house was familiar to him, and whilst in the larder he had several times heard a footstep hitting the slightly sunken floorboard at the western end of the first-floor passage – hitting it once and not returning. He walked softly past the row of doors, skirted the tell-tale floorboard and listened outside the lumber room. There was a taut silence within, broken by a frilly giggle from Miss Appleby. Noel was just debating whether to enter the room, or whether to leave them in there for a while longer, crouched amidst the umbrella stands and disintegrating taxidermy, when the front-door bell rang. It rang for a second time just before he reached the door, and he opened it to find a naval officer holding a bunch of holly.

'Oh, good-oh,' said the man, seeing Noel. He was fair-haired, with the regular features of a Forces recruitment poster and a boyish air belied by the crumpled skin beneath his eyes. 'I was just beginning to wonder if anyone were in. Merry Christmas.' Smiling, he held out the holly. 'Terribly sorry, this is all I could find to bring.'

'Merry Christmas,' said Noel, politely, not taking it. 'Do you want Miss Appleby?'

'Miss Appleby? No, I don't think so. Should I want her? Is it a rule?'

'No, I meant . . .'

'I was actually looking for Miss Simpkin. Miss Matilda Simpkin.'

The world swung like a weathercock and Noel had to put a hand on the door frame to steady himself.

'She's not here,' he said. 'And she was Doctor, not Miss. She died five years ago.'

'Oh, did she? I'm so sorry, I had no idea. And I don't

suppose you know what happened to the child who lived with her? He'd be about . . .' He paused, his gaze sliding past Noel and then jerking back to him. '*Oh!*' He gave a huff of incredulous laughter. 'I think I'm being an idiot, aren't I – it's you, isn't it? Neil.'

'Noel.'

'*Noel*, sorry. Of course. Which means . . . well, I don't quite know how to tell you this. Straight out, I suppose, bite the bullet – it means I'm your father. Here.' He offered the spiked bouquet again. This time Noel took it – or, rather, a hand that was apparently his reached out and grasped the stems; they'd been torn or twisted rather than cut, and were bound together with a length of twine. A couple of berries rolled over his knuckles and dropped to the ground.

'I know I've just given you a hell of a shock, but I don't suppose you have anything to eat, do you?' asked the officer. 'I'm straight off the ship, and they've not given us a penny in shore pay. I'm absolutely famished.'

'Yes.' Noel dragged his eyes away from the holly. 'Yes, I . . . could you wait here a moment?'

'Here? You mean, outside? Can't I come in?'

'No,' said Noel, picturing the current occupants of the lumber room. 'Sorry.'

He stepped back into the house and closed the door, and then immediately re-opened it, because what had just happened couldn't possibly have happened; the naval officer was still there, however, hands in the pockets of his duffel coat, his breath clouding the air. 'I'll be quick,' said Noel, closing it again. The house was silent, the sardines still hiding in their tin, and he raced to the kitchen, lobbing the holly into the sink, taking Vee's string bag from the hook and gathering food almost randomly – a half-full bottle of wine, the drumsticks torn from the chicken carcass and wrapped in a tea-towel, a dense wedge of fruitcake, a jar of pickled beetroot and, finally, a handful of chocolates that he shoved into the pockets of his coat as he passed through the hall again. In the drawing room, he grabbed a box of matches and some paper spills from a brass pot in the grate, and then shouted, 'Just going out!' as the door closed behind him. The officer was standing halfway down the path, looking up at the house, and Noel swung round to share his view. The low sun had reddened the bricks and blanked the windows. 'Good-looking pile,' said the officer. 'So if I can't come in, where are you taking me?'

'It's not far.' Noel walked fast, uphill towards the Heath end of the lane, skirting the vast sand-pits that had been gouged out earlier in the war and were now disused and grassy. Crescents of unmelted frost lay along their northern edges.

'Might have to slow down a bit,' said the naval man, from behind. 'I'm actually convalescing. Currently a bit of a crock, I'm afraid.'

Noel waited for him to catch up. 'Were you injured at sea?'

'No. Inglorious pneumonia while in port. Left me with a wheeze.' He paused to catch his breath, his lips purplish. There seemed nothing familiar about his face, no feature or angle that Noel had ever seen in his own mirror.

'What's your name?' he asked, abruptly.

The officer flipped a salute. 'Lieutenant Simeon Foster. Generally known as Sim. And you're Noel . . . ?'

'Bostock.'

'Bostock? Where does that come from?'

'It was my godmother's alias, when she was a suffragette on the run from the police.'

Sim's laugh turned into a cough.

'I'm not making a joke,' said Noel, coldly.

'No, no . . .' Sim flapped a hand as if to waft away offence. 'It was a laugh of considerable admiration. I came across your godmother a couple of times, and she left quite an impression. Shall we carry on?'

Noel took a path that wove through the trees, and then ducked under an oak branch that thrust out horizontally at head height. Beyond it was a clearing, the ground crisp with leaf-litter, and a ring of stones in the centre with three logs arranged as seating around it.

'We can light a fire here,' he said, already hunting for sticks. 'The Hampstead Boy Scouts use it quite often.'

'Are you a Scout?'

'No,' said Noel, with disdain.

'I was, once. I had a fight with the Scoutmaster's son, and was thrown out. Do you need some help with that? It's just that every time I lean over, I start coughing . . .'

'No, it's all right, I'll do it.'

Quickly and neatly, conscious of having an audience, Noel laid and lit a fire. The sticks were dry and the flames almost smokeless.

'That's the ticket,' said Sim, taking off his mittens and

holding his palms to the warmth. 'Very slick indeed. You're quite the woodsman.'

Noel carried on gathering fuel until he had a decent pile, and then he gathered some more, since the alternative was to sit down and engage in a conversation that was too enormous to contemplate. 'The fine young woman who gave birth to you,' Mattie had said, 'was not in a position to raise a child, and she decided that the best place for you to grow up would be here, with me, and there is not a minute of the day, young Noel – not even a second – when her decision fails to bring me joy, and I daily mouth an encomium to the soundness of her judgement. Encomium? Latin for "speech of praise", though the word is originally derived from the Greek – think of those two tongues as jigsaw pieces from which we construct the broad and colourful picture of the English language. With odd gaps for Celtic words, of course.' She had never said anything about his father, and Noel had never thought to ask.

'Well, this is a feast!' said Sim, laying the contents of the string bag along the log, and unscrewing the lid of the pickled beetroot.

'Why haven't you come to see me before?' asked Noel.

'Didn't know you existed.' He extracted a piece of beetroot with his fingers, and swallowed it whole, like an oyster. 'Do you know, when I was a little boy, I once drank a whole cup of vinegar.'

'Why?'

'Because I never could resist a dare.' He grinned and patted the seat next to him, and Noel, instead, sat on the next log, so that he could see the whole of Sim's face. There was a brightness to it that drew the eye.

'I'll tell you the story,' said Sim, between bites of chicken. 'We were docked in Gibraltar for repairs. I came down with the lurgy and the ship's doctor had me transferred to the hospital – lucky me, half-decent food and nurses flitting round, I was in clover if only I'd known it, only I was off my head half the time. When I was starting to feel better they moved me to another ward and while they were tucking me in, up came the Sister – tall, striking redhead, like Queen Elizabeth processing along the Mall, patients springing to attention, junior nurses practically salaaming—'

'Was that her?' asked Noel, the three syllables so impacted that only the question mark was clearly intelligible.

'I'm coming to that – so she stopped by the bed, took one look at me, and it was as if she'd been sand-bagged. She actually swayed on her feet. I wondered whether I'd broken out in spots or turned green, and then I realized there was something awfully familiar about her face. I heard one of the little nurses call her Sister Pearse, and the penny dropped, and I said, "We've met, haven't we? A long time ago," and she turned away and went racing off on her rounds again, but I could tell that something was up. So I thought, *Sim, old man, you'd better try and have a proper powwow with this lady*, and so when I . . .' His voice trailed away, his animated expression suddenly fixed as he looked at Noel and seemed to see, for the first time, the tense angle of his neck, his face thrust forward, the better to catch every word.

'Hang on,' he said. 'I'm doing this all wrong. I'm telling you this as if it were a mess anecdote, not a . . . a . . .' He rubbed his mouth rather awkwardly. 'What an awful fool I'm being,' he said. 'Crass. You're only a youngster.'

'I'm fifteen.'

'Still. I'm sorry. I really should have asked you first if you knew anything about your parentage. I don't want to shock you. For all that I know, your Miss Simpkin – *Dr* Simpkin – might have spun you a yarn to spare your feelings.'

'My feelings about what?'

'Well . . . that you're not . . .'

'Legitimate? I knew that already.'

'Oh. What else did you know?'

He shrugged. 'Nothing, really.'

'You weren't curious?'

Noel shook his head rather slowly. *Why* hadn't he been curious? Perhaps life with Mattie had left no empty corners for brooding in. 'I was told that my mother was not in a position to raise a child.'

'No,' said Sim, soberly. 'No. She wouldn't have been. She was terribly young. We were both terribly young.' He raised his hands to the fire again. 'So you were told nothing about me, then?'

'No.'

'I don't suppose your Dr Simpkin had much use for men. She probably thought I was a bad lot.'

'Are you?'

Sim laughed. 'No worse than anyone else, I hope. So should I go on, then?'

'Yes.'

'Well. I couldn't wangle a conversation with the sister when I was still a patient – to be frank, she wouldn't come within yards of me – but the day I was discharged, I hung around outside the hospital and caught her when she finished work and, well, there you have it . . . Of course, I'd had no idea at the time, I'd left London by then. I never knew.'

'That she was pregnant with me, you mean?'

'Yes. I must say, you're very forthright.'

'Mattie didn't believe in euphemisms. Where had you gone, then?'

'Cambridge. Rusticated after a couple of terms, I'm afraid – I'm not cut out for study.'

'Were you engaged to be married?'

'Lord, no! It was just a – no.'

'And what's her name?'

'Ida. Ida Pearse. A very fine girl.'

It was the same word that Mattie had used: 'fine' had been one of her highest accolades, the single syllable large with implications of principle, pluck, nobility.

'And how did you meet her?'

'She was in a girls' club on the Heath, run by your godmother.'

'The Amazons?'

'That's right. You know about it?'

'I recently met someone else who'd been a member. Can you tell me anything more about her?'

'Redhead, as I said. Touch of the Burne-Jones about her looks.'

Noel swiftly averted his thoughts from an image of tall, high-breasted girls wrapped in pleated grey silk descending a staircase with indolent grace.

'And she was a nurse?'

'Not when I met her. She was only . . .'

'What? How old was she?'

'Fifteen.'

'*Fifteen? My* age?' Abruptly, Noel stood up and walked stiff-legged around the clearing, switching direction aimlessly, stooping to pick up a twig, tossing it towards the fire and missing. 'And how old were you?'

'I was nearly eighteen.'

'Why didn't she tell you that she was pregnant?'

'I don't know.'

'But you talked to her. In Gibraltar. Didn't you ask?'

'It wasn't a . . . detailed conversation. She really didn't want to discuss it. But of course, once I knew you existed, I had to find out where you were. It's not every day one discovers one has a son.'

'Don't you have other children?'

'No. No, you're my sole heir.'

'Does *she*?'

'Ida? Not as far as I know. And she's certainly a spinster – married nurses aren't allowed, certainly not ones as senior as she appears to be.'

Noel carried on his circling of the clearing. A magpie was cackling nearby, and the naval officer heaved a branch on to the fire, and coughed as the sparks burst upwards, but the scene felt distant and artificial, as if he were watching from a seat at the back of the stalls.

'So who's your guardian now?' asked Sim, his mouth full of cake.

'My aunt.' The reply was automatic, simply another layer of untruth on the existing pile.

'And what's her name?'

'Mrs Margery Overs.'

'And that house is hers now, is it?'

'It's mine,' said Noel, impatient to get back to more central matters. 'I don't think I look very much like you.'

'That may be so, but you're awfully like my father at the same age.'

'Am I? Have you a photograph?'

'Not on me. Why don't you come and sit down again? Who made the fruitcake?'

'I don't know.'

'It's welcome, of course, but it's a touch solid. More anchor than life-buoy.' He looked up and grinned as Noel sat down. 'So tell me all about yourself. Where do you go to school? Who are your friends? What are your hobbies?'

'Hobbies are for people who don't read books,' said Noel, answering the only straightforward question out of the three.

'So not keen on sports?'

'No.'

'You're clever, then?'

'Yes.'

Sim laughed again. 'Good, I'm delighted. I hope you apply yourself more than I ever did.'

'What's Cambridge like?'

'I think you'd probably love it. Full of people who prefer books to hobbies.'

'Were you in the navy before the war?'

'No. Called up in '40.'

'So what's your profession?'

'I can't say I've ever settled to any particular walk of life. I tried working in the old man's office and couldn't keep my eyes open, got the heave-ho after a month or two. Definitely not the favoured son. Taught a bit, travelled a bit, always had a taste for the sea. I was thinking I might get a yacht after the war – nothing fancy, a sloop of some kind. Drift up and down the Med – you could come and be my deckhand, you could swim in the Aegean and learn to tie knots. Can you swim?'

'Yes, and I can tie knots as well.'

'Well, there we go; the perfect companion. The water there's like nothing you've ever seen – one moment it's so clear you'd think the fishes were suspended in mid-air, and the next it's an absolutely brilliant turquoise, like a kingfisher's back, and the next moment you look round and it's purple as far as the horizon.'

The teasing note had momentarily gone from his voice, the sense that every subject had to be mined for levity. For a second or two they stood together on a sun-warmed deck, hearing the soft slap of the waves.

'Homer described it as "wine-dark",' said Noel, 'οἶνοψ πόντος. Although, apparently, it's possible that οἶνοψ should actually be translated as "maroon".'

'Should it?' Sim cocked his head in thought. 'Well, now I consider it, the colour's definitely on the reddish side of purple. A drinkable Merlot, perhaps.' He grinned again, and this time, Noel found himself smiling back.

'Do you know,' said his father, licking his fingers and then screwing the lid back on to the beetroot jar, 'that was just about the best meal I've had since the invasion of Sicily. All we seem to eat at sea is tinned fish, which is apposite enough, I suppose, but – what is it? What's the matter?'

'I have to get back,' said Noel, already on his feet and picking up the jar and the tea-towel and Vee's string bag. 'I forgot.'

'Forgot what?'

'When you said "tinned fish". I left the rest of them playing Sardines. They were all in the lumber room, waiting for me to find them, but that was ages ago. My aunt will be worried about me. Or annoyed. Or both, most likely.'

'Who do you mean by "all"?'

'My aunt and the lodgers, and . . .' He felt something brush his cheek, and looked up to see a sky sagging with cloud. 'If I don't go, she'll come looking.'

'Oh, your aunt takes in lodgers, does she? Profitable business?'

'No, not really.' They left the clearing and were suddenly in twilight. Sim stumbled over a root, and took out his torch, playing it over the path ahead, before twitching it suddenly upward. 'What the hell?'

'Barn owl,' said Noel. 'Can I see you again? When does your ship embark? Though I expect you're not allowed to tell me that, are you?'

'Not even if I knew myself. Perhaps I could drop round again if I'm still on leave next week?'

'No. Let's meet somewhere else. I don't want . . .' *I don't want this spoiled*, he thought: the Aegean sunset, the yacht at anchor and Vee standing on the jetty, binoculars trained beadily on Sim.

They emerged from the woods into steady snow, the grass already disappearing. 'How about the National Gallery?' suggested Noel. 'Or, no, better than that, how about the Victoria and Albert? It's the only museum still open and, besides, there's something I want to see there. I could meet you on Monday. In the Cast Court.'

'I can try, but I shan't know if I can get there till the day before. They're always throwing duties at us, even in port. Tell you what, though, you couldn't sub me something till we meet next, could you? A tenner would come in handy. Or a fiver?'

'I think I've only got about three and six,' said Noel. 'But you can have that.'

'Not really quite enough. I don't suppose your aunt would spare a tenner for a sailor boy, would she?'

For a fraction of a second, Noel contemplated trying to sneakily access the golden-syrup tin in which Vee kept her cash.

'I'm afraid not,' he said. 'Sorry.'

The roof of the Wimbournes' house slid into view, between the trees.

'Are you limping?' asked his father.

'I sometimes do when I hurry. What if I get to the V&A for nine o'clock every day next week, then? I can always sit and read. I'll stay till midday in case you come later. Or would the afternoons be better?' Noel could hear himself gabbling, seized with the sense that his own desperate yearning for another meeting wasn't quite reciprocated – that if he didn't hook a promise in the fifty yards between the Wimbournes' house and his own, then his father might bob away again, out of reach.

'Would the afternoons be better?' he repeated, just as Vee's voice became audible, calling his name.

'Coming!' he shouted. Through the trees, he glimpsed Vee, bareheaded, with her shawl round her shoulders, turning back towards the house.

'Is that your aunt?' asked Sim.

'Yes.'

'Well, I'm jolly glad there's someone worrying about you – you'd better hurry home. And yes, I'll try to get there, no fear, wouldn't miss it for the world.' He held out a bony hand, and Noel shook it.

'Just in case,' said Noel, 'what's your ship called? So I could write to you.'

'Can't say at the moment, I'm afraid – I'm about to be transferred. I can hear your aunt again. Off you go.'

Noel turned and picked his way through the ruts towards Green Shutters. When he arrived at the gate he looked round, but his father had gone.

~

'I'm too fond of you not to tell you the truth,' said Winnie, keeping her voice low, her expression warm, yet regretful. 'We've known each other for nearly half our lives. You're a decent man. There was a time when the only thing that

I wanted was to marry you and to settle down and raise a family, but that' – her voice shook a little – 'that was before the tide of war swept us apart.'

'Oh, give *over*!' said her friend Elsie. 'I can't say that bit about the tide, Gordon'll think I've gone nuts. But I liked what you said first, the bit about half our lives – hang on.' She licked the end of her pencil and transcribed a few words on to the back cover of the *Radio Times*. 'Go on, then,' she said. 'I need something about there not being anyone else.'

'Why? Wouldn't it be simpler just to pretend that you've met another chap and fallen in love?'

'No, because I haven't, and if Gordon asks me what this other chap's called and where I met him, and what regiment he's in and where he's from, I'll be stumped, won't I? You know I can't lie the way you do. *Act*, I mean,' she corrected herself, over Winnie's protest, and then grinned and turned her attention again to the *Radio Times*, her small, neat features sharpening with concentration. She was a petty officer in the WRNS and only a little younger than Winnie, but in her current pose – sitting cross-legged on a cushion, as close to the electric fire as possible, a blanket over her shoulders and Winnie's beret pulled down over her ears – she looked about eleven, the same age as when they'd first met as fellow Amazons on a breezy hillside on Hampstead Heath. Winnie, who had been dressed in a Liberty double-breasted woollen coat with hartshorn toggles, could still remember the shock of noticing that Elsie, in February, was wearing a man's jacket and no gloves, her fingers blebbed with chilblains. Poverty, before that moment, had been something that Winnie had read about in children's stories – picturesquely smudged chimney sweeps and large-eyed matchgirls with a delicate pallor and long golden hair. She hadn't realized that cheap food could make you spotty or a freezing flat could give you ugly hands; she hadn't realized, either, that poor people weren't necessarily ashamed of their poverty. If Elsie mentioned that she'd never tasted a tomato or been to the theatre or owned a brand-new item of clothing, she stated it merely as a fact; it was Winnie who'd found the admissions embarrassing, pointing up as they did the velvety ease of her own life. One week, she'd brought a tomato for Elsie to try, expecting wonderment, and Elsie had coughed out the half-chewed piece into her palm and thrown it into a bush. 'Horrible,' she'd said, cheerfully enough. The gloves had gone down better – a pair lined with rabbit-fur, which Winnie hadn't ever worn because they reminded her of Benjamin Bunny – but their actual friendship had sprung not from patronage, but from an overheard remark.

'What's that girl called?' Elsie had whispered to Ida Pearse, one of the older members.

'Which girl?'

'The one who always knows everyfing about everyfing.'

'Oh, that's Avril Bridge. She's Winnie's twin.'

'Twins? They're twins? What, *both* of them?'

'Yes.'

'But that girl Avril, she's . . .'

Winnie had braced herself for the inevitable comparison: . . . *ten times prettier than Winnie . . . so much brainier than Winnie . . . not nearly as fat as Winnie.*

'. . . she's a right bossy old show-off, isn't she? And Winnie's ever so nice.'

A marvellous warmth had flooded through Winnie, leaving a tidemark of indelible gratitude; it had never occurred to her during her constant skirmishes with Avril – the mutual insults and sly pinches that punctuated their days – that she was actually *nicer* than her twin. The week after that, during a game of stalking, Elsie had compared Avril's looks unfavourably with those of a ferret and the bond was sealed. The club had foundered, but the two girls had continued to meet – there'd been a pedagogic element at first, with Winnie going to the library to 'help the poor girl' (as she explained to her parents) with her arithmetic and spelling; Elsie, though, was a quick study, which meant there was always plenty of time left over for whispered discussions about film stars or where babies came from (Elsie was one of nine) or the perennially enjoyable topic of how awful Avril was. Aside from the delicious interest of these conversations, the effect on Winnie's own academic performance was considerable, since she had to work hard to stay ahead of her pupil, but the most wonderful thing of all was that Elsie *admired* her. It was a balm that soothed the dents inflicted by Avril.

'All right,' said Elsie, looking up from the *Radio Times*. 'What should I say next?'

'Hang on, let me have a think – I mean, you've rather sprung this on me.' Not that she hadn't been thinking for years that Elsie had got herself a brick when she deserved a diamond. Gordon lived next door and had wooed her by the simple expedient of cementing himself to her side. 'When did you make up your mind?'

'On the train on the way up from Portsmouth, so about' – Elsie checked her watch – 'four hours ago. It happened all of a sudden, it was like – what's that thing called? – the road to Zanzibar?'

'What, with Bob Hope?'

'No, the one with the saint, in the Bible, he falls off his horse.'

'Road to Damascus.'

'*Yes.* It was like *this*' – she clicked her fingers. 'We were just crossing the Downs and they were all white and perfect, like icing sugar, and I was thinking about how Gordon wants to set a date for the wedding, and instead of feeling excited I felt dead flat, I just couldn't pick myself up, it was as if I was looking all round but couldn't see anything that . . . that *shone*, and then I heard this noise – I didn't have a seat, I was wedged in next to the heads, and there were four of my ratings in the same carriage, all in uniform, and one of them was flirting with a marine, and she was laughing so loudly that she sounded drunk, and everyone was staring and I stood up on tiptoe and caught her eye and gave her a look – just one of my officer looks, I didn't say anything – and she shut up, straight away, and I thought, *I'm good at this, I am.* And then I thought, *Why don't I chuck it in with Gordon?* and it was like . . . flash-bang!' She looked up with wonder, as if following the trajectory of a shooting star. '. . . I'd got it. I'd found the answer. I'd always thought – you know, end of the war, back to the Post Office, back to Gordon – he's a foreman at Cossor's now, did I tell you? – and I'd thought . . . *that'll* be all right. It'll be all right. And you know Gordon, Winnie. You know that he's . . .'

There was a pause.

'. . . All right,' supplied Winnie.

'Yes.'

Their eyes met for a fraction of a second and Elsie made a spluttering noise that was close to a sob, and then recovered herself. 'And I thought, *I don't want to go backwards.* And I know it's going to be horrible, telling him, but I know this is right, I know it, I *know* it. And I'm going to stay in the Wrens – that was the other bit of the "flash-bang". They're already talking about transferring girls to the Fleet Air Arm after the war, and they always need telegraphists and I could end up just about anywhere. Australia. Damascus.'

'Zanzibar!'

The whistle on the kettle began its rising shriek, and Winnie turned off the gas and refilled her hot-water bottle, wedging it between her belt and her jumper. She'd have to get ready for Avril's party soon; her pale-blue crêpe dress and a new pair of stockings were hanging over a chair.

'You could say something like: "We've been apart too long, Gordon. We've both changed." '

'But *he* hasn't changed.'

' "We've been apart too long, Gordon, and *I've* changed." '

'All right, I can try that.' Elsie transcribed the words. 'Do you think I have, though?'

'No,' said Winnie. 'Not a bit. You've always been dynamite.'

Elsie reached out and gave one of Winnie's hands a squeeze. 'You're a pal,' she said.

They had nearly reached the Tube station, picking their way across the filthy sandwich of ice and mud that covered the pavements, when Winnie spotted the van, its back door half open, the pale smear of a streetlight picking out the gilded words 'BREAD AND CAKES' on the side. She crossed the road and peered in; the interior was empty.

'What's the matter?' called Elsie.

'I'm not sure.' The row of terraced houses beside it was derelict, the roofs missing, rafters crossed like bean-sticks, but in one of the windowless front rooms she could see a torch dipping and probing, and the silhouette of a policeman's helmet.

'Wait here a mo,' she said to Elsie.

'Why?'

'That's the mortuary van.'

'It *can't* be.'

'The official one got buzz-bombed. I just want to check what's going on.'

She knocked at the open front door.

'Who's there?'

'Is that Constable Orr?' she called. 'It's Warden Crowther. From Post 9. I was just passing.'

She edged from the narrow hall into what had been the front parlour. The room stank of woodsmoke and it was crowded, striped with shadows from the constable's torch. An empty stretcher was propped upright against a wall, two Light Rescue men standing beside it with arms folded while Dr Skipton crouched next to something on the damp floor.

'What's happened?' she asked. The torch swung round towards her.

'Win? You look smart. Didn't know you had legs.'

'Back *here*, please,' said the doctor.

Winnie took out her own torch and edged the beam towards what lay on the ground, mentally bracing herself. If you had to look at a corpse, then an official relationship made all the difference – squeamishness took second place if you had a job to do, even if that job was simply to find a blanket or to note down a name or date. Here she was only a spectator. Her torch-beam slid across trousered legs and a bucket from which a set of old fire irons protruded.

'It's Jim,' she said. She could see the old man's stained tartan shawl now, and the Afghan hat. He was lying on his back with his arms crossed, like a Crusader on a tomb, his face all hollows and sharpness, the skin no longer mottled, but the dull white of putty.

'Froze to death, poor soul,' said Dr Skipton, straightening up. 'So far as I can tell, though, it's quite likely he had TB as well – I gather he had a permanent cough. Thank you, you can take him now,' he added, to the stretcher-bearers.

'How did you find him?' asked Winnie.

'Someone reported seeing a fire in here last night,' said the constable. 'I think he must have tried to light another, but snow kept coming down the chimney. Don't suppose you know if he had any next of kin?'

'I don't even know if his name was really Jim.' She shifted out of the way as the stretcher came past, one of the bearers stumbling over the bucket, the doctor following. 'He told me once he'd been gassed in the Great War and he'd had a bad chest ever since.'

She stooped to right the bucket, flashing her torch across the looted treasures within – the fire irons, the cracked front panel of a wireless, a soiled tea-cosy, a bright gilt naval button just like the ones on Elsie's uniform. Winnie picked it out and ran her thumb across the embossed anchor, and then dropped it back with the other items.

'Could you let me know if there's a funeral for him?' she asked the constable.

Outside, it had begun to snow again. Elsie was still waiting, shifting from foot to foot, her eyes following the passage of the stretcher.

'Who was it?'

'Poor old chap who lived on the streets. Half mad, wouldn't ever let us help him.'

'There'll be a few more of those when this is over.'

'Few more of whom?'

'People on the streets. Where are they all going to live when they come back?' Elsie said, her tone suddenly indignant. The doors of the bread van slammed shut and the wheels spun, gripped briefly and then slithered towards the main road, the van's rear end giving an ungainly shimmy as it turned the corner.

'You ladies going to a New Year party?' asked the constable, carefully closing the front door of the house, even as snow began to blow in through the window.

'No,' said Elsie, soberly. 'I'm off to give my fiancé the elbow.'

'*I* am,' said Winnie. 'Not that I want to. Happy New Year, Tom.'

He flipped a salute. 'And to you, Win.'

She linked arms with Elsie, and they resumed their walk.

'I wish you were coming too,' said Winnie.

'I don't. You know what I think about your sister, and anyway, what would I do at a literary party?'

'What I'm going to do: drink. If there *is* anything to drink. And Avril's house is terribly swanky.'

'Any dancing?'

'Doubt it.'

'What will they talk about?'

'Clive's friends are all Ministry bods so there'll be War Office gossip, I suppose. And there's bound to be some bookish types . . .'

'So if you forced me to summarize it, absolutely forced me – because, to be frank, asking a writer to précis his work is an act of utter barbarism. Just imagine demanding that Picasso scribble a little sketch of *Les Demoiselles d'Avignon* for you – but if, as I say, you absolutely forced me to reduce it to a single line, I'd have to suggest that it's about the impossibility of true communication between the sexes,' said the man with a paisley neck-tie, checking over Winnie's shoulder for the fortieth time in case someone more important or better-looking was standing behind her. 'I'm thinking of calling it "Thus Endymion Weeps". What do you think of that for a title? Intriguing, *n'est-ce pas*?'

'Yes,' said Winnie, not even attempting enthusiasm, her

facial muscles already fatigued by the expression of interest she'd been feigning for the last ten minutes. As far as she could gather, he hadn't even written the book yet; it was just a clanking bucket of ideas he'd filched along the way, like poor old Jim with his looted rubbish.

There was a tiny pause in the conversation, the sort of pause which might prompt someone not entirely self-absorbed to ask a question of the other person. 'Of course, it's not my *only* idea,' he continued. 'My agent was insistent that I should – oh, there he is. I say, Ivan!'

Winnie turned to see an elderly man with a large red face, and an extraordinary arrangement of long white hair, like a swirl of mock cream. 'Oh, hello, Maxwell,' he said, with a certain lack of keenness.

'Join us?'

'Yes. Of course.' Ivan glanced around in the obvious hope of finding someone else to talk to, before resignedly moving towards his client.

Maxwell resumed his monologue. 'I was just saying to . . . to . . .' He gestured vaguely at Winnie. 'That you advised me very strongly to pursue the idea of fictionally examining what I would term – in a self-coined phrase, I believe – *osmotic emotion* . . .'

Released from the post of solitary listener, Winnie edged backward a few inches, and then slowly revolved through forty-five degrees so that she was on the very fringes of – and yet not actually involved in – a different conversation ('. . . at which point I said to him, "Oh, I hadn't realized that you want the sort of poetry that can be sung to the tune of 'Knees Up, Mother Brown'," and he looked at me *daggers*'); the speaker's eyes slid over her without interest, and she was at last free to simply look around. The room was blue with cigarette smoke and completely full, and she knew no one besides her sister – twinkling somewhere at the centre of the crush – and her brother-in-law, Clive, who had greeted her briefly before being summoned away to a telephone call.

It was a long time since she'd been to a party like this, and she could feel her current self, the Winnie who drew up orders and joshed with colleagues, begin to slough away; how many times, as a gauche drama student, had she stood in just this position, sucking in her stomach and attempting to laugh at the same time as everybody else? That was exactly what she'd been doing on the night she'd met her husband; she could recall, suddenly, the taste of cheap sherry, and the dawning realization that the nice-looking young chap with the Labour Party badge was gazing at *her* and at no one else, and the precision of the memory seemed to jog something within her, so that she felt an unexpected shiver of the heart-strings, accompanied by a very definite sensation at crotch-level – a pleasurable tug – that made her shift and blush, though no one was looking at her. She had almost forgotten Emlyn as a solid being, awkward but gentle, his cold feet, the oddly biscuity smell of his hair, his ticklish middle: she'd been able to tease him into a defensive ball of arms and bony knees, begging for mercy. He'd kissed nicely, too. Last year, after a Civil Defence Social Night, she'd experienced the damp-lipped vacuum suck of the Chief Officer of Haringey Heavy Rescue, who had wanted to thank her very much indeed for her help in putting away the chairs, and it had roused nothing in her apart from the desire for a handkerchief. What if she turned her head now, and saw Emlyn?

She turned her head and saw Avril, svelte in a silver-grey dress, a fuchsia silk bow at her neck.

'Twinnie! I've been looking for you – where have you been? This is my sister, everybody.' The adjacent conversations stopped abruptly, and Winnie could almost feel the gazes shuttling between herself and Avril; Maxwell's expression was one of baffled pique. *Bet he wished he'd asked me some questions now*, thought Winnie.

'Come with me,' said Avril, grabbing her hand and leading her back through the crowd. 'Have you had a drink?'

'Yes.'

'Have another.' She plucked a glass from a waiter's tray and passed it to Winnie. 'Clive's raided the family cellars. I wish you'd said you needed a new dress, I could have weaselled one out of Saks, the head of gowns is a friend of mine.'

'What's wrong with this one?' asked Winnie.

'Nothing's *wrong*, darling, it just looks as if you climbed into a box in 1937 and have only just found your way out. Come and stand *here*.' She halted beside the empty Adam fireplace at the end of the room, and patted the mantelpiece, as if expecting Winnie to clamber up and perch on the end.

'Why here?'

'Because I want you to be able to hear my speech. Though my editor's going to say something first.' Under her words came the repeated pinging of metal on glass, and the roar of conversation gradually diminished, until only one querulous, elderly voice was still audible – 'of course what we *weren't* allowed to say was that Virginia was an ABSOLUTE BITCH . . . What's the matter? Oh . . .'

In a small clearing in the crowd, a bald man in a tight tweed suit handed his glass and spoon to someone, and turned to face the bulk of the room, his back to Winnie. There was a very long pause and then she noticed that the people around him were leaning inward, tilting their heads, and that what she had taken for the noise of someone clearing their throat was in fact a speech, virtually inaudible from where she stood.

'Is nobody going to give a SPEECH?' enquired the elderly voice, plaintively. In the corners of the room, conversation was beginning again. 'Well, if there are to be NO SPEECHES, then I shall most definitely go and find THE LAVATORY.'

The distant throat-clearing continued for a while longer and was followed by a smattering of applause, and then Avril's husband, Clive, carried a dining chair into the clearing. A moment later, Avril's head and shoulders appeared above the crowd.

'Welcome, everybody – I say, welcome!!' She was holding a little ceramic bell, and she tinkled it reprovingly towards those who were still talking. 'Quiet, everyone! I need a *reverent hush.* Pretend I'm the six o'clock news.' There was a light laugh, and silence fell. 'Thank you so much for coming,' said Avril. 'It's a stinking night, and I suspect that no one wanted to leave home, even for free alcohol and relative warmth, so I'm awfully grateful for your attendance. I'm also grateful to my editor, Allen Faste, whose invariably valuable advice to me is, fortunately, more audible than his speeches.' There was another laugh. *Blimey, she's good at this*, thought Winnie. *No wonder she wanted me to hear it*. No one was chatting now; the room was paved with upturned faces. '. . . So, yes, I know that I'm a very fortunate girl indeed to be with such a progressive publisher. Now, who else do I have to thank? Ah yes, Clive, I haven't forgotten you; little did you know that when you said "I do" in Chelsea Town Hall, you were marrying a tortured artist. I hope that it's not been . . . too painful.' She smiled downward in a way that made the man standing nearest to Winnie give an excited little inhalation.

'Lucky, lucky fellow,' murmured someone else.

'But there's another person I need to thank,' continued Avril. 'It's the woman whose experiences inspired me to write *Tin Helmet*.'

Winnie flinched, spilling some of her wine.

'Senior Warden Winifred Crowther, also known as my twin sister, Winnie – she's the one in blue, standing beside the fireplace over there—'

A hundred faces turned to look at her.

'—Winnie has lived the truth that I've merely attempted to transfer to the page; she epitomizes the gumption and bravery of civil defence workers, all those chaps who so often only stand and wait, yet who are required to act at a moment's notice, in the service of us all. But, of course, truth in fiction can only ever be the *filet mignon* to the unwieldy farmyard beast that is real life. So I would like to raise a glass to Winnie, who, while I was safely ensconced in the cosy basement shelter of Senate House, was outside, under the searchlights, wrestling with the great, dull, sweating ox of verisimilitude. To Winnie!'

'To Winnie!' echoed the party-goers.

'They're certainly NOT IDENTICAL, ARE THEY?' observed the elderly voice.

Avril climbed down, to applause, and then reappeared almost immediately, holding a copy of the book – 'I have been induced to read a short section' – and Winnie downed the remains of her wine and started to edge through the crowd towards the door, unable to face hearing about Binnie and her bed-bouncing exploits. From those who caught her eye on the way out, there were smiles of gratitude and encouragement, such as one might give to a person endowed with gumption and bravery, or, indeed, to a perspiring ungulate who was behaving well in public. She could see herself brooding for several days on the nuances of Avril's speech.

In the hall outside, she waited for the maid to bring her coat. Once again, applause sounded from the drawing room, followed by the resumption of chatter.

'Oh, Winnie, you're here! I was worried I'd missed you.'

'Clive.' Avril's husband kissed her cheek and she felt the unexpected scrape of stubble.

'I'm so sorry,' he said, clapping a hand to his chin. 'I only flew back from . . . another place this afternoon; I had to shave on the aeroplane, not ideal.'

He was wearing a grey suit and there was a greyish

tinge to his pleasantly baggy features, so that he resembled a photograph in a newspaper.

'You look tired,' she said.

'Don't we all? But I couldn't miss this, could I? Wasn't Avril simply *marvellous*?'

'Yes.'

'Absolutely luminous.'

'Yes.'

'Do you know which line she always reminds me of?'

'No.'

'The Byron sonnet. "And all that's best of dark and bright, meet in her aspect and her eyes." You know it, of course.'

'Yes,' said Winnie, wondering how long this would go on for; once Clive got on to his favourite topic, he was difficult to shift.

'How's the war coming along?' she asked, only half facetiously; he was, as Avril liked to say, *un grand fromage* at the Foreign Office.

'I suppose one could say it's progressing towards the correct conclusion,' said Clive. 'Though not altogether smoothly.'

'Were you in France today? No, sorry, I know you can't say. But how was it, wherever you were?'

'Rather windy, as a matter of fact. Have you heard from Emlyn recently?'

'No, actually. Not for a few weeks. I keep thinking that since everything's in uproar, the letters aren't getting through, or else that he's been liberated and he'll suddenly turn up on the . . .' There was an indefinable shift in Clive's expression. 'What?' asked Winnie, just as the maid arrived with her coat. Clive waited until the woman had left, and then gestured towards a door further down the hall. Inside was a small sitting room. He drew the curtains and switched on a lamp.

'*What?*' asked Winnie again, alarmed now. 'What is it?'

'Emlyn's in Stalag Ten, isn't he?'

'Ten A. Why? Have you heard something? Tell me.'

'The thing is, Winnie, we've had a report from a Red Cross delegate that POWs in camps close to the Russian advance – and that may include Emlyn's – are being moved. The delegate had actually seen groups of Allied prisoners being marched west by their guards.'

'*Marched?*'

'Yes.'

'But it's the middle of winter!'

Clive made a rather helpless gesture. 'I didn't know whether to tell you. There's no certainty about this information, obviously, and, of course, it's . . .'

Automatically, in the childish gesture always used at Post 9, Winnie found herself lifting a hand to her lips, and turning an imaginary key.

'Thank you, Clive,' she said.

He patted her arm. 'You know that if I hear anything more . . . You're going now?'

'Yes. Say goodbye to Avril from me, will you, and congratulations and all that.'

'I shall. You know, she thinks the world of you, Winnie.'

Even in her current state of mind she had to hold back a wordless puff of disbelief.

She arrived back at the flat hardly aware of having

made the journey, and immediately took the old sewing basket and the suitcase from under the bed, and opened both, and sat back on her heels, staring at the bundles of letters. The one certainty – the one *absolute certainty* – she'd had about Emlyn over the preceding four and a half years was that he was safe: out of the fighting and behind a prison fence, and safe. She didn't know when he'd be coming back, or how long he'd have to remain in the army, or what either of them would do after the war, or where they'd live, or what on earth they would have to talk about beside the advantages of parquet flooring over linoleum, but she'd always assumed that at the end of the war he'd be *alive*. And how entirely stupid that assumption suddenly seemed, as if there were rules in war, as if fairness came into it, as if a bullet in combat were the only way for a soldier to die. She'd heard dozens of stories of people losing sons or husbands in unexpected ways or stupid accidents, tanks swinging round during training, catastrophic parachute drops, traffic collisions whilst on leave, neglected colds in army camps that led to 'flu, but somehow that hadn't intruded on the imaginary cocoon she'd spun around Emlyn. He'd been invulnerable, which had meant she could stow all those stifling letters under the bed, and turn away and do other things. It had been different at first: she'd had a Red Cross postcard when he'd been captured in France and then nothing at all for nearly two months, so that when his first letter had arrived from the camp, in July of 1940, it had been like a great gasp of oxygen after weeks of holding her breath; she had read and re-read it until the creases had pulled apart, and by then she'd memorized every sentence.

She started lifting the bundles from the suitcase, each layer older than the last, until she reached those early letters, handled so often that their written surface had the texture of felt.

'Dearest darling, I can't stop thinking about you, I can't forget for a second that you're not with me . . .' The words poured on to the page, seemingly without artifice or hesitation; she remembered that, as she'd read, she'd heard Emlyn's voice, and she tried to recall it now, but though she could have described its lineaments – a trace of a Welsh accent, a teacher's tendency to over-pronounce long words (she had teased him about that) – the actual sound of it was lost to her. The phrases that had once turned her inside-out brought only a flat sadness.

'Dearest darling, there's so much that I want to say to you and yet so little to actually tell you about. Each day here is much the same as the next, up at 6.30 and then fourteen hours of petty activity and dreadful tedium . . .'

'Dearest darling, I've been trying to store up things to write to you about but most of them are so tiny and dull that they've fallen down the cracks in my memory and I'm sitting here, staring out at the compound (it's raining for the first time in a while), simply wishing that you were sitting beside me . . .'

She re-opened one letter after another. The dates shifted to August, and then to September and the start of the Blitz and, though she'd tried not to alarm him, there was a change in Emlyn's tone.

'Darling Winnie, I gather that you might all be having rather

a difficult time of it at home. I know you haven't said much, but we manage to learn odd bits and bobs along the way, and it's worrying the hell out of me . . .'

'Dearest darling, of course I'm proud of you in your new job, but do be careful. I'm sure there'd still be plenty of useful work for you to do if you went to live somewhere quieter, and it's quite painful having to sit here with little or nothing to occupy me while my dearest girl is in danger . . .'

Winnie remembered wondering what on earth she could write about, since any mention of her work, or sleepless nights, or shelters, or the myriad disruptions to daily life that stemmed from nightly bombing, led to pages of anxious admonition, and the subject matter of her own letters began to shrink, so that each one became a checklist of the same, careful topics: books read, wireless programmes listened to, neighbours' gossip, rationing complaints . . .

'Dearest darling Winnie, I'm always thinking and worrying about you, as you know, but you might laugh when I tell you what I dreamt about last night: it was that time when you were trying to extricate one of your shoes from under the bed, using the broom, and then the head of the broom came off, and we ended up having to lift the mattress and reach through the springs, in a dusty and annoying way. I woke up having made the momentous dream-decision that we must ensure we have a house with a bedroom large enough to have the bed entirely in the middle of the room, so that lost shoes can be retrieved from either side . . .'

'Dearest darling Winnie, I've been thinking further on the bedroom scheme in my last letter. Yet another advantage of the central bed would be the chance for us each to have our own

nightstand, and perhaps a bookshelf as well – and a lamp each, too. I've done a little sketch of the sort of thing I mean . . .'

The next letter was a further rumination on the subject of bedroom decor, with blinds versus curtains displacing the tense enquiries about her welfare. Was it at this point that she'd begun to lose the habit of carrying Emlyn's letters around with her and re-reading them at quiet moments? A letter largely about bedside tables, however lovingly intended, is still largely about bedside tables. She'd read each one quickly and dutifully and had quickly and dutifully written her own in reply. It occurred to her now, for the first time, that perhaps Emlyn had been as uninterested in the non-availability of pencils as she herself was in whether ceilings should be painted lighter or darker than walls. They'd no longer been writing to each other; they'd been standing back to back, talking into the wind, words lost, only a thin warmth still tangible.

'Winnie, are you there?' It was Elsie's voice, accompanied by a tentative knock.

'Just a minute.' She shovelled the letters back into the suitcase and pushed it under the bed before going to the door.

'Your downstairs neighbour let me in,' said Elsie, bringing a cylinder of cold air into the room with her. 'I wasn't sure if you'd be back from the party. Can I stay here?'

'Yes, of course. What's happened? Did you tell Gordon?'

'Yes.'

'What did he say?'

'He cried, and then I cried, and I gave him back the

ring and he said I should keep it, and we shook hands and I cried again. It was all just like a film, except then he told me he'd probably marry Cherry Parsons now.'

'Who's she?'

'Neighbour on the other side. And then I went home and saw my mum, and she's thrown me out.'

'What?'

'I told her about Gordon, and she hit the roof and said I'd end up a stringy old maid. I think she's always preferred him to me.' She gave a weary half-smile. 'Talk about burning my boats.'

'Lucky you're a WREN.'

'Ha ha. How was the party?'

'Avril made a speech about me.'

'Did she?'

'Compared me to an ox.'

'Cow.'

'No, ox.'

'Her, I meant.'

'Oh. Yes.' There was someone bawling a song in the street outside, and it was a second or two before Winnie realized that it was 'Auld Lang Syne'. 'Is it midnight?'

'Nearly.' Elsie checked her wristwatch. 'Five minutes. Haven't got anything to toast the New Year in with, have you?'

'Yes! Bottle of sloe gin – it was a present from my mother.' She fetched two mugs and poured them each an inky inch or two.

'Looks like a magic potion, doesn't it?' said Elsie, admiringly, tilting her mug. 'What'll we wish for?'

'Oh, I don't know,' said Winnie. She felt as if she were dragging Emlyn's letters along in a sack. 'Peace in 1945, I suppose.'

'Not *just* peace. I don't only want the fighting to stop, I want it to be better than it was before.'

'"O brave new world, that has such people in it!"'

'Yes, why not? If Mum's wrong and I ever do end up married with kids, I want them to have a lot more than I had – in fact, I don't even *want* kids if I can't give them a nice time: what's the point? I can't ever remember not having a sore mouth when I was little, or a bunged-up nose. I can't ever remember feeling properly full, I can't even remember having *fun*, not till I joined the Amazons.'

Winnie touched her arm. 'I wasn't teasing, honestly. I agree with you, you know I do. Peace isn't enough, it isn't anywhere near enough, we should drink to . . . to . . .'

'Happiness,' said Elsie, firmly.

'All right.' They clinked mugs.

'I taught you that toast, didn't I?' asked Elsie, gin half-way to her mouth. 'The old sailors' one?'

'I stands afore you,' said Winnie.

'I catches your eye.'

'I bows according.'

'Down the hatch!'

There was a pause, and some coughing.

'Bloody HELL,' said Elsie, tears in her eyes. 'I'll have another of those.'

'Are you looking for the RAF canteen?' called Noel, as the third grey uniform in an hour wandered into view.

The figure looked up, startled, craning his head back to see the walkway on which Noel was standing.

'Yes, actually, I am.'

'Turn left at the bottom half of Trajan's column, go out of the door, straight through the metalwork gallery and down the stairs by the cabinet of early-nineteenth-century milkmaids' bonnets.'

'Thanks awfully.'

Noel watched the small figure pass through the narrow gap between a Celtic cross and the Boy David, and then disappear from view behind a tank-sized Veronese pulpit, his footsteps audible for a few seconds longer. And then, once again, Noel was the only person in the entire, vast space. He resumed his slow circumnavigation. The walkway was more than thirty feet above ground, just below the boarded-up glass roof, and it ran all the way round both Cast Courts, affording a vertiginous view of the contents. Its balustrade was slightly lower than Noel found comfortable, and he kept his weight towards the wall, where smaller, less interesting casts were accumulating dust on a series of narrow tables: Greek porticos, Venetian well-covers, Roman inscriptions, all rendered in plaster, and cast from moulds, enabling all the culture of the Grand Tour to be delivered to those Victorians too poor, too frail or too female to make the journey to see them.

And now, of course, it was the casts themselves that were deemed too fragile to be moved, so that despite the fact that the museum façade was savagely pocked from blast damage, and that earlier in the war, a bomb had actually dropped straight through the roof and destroyed a pair of mediaeval German effigies, the two huge halls of the Cast Court looked just as they had throughout Noel's childhood, when he had played Hide and Seek with Mattie among the colossal souvenirs: 'Is that a stray cherub I spy behind the Portico of the Gloria, or have I found my godson?' The rest of the museum was half empty, with only the most resilient or least valuable exhibits left on display. The majority of visitors seemed to be airmen, and most of those appeared to be looking for the temporary canteen. Noel had so far seen no one from the navy.

'You back again?' the doorman had said to him this morning. 'You was here all day yesterday.'

'I'm interpreting the frieze on Trajan's column,' he'd replied; he'd brought his binoculars and a notepad, for authenticity, as well as a packet of sandwiches and an apple.

He ate the apple and took another turn around the room, resisting the temptation to drop the core into the open goal of the Veronese pulpit, thirty feet below; such an impulse was possibly one of the reasons why the walkway was not actually open to the public, but there were so few staff currently at the museum that he had found his way up there unchallenged, walking through empty galleries and along passageways with cryptically labelled doors. It was the sort of mild rule-breaking that came to him automatically; a combination of Mattie's lofty dismissal of the law, and Vee's attempt to glide unnoticed just beneath it. Tomorrow – if he needed to come back again tomorrow – he might bring a camping-stool with him, and wait in comfort. Though 'comfort' was the wrong term: ever since Christmas Day he had felt like the rhinoceros in the *Just So Stories*, a pinch of grit permanently sifting beneath his skin. He felt so utterly different that he couldn't believe that he still looked the same.

'Have you got a spot coming?' Vee had asked, startling him in the hall on the morning of Boxing Day. He'd been standing in front of the huge Georgian mirror, turning his head from side to side, studying his face from unfamiliar angles, hoping to surprise himself with a glimpse of paternal cheekbone or a fleeting expression that matched his father's. 'You've always had nice skin,' she'd added, carrying on past with an armful of ironed sheets, noticing nothing.

Which was, of course, what Noel wanted. His meeting with Sim was a secret which he had no intention of sharing, and yet he also found himself unable to resist using the word 'father'; it kept rolling out of his mouth and into his conversations.

'What was yours like?' he'd asked Mr Jepson. They had been studying *Daniel Deronda*, so it was not quite a non-sequitur.

'My father?' Jepson had smiled, lifting his gaze as if just spotting someone coming in through the door. 'Well, he was a quiet man, but very kind – he was a cabinet-maker; when he came home from work he'd say, "Hold out your hand, son," and he'd tap his fingers on my palm and I'd find a little toy there, something he'd whittled in his lunch-hour – a soldier, or a whistle. Or once a key fob, shaped like an acorn. I had it with me in the trenches . . .'

Noel had asked Miss Appleby as well ('My dad? Oh, he's a terrible old fuddy-duddy'), and Dr Parry-Jones ('How is this relevant to our studies?'), but not Vee, since for all her obliviousness in front of the mirror, she was unlikely to miss a clue of that size. And it wasn't as if Noel had any actual desire to know anything about Vee's father; he just wanted the topic to be voiced, present, a guest at the dinner table . . .

Mr Reddish, unexpectedly, had been the only person to turn the subject back to the questioner. 'I wonder if you can help,' Noel had said, looking up from a sticky calculation involving double-boilers of varying sizes, in *One Hundred Problems in Logic*. 'I'm currently reading a George Eliot novel about a young man who finds out that he's adopted. I need to write an essay on' – it took him a second or two to invent a title – ' "Desirable Paternal Qualities".'

Mr Reddish, lying on the bed, had removed his wireless ear-piece and placed it on the counterpane. Noel was perched at the foot-end, using the chest of drawers as a desk. 'Paternal qualities,' repeated Mr Reddish, resting his hands across his stomach, fingertips touching. A burst of static from the ear-piece resolved into the opening of Beethoven's Fifth, those four insistent beats that Morse code enthusiasts had declared were the dot, dot, dot, dash that spelled out 'V for Victory', so that now it was never off the airwaves. ' "Desirable Paternal Qualities",' said Mr Reddish again. 'As Theseus declares in *A Midsummer Night's Dream*, "To you your father should be as a god. One that composed your beauties, yea, and one to whom you are but as a form in wax by him imprinted." ' He returned his voice to more normal levels. 'Of course, as a bachelor without offspring, I can only offer thoughts based on the finer attributes of my own father.'

There was a long pause; Mr Reddish's fingers drummed his knitted waistcoat. All Noel could see of his face was the spongy nose, the empty sag of the jowls.

'He had none,' said Mr Reddish, abruptly. 'As a young lady once said to me – a young lady who was very special to me – "Your father is an extremely unpleasant man." And he *was* unpleasant – and bitter, and jealous, and lazy. He knew of my theatrical ambitions and he laughed at them. He forbade me to join an amateur dramatic society as a youth, on the grounds that it would lead to effeminacy. He began to suffer from "glass back". Have you ever heard the phrase?'

'No.'

'It signifies bone idleness in the guise of spurious infirmity. In other words, lying in bed while others work. I was the oldest in the family and had no choice but to leave school at the earliest possible opportunity. Having a moderate talent for mathematics, I became a clerk, perusing columns of figures while my youth fled. The war came and I was enrolled in the pay corps. The years passed. The velvet curtain closed for ever; the limelight gleamed, and was gone. Deadening, Noel. My soul turned to ash.' The bed creaked as Mr Reddish pushed himself upright, taking two attempts to stand. He straightened his waistcoat. 'I have no knowledge of your own paternal situation, Noel – it is none of my business – but I would say that the greatest gift my own father could have given me was his absence. And were I a parent myself, I would open the door of my house, and turn to my child and say' – he extended an arm towards the imaginary horizon beyond the wardrobe – '"The World is Yours. I will help you if I can, but you must choose your own Way."'

His arm had remained raised for several seconds, his expression poised somewhere between Wistful Melancholy and the Bright Dawn of a New Hope, and then, in lieu of an audience ovation, a V-2 had gone off somewhere – far enough away that they had felt no vibration, only caught the long, slow, dark rumble.

In the Cast Court, a woman was issuing orders. Noel looked down, and saw a very small child in a pink coat grasping the flexed leg of one of the dancing girls on the Moghul Gate as if it were a door handle. 'No, you mustn't touch,' repeated the speaker. The child took its hand away, studied the writhing figures for a moment or two and then reached out and carefully patted one of the many, many globular breasts. 'Nigel, what did Mummy say?' asked the woman. She was sitting on the bench beside the plinth of the Trajan Column, reading a magazine. Nigel let go of the breast, leaned forward and licked another of the sculptures, and his mother rose with an exclamation, and swiftly crossed towards him, pulling him away from the Gate with such speed that he lost his footing and sat down heavily on the marble floor. The wail spiralled upward, like a siren.

Noel aimed a hard stare at the back of the woman's neck. The category of 'father' might be a blank to him, but he knew plenty about Desirable Maternal Qualities. In a similar situation, rather than chastising him, Mattie might well have used the multiple bosoms on the Moghul Gate as a chance to work on the higher reaches of the two-times table, while Vee wouldn't have taken her eyes off him for a second, just in case something was accidentally knocked over or smashed, although if this had actually happened, she'd have scooped Noel under her arm and scarpered to the lower-ground exit, pursued by fist-shaking museum guards.

Of course, the child in the pink coat couldn't be more than two or three years old, and Noel had already turned four by the time he'd met Mattie. Of his life before then, in a home for children with polio, he retained only a vague memory of a room full of high-sided cots and a sense of chafing compression, the latter explained by the fact that he'd arrived at Green Shutters wearing a stiff leather corset, prescribed in order to support his affected back muscles. Mattie had taken him to a masseuse, who had suggested long walks over uneven ground, and the corset had been ceremonially burned in a brazier in the back garden, leading to a smell so pungent as to be almost visible, and multiple complaints from the neighbours. Not that Mattie had cared; 'Fearless Devotion' might have been the label for her particular brand of parenting, just as 'Fretting Fondness' might be Vee's; both styles, centred as they were on his own welfare, seemed to Noel superior to what Nigel was going to have to put up with.

The pink coat was dragged away; the court was momentarily empty and then his father walked in and, before he knew what he was doing, Noel had shouted 'Hello!', his voice cracking halfway through the word in that humiliating half-octave plummet that still happened when he was upset or excited.

The lieutenant tipped his head back – 'Are you calling me?' – and it wasn't his father at all, but a man with a pale, lipless face, who took off his cap to reveal hair the colour of a pumpkin. The sight was dislocating; Noel felt as if he'd missed a step in the dark.

'Sorry. I thought you were somebody else.' He drew back against a table laden with plaster medallions and watched the lieutenant progress around the gallery, his hair startlingly bright against the marbles and clays. Ida Pearse, the woman who'd given birth to Noel, was also a redhead, of course – a redhead, a senior nurse and a *fine girl*; he had a mother who consisted of two concrete but generic facts and a nebulous summation. He wasn't sure that he really believed in her; she was like the Princess-over-the-Water in fairy tales.

Disappointment had left him feeling hungry, and he ate one of his sandwiches: soy-bean paste with finely chopped gherkin, a surprisingly successful combination. It was, after all (he reminded himself), only Tuesday. 'I wouldn't miss it for the world,' his father had said, of their prospective meeting. There was plenty of time yet.

'You're off to the museum *again*?' asked Vee, on the Thursday morning, looking through her handbag for a missing glove.

'Yes. Where are you going?' She was wearing her best hat, the one on to which she'd sewn a jay's feather he'd found on the Heath.

'You remember,' she said. 'Brighton.'

'*Brighton?*'

'I told you.'

'No, you didn't.'

'I did, I said that I was going to the seaside for the day, with Mario, before he goes away. You're in a daze at the moment. I wonder if I should try and get you some cod-liver oil, you might be anaemic.' Vee reached for Noel's lower eyelid and he jerked his head away.

'I'm not anaemic, and that wouldn't help me even if I were. Anaemia's caused by a lack of iron, whereas cod-liver oil contains vitamin A.'

'Yes, very good,' said Dr Parry-Jones. 'Besides, boys of Noel's age are rarely anaemic, not being subject to monthly menstruation.'

'Oh *dear*,' said Mr Reddish, 'must we mention that at the breakfast table?'

Vee continued to give Noel an appraising look, and his eyes met hers and then slithered away, his expression one that she hadn't seen on him for years: sealed, almost furtive. He was never going to be like Miss Appleby (thank Heavens), blithely broadcasting every idea that fluttered through her head, but neither was he especially secretive – a straightforward question usually gained a straightforward answer – but when she'd asked him where he'd disappeared to on the afternoon of Christmas Day, he'd muttered, 'A walk,' and she'd got nothing further out of him. 'A walk' that had turned him back into the silent ten-year-old she'd first met five years before. She'd wondered, briefly, if Major Lumb's minx of a grand-daughter had seduced him in the woods, but the Lumbs' house was empty and shuttered; Mrs Lumb, apparently, had had enough of the V-2s.

Vee found her glove in the side pocket. 'I'll try and bring you back a strand of seaweed. Remember you used to have one you told the weather by?' Noel nodded, his expression softening a little. 'Everything's in the larder for this evening,' she added. 'I should be back before it's dark, it's only a little jaunt.'

She stopped to adjust her hat in the hall mirror, just as Mr Jepson left the kitchen.

'I haven't seen the sea since 1939,' he said, pausing at the bottom of the stairs. 'Funny to think of it.'

'I've *never* seen it,' said Vee.

'Really?' He said the word without derision – eagerly, as if lit by her own excitement. 'Well, I'll be very interested to know what you think. It's one of those events that happen to most people so early that they can't remember its impact. I hope it's everything that you imagined.'

'Thank you.' Though what she imagined was the illustration on the packet of desiccated coconut she'd pounced on at the grocer's (a reckless twelve points, but worth it for Noel's face when he saw it): a tropical island with palm trees and yellow sands, and a sea of sparkling sapphire. Mario had already told her the beach at Brighton looked like a quarry; she'd be foolish to expect too much.

'Last chance for a vacation,' he'd said, his voice on the telephone interrupted by the usual clicks and buzzes and sudden gaps.

'What do you mean, "last chance"?'

'They're sending us to France. Or maybe not France,

maybe Belgium or Holland or some place with flat roads, you know. We're due to leave next week.'

'Oh.'

'They've taken the trucks in for service. Can you meet at the train station Thursday? Early?'

A month ago she'd have refused, she was too busy, Thursday was the day she changed all the beds and shopped for fish – but after four weeks of odd surprises and switchback decisions and unexpected calls, she felt lighter, springier, like a flattened feather cushion after a good shaking, and all she could think of was one of Mario's favourite phrases: 'Ah, what the hell!' After all, would Mr Reddish actually *die* if he had shepherd's pie on Friday instead of something unsuccessfully masquerading as cod? And in any case, if Mario were going to Belgium or wherever, then this might be the last time that she ever saw him, and though she'd known that this interlude was bound to be short (she wasn't a *fool*) it was still painful to contemplate that when he'd gone it would be straight back to the usual: Miss Appleby mooning over her forthcoming nuptials (should the bouquet be artificial or could she get away with snowdrops and ivy?), Mr Reddish reciting 'The Flowers of the Forest' whenever they had Scotch eggs, and Vee sitting in the middle of it all, knowing that the chances were that nothing unpredictable would ever happen to her again, at least not in a pleasant sense.

A thaw had set in overnight, and at Victoria Station, water was spattering from a gap in the blacked-out roof into a cluster of buckets. The floor was patterned with filthy footprints, the air wringing with damp, and every single person in the booking-hall seemed to be coughing. Vee, looking round for Mario and spotting him almost immediately – that great head above the crowd – felt as if she could have swatted the germs like flies.

She was disappointed, though not in the least surprised, to find that he had brought half a carriage-load with him: six other GIs, a Tommy and two girls, neither of whom looked quite awake. He always seemed to accumulate an audience, so that even when an evening had begun with a quiet drink, within an hour or two there were half a dozen simultaneous conversations, and tricks with coins and beer-mats, and great gusts of laughter. 'Grew up in a big family,' he said. 'Can't stand it when it's quiet.'

'This is Margery – Mrs Margery Overs,' announced Mario, as they headed towards the platform. 'You want to know anything about Sardines, you just ask this lady. We played it at the camp last week, thirty-five people in the john, two of them standing on the sink. Came *right* off the wall, looked like Niagara.'

'Hey there,' said one of the GIs, flipping a salute. The girls glanced at Vee without interest.

'Hello, Marge,' said the Tommy, grinning. He had terrible teeth, like little brown pebbles. 'Have you heard the news?'

'What news?'

'Hitler's going to be visiting the seaside too. What's his favourite resort?'

'How should I know?'

'Braunmouth. Do you get it? Like Eva Braun. Not Bournemouth, *Braun*mouth.'

'Oh yes, very good,' said Vee, politely.

'He's told that one already,' said one of the girls. 'And we've only been here five minutes. Here, I hope we can get a seat, I'm dead on my feet. We've both just come off night-shift.'

'Where do you work?'

'The Woolwich Arsenal. Oh look, there's Horsey!' The girl waved at a long-faced GI who was leaning out of the train window, beckoning them towards one of the three carriages. It was already full, every seat taken in every compartment, everyone coughing, so that it was like entering a mobile TB clinic, and Vee found herself in the corridor wedged between Mario and the Tommy, and forced to talk to the latter, since his head was more or less at the same level as hers, while Mario was conducting a shouted conversation about the Rocky Mountains with a Canadian airman who was travelling in one of the luggage racks.

'You want to hear another?' asked the Tommy.

'Another what?'

'Go on, this'll make you laugh. It's like a riddle. Man goes up to a greengrocer's stall and he says, "Four oranges, please." So what song does the coster sing in reply?'

Vee shook her head, thinking about oranges; the glow of them, as if you could warm your hands; the peel drying on the stove-top and scenting the kitchen; the soft tear, like the noise of a ripped stocking, as you separated the segments. She'd been three away in a queue from getting some last week.

'Can't you guess?' said Private Tooth Stubs.

'No, I can't.'

'He sings "Can I? Four? Getcha?"'

'What?'

'*Can I Forget You?*' – do you see? Can I. Four. Getcha. That's the joke.'

'Oh.' She hoisted her mouth into a smile, just as the train started with a terrible lurch, and her head snapped sideways, almost knocking a fag out of a sailor's hand.

'Watch what you're doing!'

'Sorry.'

'You'll like this one,' said the Tommy. 'It's a bit off-colour, but I can tell you're the sort who don't shock easily. There's this vicar, and he's taking the collection, and he looks into the basket and there's a packet of rubber johnnies in there, so anyway, he looks along the pew . . .'

Vee leaned away as much as she could, turning her head so that one ear was pressed against Mario's chest. The padded warmth was like leaning against a lagged boiler and she could feel the rumbling vibration of his voice. Over the Tommy's shoulder she caught a glimpse of the river, and then they were back among sooty warehouses and rows of chimneys, and sudden, startling swathes of open ground, with walls like broken combs and the flash of puddles among the ruins. She saw boys running across a wasteland, and a tabby cat sitting in a glassless window, and then they were crossing a viaduct and beneath them were allotments, with a spiral of pigeons rising above the rows of winter cabbage.

The train halted for ten minutes beside a roofless school,

its playground turned into a timber yard, and then again on the edge of London, next to a ploughed field containing a scarecrow dressed as a land-girl. Rooks pecked around the furrows, undeterred. One of the Woolwich girls handed round cough lozenges that tasted of burnt paper.

Half an hour passed without further movement, and then a freight train went by with dreadful slowness, each flatbed loaded with a giant roll of cable; Vee counted forty of them before closing her eyes against incipient dizziness.

Mario was telling a story about an aunt of his who found a raccoon living in her laundry-room, and two Anzacs in the next compartment were quarrelling about someone called Beryl, and then the train started up again and crawled along for a mile or two before pulling into a siding to allow another goods train past, and the journey continued in a series of jerks and pauses so that it was almost midday by the time they reached Brighton, and Vee had twice had to take the humiliating *via dolorosa* to the lavatory – a thousand 'excuse me's and the knowledge that at least ten people directly outside the door could hear every rustle and splash. Outside the station, it was sleeting, and the road down to the sea ended in a view of coiled barbed wire and concrete barriers as large as tea-huts so they all had to straggle along the front to find the newly cleared gap in the defences, shedding members of the party to pubs and chip shops along the way, so that in the end it was only Vee and Mario who picked their way past a row of rusting swings and a closed ice-cream parlour, and on to the beach. The stones clacked and slid beneath their feet, and Mario took her arm.

'Whaddya think?' he asked.

For a moment she couldn't answer. She'd thought of the sea as a painting. She hadn't imagined the noise of it, the unchanging roar, the weight of each wave slumping on to the pebbles, the drum-roll drag of its retreat; she'd thought it would be blue, but it was the colour of wet slate; she'd thought it would keep to its own place, like water in a basin, but she was more than twenty yards from the slapping edge and her lips already tasted of salt.

'Wanna go nearer?' asked Mario. The sleet had flattened his curls and his face was raw from the cold. 'Wanna swim?' And, without warning, he picked her up and started running with her towards the waves and she had never felt so silly or so young, hanging on to her hat with one hand and gripping the collar of his coat with the other, screaming with laughter while sleet blew up her skirt and a group of sailors jeered from the promenade – and when, just feet from the water, Mario lowered her on to the shingle, she found herself lunging upward, one hand on his shoulder, to aim a peck at the great red face with its dented nose, though she only managed to reach as far as his chin. She'd forgotten the feel of stubble, like taking a thistle to your mouth.

'What's that for?' he asked.

'To say thank you!' she shouted, into the wind.

'Did I ever tell you about my brother Iggy and the crate he found washed up on the beach?'

He had, the last time they'd met, but she didn't mind. The open section of beach took only a few minutes to cross, and then they returned to the promenade and walked arm in arm towards the pier, heads down against the weather. The turnstiles at the entrance had been wired shut; beyond them was a stretch of churning sea, the planking above it removed so that there was a gap of forty feet between the land and the rest of the pier.

'To stop Ay-dolf hitching his yacht there,' said Mario. Though the Führer would still have been able to use the helter-skelter and the shooting galleries and the concert hall at the far end. Vee thought of a painting that Noel had once shown her in a book – stiffly grinning soldiers seated on a merry-go-round, the wooden horses galloping in an endless circle from one war to the next . . .

Just across the road, two of the GIs were queuing for fish and chips, and Vee and Mario joined them, and afterwards idled around the souvenir shops before meeting the others in a pub. Vee sat with a half of shandy next to a decent fire, and let the conversation roar above her, Mario – as always – at the centre, the genial uncle, larger, older than the rest. 'You didn't get conscripted, did you?' she'd asked him, once. 'I mean, you're not the right age, are you?'

'No, a cousin of mine told me they wanted truck drivers, I thought I'd get to see a few new places – you know, I didn't join so as to kill anyone and I sure as hell didn't *mean* to kill anyone . . .' It was one of the few times she'd heard him sound serious, his broad face suddenly sagging, wet washing on a line. 'Hey,' he'd added. 'Did I ever tell you about the guy who smuggled a monkey on to the troop ship . . . ?'

The sleet had turned to a pattering of rain as the party straggled back towards the station and then, just as they reached the section of open beach, there was a shift in the clouds and the sea lit up like a silver tray.

'I said I'd get Noel some seaweed,' said Vee, pausing. The water was actually changing colour as she watched, navy blue spilling across the dark surface, as if someone had kicked over a tin of paint. 'Do you mind if I have a look?'

'Plenty of trains,' said Mario.

One of the GIs came with them, and Tooth-Stubs Tommy, still grinding out his terrible jokes; the three men clattered down the series of ridges that led to the water – now much further away than before – while Vee walked more slowly, eyes to the ground, failing to find any seaweed but stooping to pick up a long, smooth shell, shaped like the spine of a book and shining as if varnished, and an odd papery oval, as light as a slice of toast, but rough to the touch. Noel would know what it was. She wrapped both objects in a handkerchief and put them in her handbag, next to the butter knife Mario had insisted on buying for her, with 'A Present from Brighton' painted on the china handle.

'Now I have to pay you something for that,' she'd said, digging in her purse for a halfpenny. 'It's just a superstition,' she'd added, 'so it doesn't cut our friendship.' For she'd weighed the possibilities and had decided, with some surprise, and maybe a twinge of disappointment, that that's what it was nearest to – a friendship. After all, in their handful of meetings, he'd never once tried it on with her; there'd been none of the usual forced steerage towards a darkened doorway (she was not inexperienced in such matters), no sudden hot breath on her neck, no fat-fingered unbuttoning or unzipping or unexpected bumping into unexpected bumps; neither, though, had there been any of the lingering looks or gentle hand-holding that (in films) indicated romantic interest; he had behaved towards her with easy, teasing good nature, in the way that a decent man might treat his sister, and Vee could only suppose that he was missing his family and that she herself was *in loco* Carmen O'Mahoney, and she wasn't complaining, exactly. It was just that at certain moments – as when she'd been leaning against him in the train; the warmth, the solidity of him – she could remember what it was like to actually want to be kissed, properly, the way she'd been kissed at seventeen or so, before her sex life had become a series of expediencies. And, at such moments, she couldn't help wondering whether her farewell embrace with Mario, when it came, might possibly run to more than an amiable arm-squeeze – might even hold a dash of fantastic promise (*Hey, honey, don't forget me, I'll be back . . .*).

The rain began to fall more heavily, and she abandoned her search for seaweed and waited under the eaves of the shuttered ice-cream hut until the stone-skimming contest ended in victory for Mario. 'The thing is,' said the Tommy, swaying close as they walked back up the hill to the station, his warm breath sliming her ear, 'I like to sink my stones and not flick 'em. If you get my meaning.' This time she didn't even bother to smile.

They heard the buzz of the crowd even before they saw it bulging from the station exits. Someone inside the concourse was using a loudhailer, the speech largely unintelligible, though as they neared the entrance, Vee caught the words 'enemy action'.

'What's going on?' she asked of a spivvy-looking type in a pinstripe suit.

'Search me. No trains, anyhow.'

'No trains?' Noel would be cross, she thought. And worried.

'I'll go see,' said Mario, wading through the crowd, Vee and the others following him like a string of barges. The amplified words became clearer. 'ALL LONDON–BRIGHTON LINES CURRENTLY CLOSED DUE TO ENEMY ACTION.'

'I'll get bloody cashiered if I'm not on duty tomorrow,' said a voice close to Vee's ear.

'Hoi!' shouted a sailor. 'You have to tell us more than that. When's there going to be a train?'

More voices joined the first, and there was a surge from behind, so that Vee was pushed towards the barriers.

'It'll be a rocket,' said someone. 'The railway bridge'll be out.'

There was another pulse of bodies, and Vee was thrust forward, pinned by her shoulders, her feet dabbing at the ground, and she reached out a panicked hand and knocked off a man's hat. He twisted round, instantly furious, the hat already unreachable as it sifted down between the elbows.

'Sorry,' she said.

'That was a three-guinea job, you clumsy cow.' He was shaped like a petrol pump, with a small round head on wide shoulders, and his hair was slicked to the scalp as if painted on.

'I said I was sorry.'

The crowd swayed forward again, carrying Vee beyond him, and closer to Mario, who was talking over the barriers to a porter. He looked round and caught her eye.

'Guy says there's a rocket on a place called Battersby.'

'Battersea, I expect. That's where all the lines from Victoria run.'

'PUSH ALL YOU LIKE,' said the announcer. 'HITLER'S CANCELLED THE TRAINS UNTIL FURTHER NOTICE, SO ALL COMPLAINTS SHOULD BE ADDRESSED TO BERLIN.'

There was a groan of protest, and then a lessening of crowd pressure as people began to move away.

'But how are we going to get back?' asked Vee.

'Itch,' said the Tommy, who'd appeared beside her once again.

'Itch?'

He stuck out a thumb in illustration. 'Mind you, they don't like stopping in the rain. You might have to show them a bit of knee, know what I mean? Want to travel with me?'

'No.'

He winked. 'You're probably right. You'll get further on your own.'

'*Stop it*,' she said. 'Stop talking to me like that,' and she was astonished to hear a firmness in her voice, a sharp finality that made him draw back, as if slapped; before she'd become respectable Mrs Overs she'd had years and years of men like Tommy Tooth-Stubs treating her like a tart because she didn't have any money or a visible husband, or maybe it was because of the way she looked or how she talked (she'd never known the exact reason – it was as if someone had daubed something indelible on her back), but she remembered how it had sometimes seemed less of an effort to simply go along with their assumptions rather than yet again having to hear the climbing complaint of her own voice. And yet here she was now, sounding like Edith Evans.

'Keep your corsets on,' muttered the Tommy, but he looked as if he'd just bitten into a crab sandwich and cracked his tooth on a piece of shell.

Vee turned away, searching for Mario, and found herself instead staring at an object held in front of her. It had once been pearl-grey felt with a maroon silk ribbon, and now looked like something fished out of a blocked drain.

'Three guineas,' said the man with the round head. 'You owe me.'

'It was an accident.'

'*Three guineas,*' he repeated, pushing his face towards hers, and she took a step back and stumbled over someone's foot, turning her ankle and falling sideways, her out-flung hand desperately grabbing on to something that turned out to be Hat Man's tie.

'What the HELL!' It was Mario's voice, roaring across the crowd. 'Did you just hit that lady?'

The answer was strangulated.

'Did you just HIT her?'

'No, he didn't, I tripped, I'm all right!' shouted Vee, from below, her voice lost among the damp overcoats. She'd landed on one knee, her shoe half off, and she was still crouched, struggling to replace it when the fight started, all pushes and grunts and lurches, the odd smack of flesh on flesh. It was a station porter who pulled her out of the crowd, and she straightened to see a heaving knot of men, khaki serge, grey flannel, red faces, a split shoulder-seam showing a crescent of pale blue shirt, Mario's head pushed back at an angle by someone's hand under his chin, and then a whistle blew and two coppers elbowed past, followed by a third. The knot unravelled, an airman dodged towards the exit, his nose streaming blood, and then the struggle was over and Mario and Hat Man and an indignant-looking American sailor were being arrested, and everyone was talking at once, even Vee, though the phrase 'It's all been a mistake, Officer' felt chillingly familiar in her mouth, and God knows it had never done her an ounce of good in the past. In any case, she thought, if anyone could talk his way out of custody, it would be Mario, who, by the time they had reached the police station two hundred yards away, had already recounted the story of a friend of his who had stumbled during a St Patrick's Day Parade and accidentally punched a police horse. He looked round for Vee as they filed up the steps and under the blue lamp. 'You gonna wait? You don't have to.'

'Of course I'll wait,' she said. No one in her life before had ever swung a fist on her behalf. Besides, she had no idea how to get home on her own.

Noel stayed up until midnight. After finishing an essay entitled 'The Structure and Properties of the Metallic Elements' for Dr Parry-Jones, he laid the table for breakfast and then took *The Complete Saki* up to bed with him. The house was quiet, except for the usual creaks and ticks, and the cycle of Mr Reddish's snore in the next room, starting each time with a gentle snuffle and building gradually to something that sounded like a death-clash between rival wild boars, before subsiding, for a golden minute or two, into silence. 'I expect there's been a problem with the trains,' Mr Jepson had said, when Vee hadn't returned by supper time. Mr Reddish had suggested the same thing, while Miss Appleby, arriving home late herself, had exclaimed, 'Ooh, isn't she back yet? The naughty girl!', which hadn't been helpful.

His favourite Saki story, 'The Lumber Room', failed to deliver its usual dose of vicious charm, and Noel got out of bed again, turned off the reading lamp and opened the shutters; it was a clear night, the Vale of Health magnesium-grey under a three-quarter moon, the puddles in the empty lane like drops of mercury. He stood for a while, growing steadily colder, and then fetched the eiderdown from the bed and sat swaddled on the window seat, staring downward. He'd spent much of the day in a similar pose in his eyrie above the Cast Court, a chemistry textbook open on the parapet in front of him for those times when the gallery was empty. It had been the fourth day of his vigil, and once again, his father had failed to appear; the hours had passed extraordinarily slowly. He'd seen a group of Sikh soldiers taking snapshots in front of the Moghul Gate, and a sailor tapping cigarette ash into a marble satyr's mouth. Mid-afternoon, a couple had entered the small room at the base of the Trajan Column, and had remained in there for far longer than a general interest in the structure of the hollow interior would warrant, and just after that, a V-2 had dropped somewhere to the south of the museum, and the glass in one of the high windows had rattled in sympathy, like a distant road drill. 'Came down near Clapham Junction' was the verdict of someone Noel had overheard on the Tube home.

Walking back from the station to Green Shutters, he had come to the conclusion that he really should tell Vee about the Christmas Day meeting – partly because he *ought* to, partly because the encounter was beginning to assume an almost hallucinatory quality in his memory, and if he actually spoke Simeon's name, and had to respond to the fire-hose of questions, exclamations and horrified squawks which would undoubtedly follow, then the whole thing might become more concrete again, but also because he missed talking to her, missed the syncopated rhythm of their conversation, their own peculiar patois, evolved to span the gap between them, like the Canary Islanders Noel had once read about, communicating across unbridgeable ravines with a language of whistles. Of course, they hadn't actually had a proper sit-down talk for weeks, not since the arrival of the Great Yankino, King of Garrulity, with his giant head, and hay-load of hilarious anecdotes. No doubt he'd organized an enormous game of Hunt the Thimble on Brighton seafront, and Vee was still searching the underside of the pier.

Noel kept his eyes on the muddy lane and mentally listed all the most mundane reasons possible for the delay, and then thought, for the twentieth time, about the V-2 that he'd heard, and wondered why she hadn't tried to telephone, and was impelled to put on his slippers and go back downstairs to check if the line was working. He lifted the receiver, hoping for the silence that would explain Vee's failure to ring, and heard instead the usual echoing crackles, and that was when he began to feel afraid, the feeling knifing out from the past, from a night half his lifetime ago, when Mattie had lost herself entirely and had unbolted the door and wandered into the darkness. The events that had followed – Noel's removal to his aunt and uncle in Kentish Town, Mattie's death in hospital, the new school, the evacuation to St Albans – had been compressed in his mind to a single blurred journey, like a train carriage diving into a tunnel, the view extinguished, the voices of strangers inaudible beneath the roar of the engine, the faces in the half-light as featureless as plates. And then, with sudden and perfect clarity, the recollection of seeing Vee, red-faced, running to catch a bus with an empty collection box in her hand while a man shouted threats at her from an open front door. That was when his second life had begun, flimsy and makeshift initially, before a slow tide had caught and turned it, pulled it gradually towards the solid anchor of the first, and the two had abutted, so that now Green Shutters was as much one as the other, and a clatter in the hall might be Mattie trying to juggle conkers or Vee dropping a box of cotton reels, and to find the door unbolted again, to find himself for the second time searching hopelessly in the dark, was hideous.

He replaced the receiver and knew that he wouldn't

sleep. A narrow strip of moonlight lay across the floor, bisecting the chessboard. Pushing the shutter closed, he turned on the light and set out the pieces – the pawns with their polished heads, the black king who bore the tooth-marks of a visiting dog, the rooks (or castles), into whose crenellated tops one could wedge a little finger, and wear like a Balinese dancer's nails. He started by playing Mario and beat him by a fool's mate in three, and then set himself up against Genevieve Lumb, and let her win. Mattie was always a more difficult proposition; she began with pawn to e4, an obvious Sicilian defence, but she'd caught him out before now. He turned the board again and studied it, elbows on knees, hands clasped to stop them trembling.

He was frying bacon when Vee walked into the kitchen, her footsteps inaudible under the sizzle. 'I'm back!' she said. 'You won't believe what happened!' and Noel turned, relief flapping across his face, to be replaced almost instantly with something darker, and Vee knew straight away that she'd been wrong to predict that he'd be merely cross and worried, because it was far worse than that.

'*Why* didn't you telephone?'

'Well, that's the thing, I never had a chance, because – well, it's quite a complicated story, but it all started with somebody's hat . . .' She was half laughing, just from nerves; Noel's expression was that of a hanging judge. '. . . You see, we'd just got back to Brighton Station when they made an announcement—'

But Noel, hearing only the laugh, had already jerked the pan from the stove.

'I have to go,' he said, not looking at Vee. From the corner of his eye he could see that Mr Jepson had entered the kitchen.

'Go where?' asked Vee.

'It's not actually any of your business,' said Noel, walking past Mr Jepson and into the hall, taking his duffel coat from the hook, and opening the front door, something that took a couple of tries, since it was rarely used and the wood always swelled in the winter. Outside, it was bright and sharp, the sky wiped clean by the rain, a female blackbird poking around on the front lawn.

'Noel!' called Vee, from the hall, but he marched straight along the front path, startling the blackbird, unlatching the gate with such force that he skinned a knuckle, and slamming it with ferocity behind him. Funny; she'd thought it was *funny*. Last night, he'd played three more games of chess and then had rearranged all the books on the drawing-room shelves in alphabetical order, before getting dressed and walking along the lane in the moonlight, owls twitting, another V-2 exploding somewhere out west, ignorant armies clashing by night all over Europe and North Africa, everything split, fractured, missing, irreparable, and then he'd turned back to see dawn breaking over Highgate in the usual way, a streak of khaki-yellow like a wiped nose, and had gone home to begin on the lodgers' breakfast, and while he'd been spooning the tea into the pot it had occurred to him that if Vee were dead – and he knew she might be dead, he couldn't pretend it wasn't possible, unspeakable things happened all the time – she would probably want a Methodist funeral, a ceremony about which he knew nothing whatsoever; a knitted coffin cover, probably, and a tombola to choose the hymn numbers, and a plot with a wooden marker at the new end of Highgate Cemetery, the bit that looked like a corner of a school playing-field. And then, just as he was placing a jar of her favourite Virginia stocks on the newly filled grave, in she'd waltzed, laughing, and his stomach, which had felt like a knotted balloon since the previous afternoon, had untwisted itself and he'd tasted acid. He could still taste it an hour later, arriving at the Victoria and Albert Museum ten minutes before opening time. There was already a queue: three matelots, a very old lady carrying a string bag filled with stained newspapers, and a naval officer. Simeon.

'You've hurt your foot,' said Mr Jepson, from the hall. Vee closed the front door and looked down at herself. Her left ankle sagged like bread dough over the top of her shoe, the stocking laddered in three places.

'I turned it,' she said. 'I'll give it a soak in a minute – you don't happen to know where Noel's off to?'

'I don't, I'm afraid. Would you like me to try and catch up with him?'

She hesitated and then shook her head. 'No, thanks – probably better to leave him. He'll come round.'

'Morning, Mrs Overs,' said Miss Appleby, clattering down the stairs, and then coming face to face with Vee and performing a double-take of music-hall proportions. 'Ooh, can see *you* had a good time,' she said, giving a distinctly sisterly wink before carrying on towards the kitchen, and Vee, rather stunned, turned and saw herself in the hall mirror, eyes like boiled onions, hat askew, her hair down at the back, no lipstick, a streak of powder on her neck, the skin of which was already blotchy with an incipient blush. 'There was a V-2 on the railway lines,' she said, rubbing at her throat. 'I've been travelling all night, trying to get home, I knew he'd be worried.'

'I thought it would probably be something like that,' said Mr Jepson. 'I said as much to Noel. As did Mr Reddish.'

'I don't know what Miss Appleby was implying,' said Vee, though obviously she did; it had been about as subtle as a dropped fire-iron. 'I'm not that type of woman.'

'Of course not,' said Mr Jepson. 'And the corporal's—' He checked himself, his mouth staying open but no sound issuing from it, so he looked like a stuck film.

'What?' asked Vee.

Jepson unstuck himself. 'Just that . . . well, I'm sure you know.'

'Know what?'

It took a couple of attempts for him to answer, his voice creaking as it emerged. 'That Corporal O'Mahoney's not that type of man.'

For a moment she didn't understand, too tired to connect two thoughts that didn't seem to fit together.

'I think there's tea,' said Jepson, rather hurriedly. 'Would you like a cup?'

'You're not saying he's a – a pansy? But he's not like . . .' Her mind jumped back to poor Ronald Cuffley in the village where she'd grown up, who'd never been like the other boys, a lamb among bullocks, and who after Eddie Clare had accused him of trying to touch him where he shouldn't, had been pushed over and rolled in cow-pats, tripped, punched, smacked, taunted, week after week, year after year, until one day he'd drunk Brasso and his mother had stood in the road outside the church on Sunday and shouted at everyone that they were no better than the beasts of the field. 'The corporal's not like that,' she said.

Jepson was silent. Vee removed her hat and looked back at the mirror, smoothing her hair.

'Yesterday he got into a fight because of me,' she said. 'He thought someone had knocked me down, and he ended up being arrested. Does that sound like a pansy?'

Jepson looked down at the space where the hall carpet used to be. 'The only man in my battalion to win an MC was an invert,' he said, quietly. 'But I really shouldn't have said anything.'

'No,' said Vee. She remembered her silly little daydream of a farewell kiss and a promise: *Hey, honey, don't forget me, I'll be back* . . . She hadn't even seen him to say goodbye. After she'd been waiting for over an hour in the police station – standing up the whole time because the only bench in the place was not only sticky but occupied by a man who was spitting bits of tooth into a handkerchief – two US military policemen had walked in, both wearing those huge white hats which had earned them the nickname 'Snowdrops', but which reminded her far more of the toadstools in *Fantasia*. They'd been ushered into the back somewhere, another hour had inched by, and then the police officer at the desk had beckoned Vee over and asked if she was waiting for the GIs, and if so, they'd gone out the other entrance with the toadstools and were being taken back to their camp. 'They look after their own, that lot,' he'd said, before turning his attention to a lost-dog report.

She'd intended to ring home, but someone had pulled the receiver off the only telephone-box she could find, so instead she'd found her way back to Brighton Station, where the odd train was running again, and had taken the first that was going in the general direction of London, and which, after stopping every twenty-five yards, had deposited her in a bomb-site called East Croydon at half-past two in the morning. Eventually, there'd been a bus, the first of four, or five – she'd lost count. She'd slept maybe ten minutes the whole night. Her head felt stuffed with sand.

Mr Jepson was still standing there, looking apologetic. Vee turned away and began to unbutton her coat with hands that were clumsy with cold, and somehow managed to drop her handbag. There was the bright, precise noise of breaking china. She picked up the bag and looked inside at the pieces of the knife handle, the razor fragments of the narrow, subtly coloured shell she'd brought back for Noel. 'Well, that's that,' she said, and went upstairs.

His father looked thinner, and there were yellow crusts on the lashes of his right eye. 'Are you still ill?' asked Noel, once they were inside the museum. 'I was beginning to think that you must have embarked.'

'On the mend, now. No, I was visiting relatives in the North Country.'

'Your father?' asked Noel, remembering the purported resemblance between himself and his paternal grandfather. Simeon shook his head without replying. He had lost the bounce and lustre of their first encounter.

'Not a lot to look at, is there?' he said, glancing around the entrance hall, empty apart from a heavily sand-bagged statue of St Paul. 'Tell you what, I could do with a cup of coffee.'

'There's only the service canteen in the basement,' said Noel. 'I'm afraid that they wouldn't let me in.'

'Pity. Would you wait while I went in there? I wouldn't be long.' To avoid breaking a note, he borrowed a half-crown from Noel and disappeared through the swing doors. There was nowhere to sit in the corridor outside. Noel leaned against the wall, and watched the curators come and go through the staff-room door. One or two nodded to him – he was, he supposed, a familiar sight by now and, moreover, he'd asked several of them over the course of the week about the carved roof boss he'd seen in the ruined church, which had supposedly been sent to the museum. No one had known anything about it.

'Still here?' asked his father, wiping his mouth with a handkerchief as he re-emerged. 'Where shall we go now?'

'Would you like to see the Cast Court?'

'Not particularly.'

'The armoury corridor? They have a display of Tudor sabatons – it's extraordinary to see how small men's feet were in the sixteenth century.'

'Is it? Sorry, it's just . . . when I was fifteen, you couldn't have got me near a museum – I'd rather have done almost anything else. Still, we can't all be the same, can we? Lead on, Macduff.'

The heartiness of the last two sentences was belied by a toneless delivery, as if they were being read by a bored actor, and the thought came to Noel (like an ice-cube dropped down the back of his neck), that perhaps his father had only come to the museum because he'd had nothing else to do that morning, rather than out of any desire to meet him again. Perhaps that first encounter on Christmas Day had been enough for him, a simple assuagement of curiosity; or perhaps he'd been disappointed – had been hoping for a different sort of boy: rowdy, vivid, sporting; maybe that's what a father required: a replica.

'What did you do, then?' asked Noel. 'At my age?'

'I suppose, when I wasn't at school, I rampaged around with pals. Or hung about near the girls'-school entrance.'

'I have a girlfriend,' said Noel, with attempted casualness.

'Glad to hear it. Is she pretty?'

'Do you know the da Vinci portrait of the *The Lady with the Ermine*?'

'You mean she's on the po-faced side? Like Mona?'

'No. I mean . . .' Noel weighed the public embarrassment of uttering the words 'gamine yet possessed of soulful depths' and then realized that Sim wasn't listening anyway, or even looking towards him, and that his face in repose looked not only ill, but glumly exhausted, the expression of someone in a hopeless fix, a man trapped in a muddy hole.

'We could do something else,' said Noel. 'We could go to . . .' He groped for a destination that his father might find entertaining, but the night without sleep had sanded his thoughts down to nubbins and all he could think of was the seaside, Vee gallivanting along the prom while he sat in the dark, tearing at his fingernails. 'The Serpentine,' he said. 'We could take a boat out, if it's not still frozen.'

'Somewhat of a busman's holiday for me,' said Simeon, rousing himself. 'Besides, I'll have to head off pretty soon, old chap.'

'But you've only just arrived.'

'Duty calls. In any case, shouldn't you be in school?'

'I'm playing truant.'

'Wagging off, we used to call it. You'll catch it from your aunt.'

'No, I won't.' The morning's fury rose again, gusting around his skull – as if Vee would have any right to lecture him about anything. 'She's not even my aunt, anyway,' he muttered, and Sim, who had begun to move away towards the stairs, looked back at him, curiously.

'Isn't she?' he asked. 'How come?'

Noel felt his face grow cold. 'No. That isn't . . . I didn't mean that. Of course she is.' A box of secrets, locked for four years, and idly, carelessly, he'd let it fall; even without opening the lid, he could hear the pieces rattling. 'It was just an erroneous interjection,' he said, panicking. 'A semantic error. Axiomatic of fatigue.'

'However tired I was, I don't think I'd say my aunt wasn't my aunt,' said Sim, and for the first time that morning, his attention seemed fully fixed on Noel. 'So if she's not actually your aunt—'

The canteen doors swung open and a group of Highlanders walked out in a miasma of sweat and bacon. His father waited until they'd gone past.

'—so if she's not actually your aunt, then who is she? What's her name again?'

And because Noel had momentarily been back in the world of dodge-and-run, he hesitated for just a tiny instant, to stop his lips from pursing to form the word 'Vee'.

'Margery Overs,' he said, slightly too loudly.

There was a pause.

'Are you absolutely sure?' asked his father, and although he was smiling, Noel could almost hear the clink of handcuffs because the smile was a little too interested, and his own hesitation had felt as much a confession as a signed statement and a mug-shot. No longer trusting himself, he nipped his tongue between his teeth, and nodded, just as a cheer came from the canteen. Chairs scraped, there was a scramble of footsteps, and the corridor was suddenly filled with jubilant Poles.

'Varsaw liberated!' said an airman in answer to Sim's question, and Noel said '*Gratulacje. To jest dobre*,' and was immediately kissed on both cheeks by a succession of officers, one of whom gave him an unopened bar of chocolate and two packets of cigarettes.

'Good God,' said Sim, as the Poles disappeared up the stairs. 'I can see you're a useful chap to know. So, shall we go to the Serpentine?'

'But I thought you had to leave.'

'Well, perhaps I could stay for a little longer. After all, I've missed fourteen years of being your father.'

'Fifteen.'

'Fifteen, sorry. Now tell me, this . . . this "aunt" of yours, does she take care of you properly?'

'Yes.' Involuntarily, Noel raised a hand to his hand-knitted scarf, the colour of verdigris. 'Yes, she does. And I'm afraid I really do have to go. You're right about playing truant. I mustn't. She'll be angry.' Even to his own ears, the excuses sounded false, the short sentences like a series of coded telegrams which, given more time, his father couldn't fail to decipher. And Noel knew, now, that he couldn't have both Simeon and Vee, and that the choice between them really wasn't a choice at all.

'Take these,' he added, thrusting the chocolate and cigarettes at Sim, and then he turned and ran – actually ran – because he couldn't stand the prospect of hearing Sim calling after him, as Vee had done that morning. Or, even worse, perhaps, *not* calling after him.

Outside, the brief thaw was over, the sky cloudless but the air like a clamp, the water in the gutters already beginning to freeze. Noel ducked into a café to buy a cup of cocoa and then came straight out again, having realized that his father had forgotten to give him the change from the half-crown, so that all he had left was twopence for the Tube. He took the District Line to Embankment and then fell asleep in the relative warmth of the Northern Line, waking with a start to find the train drawing into Highgate, which meant that not only was he on the wrong branch, but that a day which had begun with an imaginary visit to Vee's grave had now deposited him just half a mile from the cemetery in question. It seemed almost an invitation, and one that slotted perfectly into his current mood; it was a while since he had been there.

A party of mourners was straggling up the main path and Noel stood aside to let them pass; they were an oddly disparate bunch, headed by an elderly lady with the profile of a Sitwell, and a vicar still wearing his surplice and carrying the Book of Common Prayer. Next came a knot of solidly upper-crust Wimbourne-types, discussing someone called 'old Eggy', followed by a silent group of working men, black armbands on their jackets, and then a middle-aged woman, arm in arm with a tiny, ancient father, both of them speaking Greek.

A few yards behind the others, a plump young woman in a grey coat and beret had stopped to read a tombstone. She looked up as Noel approached, and said, 'Oh, I know you, don't I?' and offered a mittened hand. 'Winnie Crowther – we met by the ruined church. I'm the warden who wrote you a letter.'

Wonderingly, he shook it. 'Noel Bostock. You knew Mattie.' And the trajectory of the day, which had started low, and had sunk even further, seemed to rise a little.

She was looking comically shocked. '*Mattie?*' I wouldn't have dared to call her that. She was always Miss Simpkin to us.'

'She was my godmother. I was actually just about to visit her grave.'

'Oh, may I come?'

Involuntarily, Noel glanced back up the hill at the other mourners.

'No, I'm not strictly *with* them,' said Winnie. 'The grave-diggers took advantage of the thaw – one big hole, I'm afraid. I was here to pay my respects to an old chap who died in my sector.'

'From a V-2?'

'From the cold, as a matter of fact.' There was a pause. 'If you'd rather visit the grave on your own, then of course I won't intrude.'

'No,' said Noel, quickly. 'I'd very much like you to. I don't know anyone else who actually knew Mattie,' and he set off at an assured pace, taking a side-shoot off the main path that passed between ranks of tilting Victorian headstones and pausing beside George Eliot's grave, on which someone had placed a mouldering copy of *Middlemarch*.

'Have you read it?' asked Winnie.

'Yes. On the whole, I preferred *Silas Marner*.'

'I acted in a production of that, once.'

'Playing Effie?'

'Not a chance. My character was called "Woman with Firewood".'

Noel laughed, for the first time in what felt to him like a couple of decades, and Winnie thought what a nice, odd boy he was, with a face that would never be handsome but which was nonetheless appealing; watchful, yet droll. 'So you must have visited Green Shutters when Miss Simpkin lived there?'

'I lived there with her,' said Noel. 'From the age of four. Here it is.' He stopped by one of the newer graves, hard by the fence that separated the cemetery from Waterlow Park and overhung by elms, their brushwood bursting between the chestnut stakes. Winnie started to say something, and then exclaimed, and crouched beside the headstone to examine it more closely. Carved into the drab granite was the inscription:

MATILDA SIMPKIN
Spinster of this Parish
October 21st 1870 – December 7th 1939
A virtuous woman is above rubies

But stencilled in black paint underneath, in very large letters, were the words:

FAITH AND DARING

'**DR**' had been added in the same lettering in front of Mattie's name.

'Did you do that?' asked Winnie.

'No. It's been there for as long as I can remember, and it's renewed every now and again. I always imagine that it must be one of Mattie's old comrades, sneaking in at night.'

'I think that's wonderful. Where does the quote come from? I don't mean "above rubies" – the other one.'

'It's from the last verse of "March of the Women". "Life, strife, these two are one, Naught can ye win but by faith and daring."'

'I remember it!' said Winnie. 'We used to sing it in the Amazons – there was a line about laughing, wasn't there?'

'"Firm in reliance,"' recited Noel, with measured rhythm, '"laugh a defiance, laugh in hope, for sure is the end—"'

Winnie's firm contralto picked up the song, joined for the last few words by Noel's more tentative baritone. '"March, march, many as one. Shoulder to shoulder and friend to friend!" Oh my goodness,' said Winnie, grinning. 'I can almost smell the woodsmoke. Those campfires! We were such a motley bunch . . .'

Noel bent to pull away some dead couch-grass from around the headstone.

'Do you remember someone called Ida Pearse?' he asked, over his shoulder.

'Yes. Yes, she was one of the older girls – a sort of leader. All of us little ones thought she was marvellous – like an ideal big sister. Do you know her, then?'

He looked back towards his task. 'I know *of* her,' he said.

'I liked her especially because she was very good at quietly snubbing my twin sister when she got above herself. In fact, I remember early on that Miss Simpkin – *Dr* Simpkin – had to tell people off for being snobbish about the fact Ida was her char, but after a while no one cared in the slightest about what Ida did for a job, because it was obvious she was capable of anything.'

Noel walked a few steps away and sat on the flat plinth of the Rockwell family tomb. The cold shot straight through the seat of his trousers, and he stood up again.

'She was Mattie's char? Working in Green Shutters?'

'Yes. What's she doing now? Do you know?'

'She's a nurse – a hospital sister, in Gibraltar.' But he spoke distractedly, because the past had just been pulled apart and rearranged, so that his mother and Mattie and Vee were no longer separate links in a chain, but overlapping, and his godmother was talking to young Ida in the hall, while Ida stood mopping the same flagstones that Vee cursed daily ('What I wouldn't give for some nice, flat linoleum . . . '). And when he himself was standing at the kitchen sink, peeling potatoes and idly glancing out at a chaffinch in the apple tree, he was not only seeing just what Ida had seen at the same age but probably using the same potato peeler, possibly even with the same capability. He looked appraisingly at his hands – the right a little larger than the left, the nails narrow, the knuckles prominent.

'I haven't said something that I shouldn't, have I?' asked Winnie.

'No. Not in the least.'

Though she could see from his face that a whole dish of thoughts was simmering away. 'I could tell you some more about Ida and the Amazons if you'd like,' she said. 'Shall we walk a bit, though? I'm turning into an icicle.' She let Noel lead, and he took her on an intricate circuit of the cemetery, so that her Amazon tales were interspersed with brief and fluent accounts of his favourite incumbents ('. . . and he wrote "Abide With Me", which Mattie always said had the perfect rhythm for when you were trying to crank a recalcitrant ambulance engine').

'You do sound like her, you know,' said Winnie, as they re-joined the main path.

'Do I?' For a second, he looked startled. 'Oh, you mean Mattie?'

'Yes. In terms of your vocabulary, I mean – you don't have quite her volume. My friend Elsie, the Wren I was telling you about, told me that when she has to give commands she always pretends to be Miss Simpkin. She says it gives her confidence.'

' "Skill and confidence are an unconquered army." '

'Let me guess. Millicent Fawcett?'

'I *think* it's George Herbert.'

'Do you know, I actually recited one of your godmother's quotes when I met up with my twin before Christmas: "Say not the needle is the most proper pen for women." '

'Thomas Fuller,' said Noel, back on firmer ground. 'Is this the twin that Ida Pearse used to snub?'

'Yes,' said Winnie. 'Unfortunately, it didn't have a permanent effect.'

'Is she a warden too?'

'No, though she writes about them as if she were.'

'In what?'

'In a new novel called *Tin Helmet*. It's doing terribly well, so she tells me. Reprinting already.'

'Is it good? Should I read it?'

Winnie hesitated. 'How old are you, again?'

'Fifteen.'

'Well, it's a bit . . . I mean, it's quite . . . risqué . . .'

'Oh, I see,' said Noel, making a mental note to buy it at the earliest opportunity.

'So who looks after you now?' asked Winnie. 'Not Miss Lee, surely?'

'Miss Lee?'

'Your godmother's companion.'

'Oh . . . no.' There was a photograph of Florrie Lee on the wall of the drawing room, neat and alert behind a well-organized desk. 'No, she died before I ever lived there. My aunt takes care of me.' And how many times, he wondered, had he used the word 'aunt' over the last few hours? *Aunt.* It had almost ceased to make sense as a syllable. *Aunt, aunt, aunt.* Was it even a word? 'I call her Mar,' he said, and found himself yawning, hugely. 'Sorry. I had a sleepless night. I ought to go home, really.'

'Did you hear the Kilburn rocket?'

'I heard a crump at around five o'clock. How much longer do you think they'll go on for – do you have inside information?'

She shook her head. 'Nobody seems to know. I've been told that the Germans keep shifting the launch sites as the Allies advance.' She noticed a speck on her sleeve, and brushed it off. It was immediately replaced by another. 'Oh, damn,' she said. 'Snowing again.'

They both looked back over the sloping ranks of crosses, already partially obscured, as if by a fine net curtain, and Noel thought about the last lines of Joyce's *The Dead*, which Mr Reddish had recently recited over supper in what he claimed was a Dublin accent, and Winnie thought about Emlyn. There had been no further news, no letters, nothing to grasp on to except occasional, dreadful weather reports from northern Germany. Strange to think that one might hope for the chance of reading a list of speculative paint colours for a non-existent dining room.

'I should cut along now, too,' she said. 'Thank you for my tour.'

They shook hands again, and Winnie walked back up the hill towards Highgate Tube, while Noel headed in the opposite direction for half a mile, before taking a narrow passage that ran between two stucco houses and emerged at the edge of the Heath. The only noise was the faint pitter of snow. The grass was already covered, though the layer was still so thin that when he turned to watch a group of rooks lifting lazily above the old gun emplacement, he could see the long, straight line of his own footsteps, like a green zip fastener across a white gown. And it occurred to him then that he'd forgotten to mention to Winnie his attempts to find the Green Man at the V&A, and that this omission might mean that they might speak again at some point, and that he could hear more about Ida Pearse, who could stalk with the panther skill of the Last of the Mohicans and quell bullies with a single glare . . .

The reporter who usually attended North London Crown Court for the Monday sessions had gone down with 'flu, and Jepson had volunteered to take his place. He'd been hoping for spivs or fraudsters but had been landed with an interminable case based on the illegally high percentage of sugar that a Palmer's Green confectioner had been using in his fruitcakes ('The cook's hand may have shaken when putting in the sugar,' said Mr Harry Ricketts, defending . . . '). By lunch-time, he was having to pinch his arm in order to stay awake.

Brookes from the *Evening Standard* was off to Islington to review a pantomime ('Goldi-fucking-locks and the three moth-eaten fur coats from the director's gran's wardrobe') and the youngster from the *Muswell Hill Advertiser* was so new and conscientious that she was spending the entire lunch hour transcribing her notes, so Jepson sat alone in the window seat of a cold little restaurant, its floor footprinted with melting slush, and ate stewed oxtail (not a patch on Noel's) while reading a rather racy new novel about air-raid wardens, borrowed from the arts desk.

He was waiting for the bill when he noticed his landlady on the opposite pavement, peering into the fogged-up window of a café. She stepped back, looked up at the street name and then at the name of the café, before once again edging up to the glass. The whole set of her shoulders signalled uncertainty. When she half turned, he lifted a hand, but her eyes scraped past him, unseeing. He had not, in any case, had anything approaching a conversation with her since their exchange about Corporal O'Mahoney three days before. *You're an idiot*, he thought to himself, for about the fiftieth time. There'd been absolutely no need to actually tell Mrs Overs what had seemed fairly obvious to him – attuned as he was from decades of court-reporting – even before he'd spotted O'Mahoney just after New Year, exiting the woods at the top of the Heath a step or two ahead of a flushed-looking airman; she'd clearly had the time of her life with the corporal, had laughed her head off and dropped ten years and skipped around like a schoolgirl, and where was the harm in that? – it had been finite; she wasn't going to end up pregnant in the middle of Nebraska, with coyotes tugging at her washing, like half the girls in Norfolk. And God knows there'd been no malice in the man: he'd been bonhomie personified, had shaken up the house like a snow-globe and made Jepson feel like the dreary bore that Della had always labelled him.

He watched Mrs Overs touch the handle of the café door as if there were a chance it was electrified, and then spring aside as the door opened, emitting an elderly man, and a gout of steam. She caught it before it closed again, and went inside, and Jepson, drawn by curiosity, paid his bill and crossed the street.

From the pavement, he could see her seated at a table against the side wall, her posture rigid, her hands clasped, her eyes fixed on the entrance. It took him a moment to define her expression, and when he realized, with a jolt, that it was *fear*, he was through the café door before he could think about it.

'Good afternoon,' he said, taking off his hat as he approached, threading between the cramped grid of tables.

Her eyes widened and then darted past him towards the door again. 'Afternoon.' Her voice was all air.

'I was passing, and saw you here. I'm working at the Courts today.'

'Oh.'

'Would you like a cup of tea?'

'I've ordered. Thank you.'

'Could I . . . ?' He indicated the other chair at her table.

'No. Sorry. I'm waiting to meet someone.' Her speech

was staccato, terrified, but she forced a dreadful smile. 'Thank you very much,' she added, turning her head so that she was looking away from him and towards the yellow-painted wall by her shoulder, its surface slick with condensation.

Jepson hesitated, and then sat at the table immediately behind, so that he was back to back with her, their chairs almost touching. He heard her tea arrive, and ordered a pot for himself.

'Please could you go,' said Vee, when the waitress had left.

'I shouldn't like to walk off without knowing why you look so frightened. Is there anything I can do to help?'

'No.'

He could hear her spoon tinkling in the teapot, mashing the leaves.

'I've often had conversations in this way,' he said, turning his head slightly, talking along the wall, his speech clear but quiet. 'I do it when I need to interview someone who'd rather not be seen to be talking to a reporter. You can put a hand to your mouth – I have pretty good hearing, despite everything.'

'I don't need you to stay, Mr Jepson.'

'What if I give you my promise that if the person you're waiting for arrives, I'll leave immediately and say nothing at all, then or in the future. Would that be acceptable?'

She didn't reply, but he took the silence as assent, and when his tea came, he ordered a jam roll and custard, to give himself an excuse to stay longer. And he speculated on why she might be frightened, though the exercise made him realize that despite almost a year in the same house, he knew nothing about Margery Overs beyond the basic facts of her everyday life; that she worried about money, loved going to the cinema, attended chapel apparently out of habit rather than obvious religious fervour, and danced to the wireless when she thought no one could see her; that she was a good needlewoman, and dressed well on very little; that she noticed everything; that she moved and spoke quickly and that even her laugh was abrupt. She was a widow, but never mentioned her husband; she was Noel's aunt, but never mentioned his parents – the social and educational mismatch between her and the boy was striking, but so, too, was their closeness. As a landlady, she was unusual, lacking the territorial instincts of her breed; there was little division of the house between 'mine' and 'theirs', so that Green Shutters, despite its cavernous cold, felt far more of a home than the lodgings he'd lived in as a young man; far more of a home, in fact, than the flat he'd shared with Della.

If Jepson's reporter instincts had noted anything, it was that Mrs Overs always acted as if she had fifty things that she wanted to say but was forcing herself to hold back at least forty-seven of them. Some of those were bound to be secrets; everyone had secrets.

The jam roll, somewhat lacking in jam, arrived and was eaten. The weak tea was sipped. The café, busy when he'd entered, fell into a mid-afternoon lull.

Vee, still glancing up every time the door opened, could sense Jepson just behind her, though she was careful not to turn her head. The letter she'd received had not specified an exact time, only that she should be in the Rose Café from two o'clock onward, and that she was to bring payment in a paper bag rather than an envelope. *'As I know what you look like, there is no need to describe myself.'* For a mad moment, when Jepson had doffed his hat to her, she'd thought that he must be the mysterious letter-writer, blackmailing her from within the house, but it had turned out that he was just being unwontedly kind. Unwantedly. Though she was quite glad, now, not to be alone in the café during the wait.

She leaned an elbow on the table and put a hand to her lips. 'Shouldn't you be at work?'

'I can get the notes from the other reporter, later on. Besides, it was a very dull case.'

'Was it?'

'It revolved around Clause 5 of the National Emergency Confectionery Law of 1939. The sort of thing that ends up as two paragraphs on page seven.'

Vee stiffened as the café door opened again, and then relaxed at the sight of two women with shopping. For the umpteenth time, she checked her handbag, wedged between her feet. It contained Dr Simpkin's jewellery, rolled in a piece of oil-cloth and placed in a paper bag: a garnet brooch, a ring that might be a sapphire, a necklace that looked expensive. She had kept back some of the other items in case the blackmailer asked again, because she knew that's what blackmailers did. *'I am aware that you are not actually Noel Bostock's aunt, and that you are therefore living in Green Shutters under false pretences and using an assumed identity, something that would certainly be of considerable interest to the police.*' She'd opened the letter in the kitchen and had almost dropped dead, her heart jumping around like a clockwork monkey, the cheap paper gripped so tightly that her thumbnail had gone straight through the signature. *Yours sincerely, A concerned observer.* Thank God she'd been on her own, because it had been minutes before her lips had stopped trembling – and yet, beyond the shock, there had been an awful sense of inevitability; she'd spent half of her life waiting for one axe or another to fall.

'You could tell me about an interesting case,' she said to Jepson. 'To take my mind off.'

'All right.' He thought for a moment. 'Last month I reported on a woman who received a summons for failing to comply with a Ministry of Labour direction. She was supposed to report to a factory as a trainee, but she said she was already doing work of extreme national importance.' He left an enticing pause.

'What was it?' asked Vee.

'Spiritual healing. Using her nose.'

'Her *nose*?'

'She'd stand in front of the person and smell which parts of them required healing. And then she would take a scent bottle – one that had been blessed – and squirt that particular part. She had numerous testimonials from satisfied customers.'

Vee was assailed by the jealousy she always felt when learning about people who made easy money, apparently legally. 'Did they say what sort of scent it was?' she asked.

'Cedar, I think. I rather suspect it was a moth spray.'

Vee almost laughed, and then remembered where she was, and why she was there, and it was as if someone had dropped a cinder block on her heart. 'Oh dear God,' she said, involuntarily, and covered her face with her hands.

'I wish I could help you,' said Jepson, half turning.

'You can't.'

'You know, there isn't much I haven't seen or heard about – I've covered crime and scandal and cruelty and extortion, and I can't think of anything that shocks me any longer. Are you being dunned for a loan? If you need some money, I could help you out.'

From the corner of his eye, he saw her shake her head.

'Or is someone threatening you in some way?'

She straightened, as if jabbed in the back. He spoke even more softly. 'Are you being blackmailed?'

The door opened as he said the words, and Vee flinched so violently that the table jerked forward and her empty tea cup fell over.

'Can I get you anything else?' asked the elderly waitress, rather crossly. By the entrance, a small girl and her mother were shaking snow off their matching tam-o'shanters.

'Another tea, please,' said Vee, her voice wavering like a musical saw.

'I'll have a cocoa,' said Jepson, and then, as the waitress left, he turned his head towards the wall again. 'It's much commoner than you might think – there's a case in the paper every week because nearly everyone has something they'd rather keep hidden. Often it's not even a past crime, it's just something quite ordinary – a shameful moment – and half the time the blackmailer has no intention of actually exposing the victim, because they'd end up in trouble themselves. My advice would be: don't.'

'Don't what?'

'Pay up.'

There's the voice of someone who's never heard the policeman's knock, thought Vee. 'Easy for you to say,' she said.

'You might think that,' said Jepson, 'but I spent twenty-four years in a marriage that should have ended in five, because I was blackmailed. Not for money – well, it was partly for money, I suppose . . .'

Footsteps approached. 'One cocoa. One tea,' announced the waitress. 'You do know that we don't charge extra if you want to sit at the same table,' she added, tartly.

Vee gave her a look. 'Go on,' she said, once the waitress had left. 'If you can, I mean. If you want to.' She kept her eye on the window, on the passers-by, bulky with scarves, heads down against the snow, and Jepson ran a finger over his moustache and wondered why he had just told someone he scarcely knew a fact that he had never told anyone else, and he thought that it was partly because he wasn't having to look her in the eye. An inadvertent confessional; the Catholics knew a thing or two.

'So what was your wife's name?' asked Vee.

'Della.'

'Where did you meet her?'

'On a tram, not long after the war – I gave her my seat. I was very young, and she was a few years older and she was worried that she'd never find anyone, like half the girls of her generation, I suppose – and I had a profession, and prospects.'

'What did she look like?'

'Delicate. Dainty.' A porcelain shepherdess, he'd thought, the mud of the trenches still in his eyes. She had seemed like a miracle; he had thought that no one would ever want him.

'And what happened?'

'Oh . . .' He'd never tried to frame it in words before; it was like using a rusty typewriter. 'She was disappointed. I disappointed her. Time went by and we didn't have the children we'd hoped for. And I worked irregular hours and it wasn't as . . . as important a job as she'd thought. She felt I'd let her down; she was bitter.' The missing ear, which hadn't seemed to matter at first, had become the focus of her misery. 'That's the reason you never listen to me,' she'd said. Shouted. Involuntarily, he placed a hand over the ugly crinkle of scar tissue. 'I wanted a divorce, but Della refused – she said that she couldn't manage on her own, that it would be humiliating. She said that people would either pity or despise her.'

'Only rich women can get away with divorce,' said Vee.

Jepson, startled, looked round at her. 'But I would have made sure that she always had enough money to live on . . . Anyway, eventually I decided I couldn't stick it any longer,' he said, turning back again. 'I told her I was going to move out.'

'And is that when you were blackmailed?'

'Yes.'

'But who by?'

He made a harsh noise, like a heel scraped along the floor. 'By Della. She said if I left, she would put her head in the gas oven.'

There was a shocked pause.

'Do you think she would have?' asked Vee.

'Oh, yes,' said Jepson. 'Yes, she'd have done that.' There had never been much of a gap between Della's emotions and her actions. He had learned to expect violence in both: her knuckles jabbing at him in frustration – always the head, the ear. He thought with crawling horror of that moment in the kitchen at the Methodist Christmas party, when Mrs Claxton had shot out a hand and for a second it had been Della, and he'd cringed and covered his head, as he'd done so many times, for so long.

He wondered, now, how he'd endured it. There had, he supposed, been odd weeks of almost-normality, odd days of ordinary companionship, an occasional smile that had met with another; the years had slithered by and somehow he'd divided himself, so that at work he'd remained the dependable Jepson, diffident but well liked, and at home he'd been something hopeless and shapeless, a glove puppet playing the same character for every performance, Judy to Della's Punch. And then, abruptly, it had ended.

'It's a rotten story, really,' he said. 'Two miserable people who shouldn't have been together.'

'So when did your wife pass away?' asked Vee.

'Pass away? No, Della's living in Stevenage. She left me. A cousin of hers died and willed her a house and nine thousand pounds, and she was gone the week after. You were right about rich women; she's already filed for divorce.'

'No!'

Vee, gaping, swung right round to look at him, and he managed a wretched half-smile. 'Ridiculous, isn't it?'

'But what a – a – well, I won't say what I think of her.'

'No, don't,' said Jepson, looking down at his hands. He wanted to simply leave that part of his life behind, now, like the south-coast train of his childhood, holiday-bound, dividing at Haywards Heath, one part carrying on to the crowded seaside, the other swinging eastward, to the open light of the Downs. 'There,' he said, looking up again. 'I've told you my tale.' And if he hadn't told her the whole of it, it was still more than he'd ever vouchsafed to anyone else.

Vee remembered where she was, and turned her gaze to the door again. 'It's not the same for me,' she said. 'For a start, I don't know who wrote the letter, and if that person ever decided to tell the . . .' She paused. 'The thing is, I wouldn't want you to think I'd done anything *wicked*.' Because, after all, which commandment had she actually broken by pretending to be Noel's relation? There was 'Thou shalt not lie,' of course, but that had never seemed like a truly enforceable rule, since if it were, it would result in a hell stuffed not only with murderers and adulterers but also people who'd told the man from the rates that they hadn't heard the knock because they'd been in the outside lav.

'Of course it wasn't wicked,' said Jepson.

'How do you know?'

'Because you're not a wicked person.' He said it simply, just as someone might say, 'You're not wearing gloves,' and Vee felt a bizarre rush of pride.

'I did it for a proper reason,' she said. 'I almost *had* to do it.' The snow was beginning to turn to sleet, clumps of ice sliding down the window. 'But what good will it do if I tell you?'

'You might feel less anxious,' said Jepson. 'You know – a trouble shared. And I might be able to help you, or at least to give you some advice.'

When was the last time she'd trusted another adult? She wanted to search his face, but all she had was his voice. 'What's your full name?' she asked.

'Pevensey Gerard Arthur Jepson.'

'*Pevensey?*'

'My parents met at Pevensey Bay. I was always called Gerry.'

'Gerry Jepson.' There was an unlikely hop and a skip to the name.

'And I believe I know yours,' said Jepson. 'It's Margery, isn't it?'

Vee's mouth was suddenly very dry. She took a sip of cold tea and set the cup down again. 'No,' she said. 'No, that's not my real name.'

The photographer from the *Picture Post* had wanted to pose Avril in front of a bombed-out building, but snow had given way to sleet, and at three in the afternoon it was already beginning to darken, so he had moved his camera and a plug-in light into Post 9 and was using the six-foot-by-six sector map as a backdrop. Avril, dressed in a tightly belted navy siren suit, her hair in a victory roll, was standing with studied casualness, hands in pockets and a warden's helmet hooked over one elbow, the shadow of her profile projected dramatically across the web of streets.

'Any other props?' asked McLennan, who had arrived in a cape. He was, as Avril had whispered to Winnie, a well-known 'society' photographer, and his expression on looking around the interior of the Wardens' Hut was that of a sculptor forced to model the *Venus de Milo* out of used chewing-gum.

'Any what?' asked Smiler.

'Props. Objects of some description that would shout "Wardens' Post" to an observer.'

'Well, I can get you a sign that says "Wardens' Post",' said Smiler. 'There's one outside.'

'Something less on the nose, perhaps?'

Winnie opened the store cupboard and scanned the shelves. 'Gas rattle? Tilley lamp? Telephone book? Sandwich box?'

'That's mine,' said Basset.

'You haven't seen my *Iliad* in there, have you?' asked Polesworth.

Star-fever had hit the Post and several of the wardens had turned out to watch the photographic session, whether on shift or not. Avril had been tremendously gracious, distributing kisses and handshakes all round – 'Oh, I've heard all about *you*,' she'd said, roguishly, to Smiler, and his leathern features had almost dimpled. Addy had made her a cup of tea and Polesworth had actually brought along a copy of *Tin Helmet* for her to autograph.

'What about a blue flag?' continued Winnie, poking through the cupboard. 'For use during an incident. Or a whistle on a string? Or a folding canvas screen? We put them up to hide the WC in the shelters.'

The session continued without additional props. After Avril had been photographed in a variety of poses – gazing clear-eyed just to the right of the camera, pensively biting her lip and (less successfully) smiling modestly – it was Winnie's turn.

'Just begin by standing comfortably together,' said McLennan. 'Give me a moment to move the light.'

'No stains on this, are there?' asked Winnie, glancing down at the uniform tunic she was wearing over her slacks. She had polished the buttons that morning, and brushed the matching beret.

Avril shook her head. 'No, you look awfully smart. You know that *Picture Post* want you for the interview as well?'

'Really?'

'They love the twin angle, apparently. It's on Sunday afternoon at our house. Can you come?'

'I'd have to swap shifts.'

'I'll cover for you, Shorty,' said Smiler.

'There,' said Avril. 'All sorted. Is that what your colleagues call you? Shorty?'

'When we're not calling her Chief,' said Basset, with a tone of slight reproof.

'Link arms, please,' said McLennan. 'Lean your heads together. Could you bend your knees a little, Mrs Astley-Grey, to even up the heights?'

'Do call me Avril.'

'Actually, it might be preferable if we had something for Wendy to stand on.'

'It's Winnie.'

As she spoke, there was a noise like the snap of a dried stick, followed by a directionless rolling boom, which shook the floor and set the overhead light-bulb swinging on its wire.

'Near-ish,' said Basset.

'Ring up Control, would you?' asked Winnie. 'See where it is. And someone take a gander outside.'

'You're all splendidly calm,' said Avril, as Smiler and Polesworth left the hut. 'And talk about being in the right place – it's like getting appendicitis while you're in the doctor's surgery.'

'*Could* someone straighten the bulb so we can get back to the business in hand?' asked McLennan. 'I have a reception at the Russian Embassy at seven.'

The rocket, it turned out, had dropped over a mile and a half away, well out of their sector. 'On a bus garage,' Basset reported back, after a second call. 'Hell of a mess.'

'And now could we have Mrs Astley-Grey sitting on the edge of the desk, showing a page of her book to Wanda?'

'It's Winnie,' said Winnie yet again, staring at a passage which contained the words 'the oiled-silk skin of her thighs' and trying to adjust her features into an expression of rapt interest. It jolted her right back to drama school – to that moment during a first-year party when she'd realized that her ability to act on stage didn't extend to real life, and that while there were girls in her year who could apparently dilate their own pupils to order, she herself had difficulty even feigning a genuine-looking smile at someone she didn't like.

She remembered telling Emlyn about it, not long after they'd met: 'Well, that's a good quality, isn't it?' he'd said. 'I'll always know what you're really thinking.' Though now, of course, it was more than four years since he'd had any idea what she was really thinking; nearly half a decade of mutual opacity. She'd been trying to remember the contents of the last letter he would have received from her and could recall only a rather perfunctory account of what she'd been listening to on the wireless. '. . . On the other hand, the Dorothy L. Sayers adaptation was pretty good, though I guessed the murderer about a quarter of the way through . . .' Hard to imagine anyone pressing that to their heart, except as insulation.

'Only one more left on the film,' said McLennan. 'How about something amusing – both of you playing Tug-o-war over the warden's helmet?'

'No,' said Winnie and Avril, simultaneously.

'Could we have a photograph of all of us from Post 9?' asked Winnie. 'We've never had the chance before.'

They bunched together in front of the map, Winnie and Avril at the centre.

'Say "Cheese" everyone!' said Avril.

'Cheese? Where?' asked Smiler. 'Which lucky bleeder's got some cheese?'

McLennan packed up his camera and hurried off into the gloaming, followed at a more leisurely pace by Smiler and the others – 'We might nip into the Fox and Grapes, and then again, we might not' – leaving only Winnie manning the Post.

'What, all on your own?' asked Avril.

'Basset's back at six. Besides, I'm used to my own company.' The casual phrase came out sounding like an elegy, and Avril pulled a sympathetic face. 'You do know, darling, that Clive's keeping his ears pricked for even the tiniest bit of news. He'll tell you the very second he hears anything.' And instantly, all the worry that Winnie had been keeping firmly pegged was up again and waving, flapping round her like hung sheets in a gale. 'Oh, please, let's talk about something else,' she said, dragging the desk back to its normal position, and handing the copy of *Tin Helmet* to her sister. 'Are you going to write another book?'

'Oh, I have to, I don't have any choice; my publisher's an absolute martinet and he says it's essential I build on my success. I'm thinking about short stories this time. The Home Front from different angles: the country housewife, the Ministry Man . . .'

The woman whose husband's in a POW camp, thought Winnie, with absolute certainty.

'I've already thought of a—'

The air in the room folded into Winnie's face like a concertina, and then retreated, pulling out of her lungs with a tidal suck and opening the door as it left, revealing the empty cement path up to the square, footprints visible in the sludge.

The door slammed shut again, with such force that a cobweb was shaken loose from the frame and moved not down, but sideways, parallel with the ceiling, as if borne on an invisible tray, and Avril's book, which had been on the desk, was on the rug, which itself was pleated against the far wall, exposing the concrete floor of the hut. A chair had swivelled on the spot. The map had been torn from the wall. Avril's face was taut, her eyes enormous.

'Rocket,' said Winnie, her mouth moving, but no sound emerging, not enough breath left inside her to make a noise. She hit herself on the chest and tried again, a mousy squeak. 'Rocket overhead, right overhead. Stay here. *Here.*'

She grabbed her oilskin from the hook, and then her helmet, and opened the door into a cloud of stinging hail, minute chips of razor ice that weren't ice at all, she realized, pulling on her coat and running up the path: the air was full of tiny fragments of glass.

On the south side of Deddington Square, the roofs and all remaining windows were gone. Mr Iles from the ground floor of number 12 had come outside and was standing with his hands on his hips, looking up at the empty sky, as if admiring a cloud formation, and Winnie ran past him and along Fig Passage into another street of roofless houses, the road paved with slates, someone already sweeping the glass from their front path, and ahead of her was Longford Row, more rafters like toast-racks, someone shouting, and now there was smoke in the air; Archer Street, the houses shorter with every few yards, no roofs, no upper floors, no fanlights over the front doors, and then there was her colleague Polesworth, covered in dust, leaning against a gatepost, the bare outline of the Fox and Grapes behind him, more air than brick.

'They're under there,' he said, his gaze twitching past

her towards the pub. 'I'd changed my mind, decided to go home instead. They're all under there.'

Winnie gripped his arm, trying to orientate herself. The pub had been part of a long, curved terrace which faced an identical terrace across an eye-shaped communal garden. And now there was no garden, just a vast crater at least forty feet wide, a water main playing like a fountain at the far end, a faint smell of gas, the terrace on one side an arc of humped rubble, while on the other, four storeys had been reduced to two and a woman was screaming, a shrill, unwavering noise, like a railway whistle. Smoke was rising from a couple of the ruined houses, a shimmy of flame just visible.

She dragged her gaze back to Polesworth. 'Do you think you can get to the Post and phone Control?' He nodded, his eyes clear, though his face was bleeding from a dozen tiny nicks. 'My sister's still there – send her back with the field telephone and the incident flags and lamps. And the census cards for the sector. Do you want me to come back with you?'

He shook his head and left, and Winnie ran across to the gaping wall of the pub. The upper floors had collapsed into the bar-room, which had itself collapsed into the cellar, and she was confronted with a choppy floor of brick and plaster, spiked with broken laths, half a table sticking vertically out of the rubble. On the opposite wall, a tin plaque bearing the Guinness toucan glinted in the last of the light. Two men were already making an attempt to dig.

'How many people were in here?' she asked, castigating herself for not having checked with Polesworth.

'Five or six,' said one of the men. 'They'd only just opened. Three of them were your lads, and then a couple of old boys. And Alice at the bar.' He pulled at one of the larger pieces, causing a small avalanche of plaster dust, and the creak of bending boards.

'Stay off it and wait for Heavy Rescue,' said Winnie, sharply. The chances were that no one was alive under there, but you never knew, you *never knew*: there was luck of all kinds in every raid. Addy had survived a blast that had killed the man next to him, Smiler had been blown into a cellar and come up cursing. She could already hear a fire-engine bell approaching.

'Win, you in charge?' It was Constable Orr, and with him were two of the Boy Scouts who acted as messengers during incidents.

'I think I must be. There's a fire mid-terrace on the west side of Ashington Gardens – the engine'll never get round the front. Can you head them off before they get stuck and direct them up the back alley?' She groped for the name of the taller scout. Toby. *Terry.* 'Terry, I need a working telephone – could you knock on doors until you find one and then fetch me straight away. And I need someone to run to Post 8. It's not their sector, but tell them we're down to two at Post 9 and we can do with all the help we can get.' As she spoke she was mentally listing the immediate requirements: Heavy and Light Rescue, fire brigade, gas board, water board, searchlights – there were maybe another twenty minutes of daylight left. The fact that the V-2 had fallen in the afternoon was a partial blessing – there were fewer people at home and those who were there were downstairs, protected from the scalping force of the wider explosion, though more liable, of course, to be buried.

'Win?' It was Doreen Hurst from the next sector – off duty, judging by the fact she was wearing lipstick and a mouton coat. 'I was just passing. I've heard about Smiler and the others. What can I do?'

'Nothing here, but we're going to need another incident post at the other end of the crater, otherwise there'll be endless traffic jams, so you can set that up. If Polesworth's well enough, he can come and give you a hand; if not, we've got to get someone from your own sector. See if you can find a clear route for vehicles in and out of the east side of the square, and somewhere for them to park up. I'll get one of the messengers to bring you a mac and a helmet.' She pulled out her notebook and started on a list. Terry was back, and she followed him to a house at the far end of Archer Street, which, despite having had its entire front hedge blown into the parlour through the bay window, had a working telephone.

'Someone's here for you, Warden,' said the Boy Scout when she emerged from the house, and there was Avril, holding a couple of lanterns, a laden canvas bag over one shoulder.

'How's Polesworth?' asked Winnie.

'He seems a bit shaky, but he says he'll come back to help. How about the others?'

'Won't know until Heavy Rescue arrive. The rocket we heard earlier is using up half the resources – the Borough Incident Officer's over there, and the mobile office, but they said they'll divert anything that isn't needed our way. Meanwhile, they're liaising with Holloway. I'm going to use this house as our Incident Post so can you get a lantern lit before you go?'

'Go? I'm not going, I want to help.'

'Terry, there's a spare warden's coat and helmet in Post 9. Take them to Doreen Hurst, who'll be up at the far end of the square, trying to set up a post – you know her, don't you? Don't try to edge round the crater, go round the back of the houses. Take the field telephone and one of these lamps and flags as well. And ask Doreen what she needs.' He shot off again, a good lad.

'I want to help,' said Avril again.

'All right, but you have to do as I say. I mean it, Avril. If people just muck in, all we get is enthusiasm and chaos and everyone doing the same thing.'

Avril started to say something and then saluted. 'You're in charge, sis.'

'We need somewhere for people to go who can't get back into their houses. Go and find the vicar of St Agnes – his name's Howells – and ask for the use of the parish hall as a rest centre. End of this road, turn right, the church is halfway down; he'll be somewhere around there. When you've done that, come straight back to me.'

Avril ran.

Within forty minutes, the streets around the crater were seething with vehicles. Torch-beams flicked across the ruins, and the hiccup of a generator indicated the arrival of a set of floodlights loaned by the US Navy. During the Blitz they'd had to do all this in near-darkness, the digging teams of Heavy Rescue erecting canopies to conceal their lights; now, as daylight brilliance suddenly bathed Ashington Gardens, Winnie saw a flock of starlings rise in confusion, circling and banking in the broad white beams, their shadows interweaving across the broken terraces.

'WVS canteen has just arrived,' said Avril, breathlessly. 'They want to know where to park.'

'Here, if they can,' said Winnie, jerking a thumb towards the pavement opposite the Incident Post. 'It needs to be visible. It's going to be a long night.'

She kept catching glimpses of the digging team through the perforated walls of the Fox and Grapes, the small, patient movements which always seemed so slow, and yet were the only way to burrow through the compacted mass of masonry, its surface already slimy with damp. Most of the Heavy Rescue boys were from the building trade – you'd see them tapping the rubble, hearing its hollows and struts, gauging its instability, choosing their careful route into the interior.

Two survivors had already been found in Ashington Gardens, a mother and child furred with plaster dust and blank with shock, saved by their kitchen table, but there were at least fourteen others missing on the east side of the Gardens, and more in Archer Street. Twenty-eight casualties had been treated on the spot and thirteen taken to hospital. Eight deaths had been confirmed. Winnie was using the top of a garden wall as a makeshift table, the searchlight as her desk-lamp, as she checked rapidly through the census cards, thankful that she had always insisted that they be updated weekly, her wardens noting which families had left London, or had returned, or left again, or if a resident was in hospital, or whether previously abandoned flats were housing temporary workers, or which soldiers were home on leave, so that now the rescue workers were not just digging blindly, or speculatively.

The Boy Scouts were back, spring-heeled, tireless. 'Gas board want a word with you, Warden,' said Terry. 'They think you should evacuate Wixell Row. They're outside number 17.'

'Right-oh.' She tucked the cards into her jacket pocket.

'Anything you want us to do?'

'Yes. Polesworth's inside – ask him to phone Control and check that casualties should still be sent to St Mary's, only we're hearing from the ambulance drivers that it's getting full.' She was walking away as she spoke, skirting the WVS van that was slowly crunching over a surface of shattered roof-slates. 'And get yourselves something from the canteen truck.'

'What about you, Warden?'

'Tea and a slice, please,' she said, breaking into a jog.

'. . . so they hired a car,' said Jepson, 'quite a swish one, and called at various shops, and explained, using official language, that they were Board of Trade inspectors and that there were counterfeit coupons circulating in the district. So the shopkeepers would get out the coupons, and the thieves would examine them very carefully – they even had a magnifying glass and what they claimed was a special rubber that only worked on genuine ink – and they'd declare that at least half the coupons were probably forged, and would have to be checked by an expert at the office, and then they'd issue a receipt, and promise to return.'

'And then they'd never come back!' said Vee, riveted.

'That's right.'

'So how did they get caught?'

'From what I remember, one of them got collared for something else, and confessed.'

'And they went to prison?'

'Oh, yes. Hard labour on the Isle of Wight.'

'Oh,' said Vee, suddenly breathless. They were still sitting back to back, but she'd been so caught up in Jepson's stories – told with great journalistic flair and economy – that she'd briefly forgotten her own peril and had half turned towards him. She snapped her gaze back to the door again, but no one new had come in for a while. The V-2 that had rattled the window an hour or so before seemed to have frightened off shoppers, though it had dropped far enough away not to have caused any local damage – Jepson had nipped out to check, and had returned with the reassuring news that it was west of them, and nowhere near Noel, and home.

'I had someone who worked at the Board of Trade as a lodger once,' said Vee. 'Mr Titus. He was a good payer, but he never cleaned his teeth and his breath smelled so bad that Noel used to call him Titus . . . something . . . oh, what was it? A word that meant "stink" – he said it was ancient Greek, and it rhymed.'

'Mephitis?'

'Yes, that's the one. Titus Mephitis.' She hadn't ever

heard Jepson laugh before, and the noise was amusing in itself – a breezy giggle, quite at odds with his usual gravity. Vee aimed another look at the door. It was nearly five o'clock and already dark.

'What time was he supposed to arrive?' asked Jepson.

'After two. That's all he put. Though I suppose it might be a she – I never thought of that.'

'Do you have the letter with you?' asked Jepson. 'I know you've told me what's in it, but handwriting can be very revealing.'

Vee took the envelope from her handbag and passed it behind her. She heard the rustle as Jepson extracted the single sheet of paper, and the pause as he read the pencilled lines.

'Oh,' he said, his voice light with surprise. 'Yes, I'd say that's a man's handwriting – and an educated man, at that – but the thing is, there's hardly anything here.'

'What do you mean?'

'There are no details at all, nothing concrete, no reference to St Albans, no mention that Noel was your evacuee. He doesn't even know your real name.'

'How can you tell?'

'Because he'd almost certainly have used that knowledge to frighten you. The phrase "I am aware that you are not actually Noel Bostock's aunt" is terribly non-specific. Any blackmailer worth his salt would have begun the letter with . . .' Jepson lowered his voice to a whisper. ' "Dear Vera Sedge" and put you straight on to the back foot.'

It was years since she'd heard her full name spoken, and

she hadn't missed it. 'Vera' had always sounded to her like the low moan of a cow waiting to be milked. 'So you don't think it's someone who knew me in the past, then? Someone who moved to London and spotted me?'

'Judging from this, I'd say not. I think the letter's a clever guess – someone who's picked up a hint in some way and is attempting to put two and two together.'

'But what sort of hint? I'm always careful, and I know that Noel wouldn't ever . . .' She thought again about what Jepson had just said. 'Putting two and two together – you mean that someone looked at me and looked at the boy and thought we didn't fit and started wondering?' Because she'd never lost her awareness of this – the clang of her own accent against the precision of his, the way that he spoke sentences with the ease of a croupier shuffling a deck, while she doled out words from a sticky pack.

'I think you fit together very well,' said Jepson. 'Matching jigsaw pieces don't have to look identical. He was lucky to find you.'

He'd said little when she'd given him a carefully filleted version of her story – how she'd done a flit from St Albans to keep Noel with her, leaving her mother and her own grown-up son, Donald, behind (not that either would have begged her to stay; in fact, she had her doubts whether they'd even noticed she'd gone, but she hadn't mentioned that bit). How she'd pretended to be Noel's dead aunt, Mrs Overs, so that he wouldn't end up in a children's home.

'But however did you get Mrs Overs' identity card?' he'd asked, before adding, 'No, don't worry, I don't need to know, I'm just being nosy,' so she hadn't had to invent anything to avoid telling him that she'd extracted the forged document from Donald's father by something really quite similar to blackmail. Some things were best left alone. And now Jepson had said something so kind, so unexpected, that she was momentarily speechless. *He was lucky to find you.* She'd never thought of it that way round.

'Anything?' asked the waitress, back yet again.

'I couldn't,' said Vee.

There was a pause.

'We're not a waiting room,' said the woman, acidly.

'I'll have fruit loaf and another cocoa,' said Jepson, who seemed to have hollow legs.

'Just warning you, we close at six.'

'I've had a thought,' said Jepson, as the waitress moved away again. 'I suspect that most blackmailers are cowards. If he were to arrive and find that not only were you accompanied, but that your companion was prepared to vouch for your identity, I should think he'd throw in the towel.'

'You'd do that?' asked Vee, astonished.

'Vouch for you? Yes, of course.'

She couldn't fit the idea into her head: another adult offering to help her out of a hole, gratis.

'Why?' she asked, before she could stop herself, but Jepson had already stood up, picked up his hat and coat and moved across to her table. He put the hat back on, and then politely lifted it.

'Good afternoon, Mrs Overs. Is this chair free?'

'Yes,' she said, too startled to play-act. 'But if he comes in, what will you do?'

'I'll say, "I'm a very old friend of Mrs Overs. I've seen

the baseless and threatening letter that you wrote to her, and as a journalist I'm keen to hear your side of the story before I go to the police."'

'You'd really say that?'

'I would.'

Vee put a hand over her eyes. It took Jepson a moment to understand why, and another for him to locate a handkerchief.

'I'm sorry,' he said. 'I didn't mean . . .'

'I'm all right,' she said, waving the handkerchief away. She removed the hand from her face and sat upright, blinking rapidly. 'I'm not used to it . . . I mean, I've always had to work out how to do everything by myself. It's unexpected. Thank you.' She said the last words with a nod and a stab at a smile.

'You're welcome,' said Jepson.

For a while, they sat together in silence; for once, Vee didn't feel the urge to fill it.

'You asked why,' said Jepson.

'Oh, no, you don't have to say.' She was suddenly worried that it was pity, or Moral Duty.

'Teaching Noel has been one of the great pleasures of my life,' he said. 'And now that I know his story, I can't bear to think of what would have happened if you hadn't chosen to do what you did. But more than that, I'd forgotten what it was like to look forward to coming home after work – to return to somewhere pleasant. So I suppose you could say that this is my thanks. The past year has been . . .'

He said something that she couldn't quite hear.

'It's been what?'

'Balm,' he said, looking down.

'One cocoa. We're out of fruit loaf, but I've brought you the end of the jam roll,' said the waitress, clunking the bowl on the table behind.

'Over here, please,' said Vee.

'Oh, all change at Crewe, is it?'

The woman shifted the cup and bowl across. Jepson was still looking at the table-top, running a finger over his moustache.

Poor chap, thought Vee, surprising herself; her own worries had a tendency to jostle aside sympathy for others.

'My mother was very fond of that Bible verse,' she said. 'Still is, I suppose. "Is there no balm in Gilead? Is there no physician?" I always remember sitting in chapel and thinking that Gilead would be a nice name for a boy, but then I ended up calling mine Donald.'

'Why?'

'It was after a character in a book we read at school. Donald Farfrae.'

'From *The Mayor of Casterbridge*? You like Hardy?'

'That's the only one of his I ever read. Nobody was very happy in the end, from what I remember.'

'No – well, I suppose he might have considered that unhappy endings were more true to life. Though, personally, I prefer Dickens, where everything turns out well.' He smiled at her, rather shyly, and Vee felt suddenly very flustered.

'We'll miss supper,' she said, looking at the café clock. 'I don't know what excuse I'll give to Noel. He's been out of sorts since Christmas, I can't do anything right. He didn't take to Mario, of course – and I know I scared him when I couldn't get back from Brighton. I can't talk to him as well as I used to. Do you think it's his age?' And she thought of her son, Donald, who had walked out of earshot somewhere on the road between jolly boy and silent adult.

'I expect his age is a good part of it,' said Jepson. He ate the jam roll neatly and at speed, but pulled a face after sipping the cocoa.

'We're closing,' announced the man behind the counter.

'It's on me,' said Jepson, taking his wallet from his pocket. 'Really,' he added, firmly.

They stood for a few minutes in the street outside, the pavements empty, the other shops already locked and shuttered. Someone was singing 'Roll Out the Barrel' in the pub on the corner – a slow and phlegmy rendition that made Vee want to clear her throat.

'Would you like to wait a little longer?' asked Jepson.

'Do you think I should?'

'No. I imagine that he lost his nerve and decided not to go through with it.'

'But what if he sends another letter?'

'Then I'll come with you to meet him and we'll send him packing.'

'But what if—?'

The pavement began to vibrate, and they both turned to see a bulky vehicle moving along the street towards them, the dim blue bulb of the streetlight revealing a crane jib affixed to the flatbed of a lorry. It juddered past just as an ambulance bell became audible, heading west.

Vee met Jepson's eye. 'I think we should go home,' she said. ' "Sufficient unto the day is the evil thereof." '

'I think you're right.'

It wasn't until they boarded the bus back to Hampstead that she saw he was looking faintly amused.

'What's so funny?'

'Nothing,' he said, waiting until she was seated before sitting down himself. 'It's just . . .'

'What?'

'You and Noel. Always quoting.'

'Oh.' She found herself smiling. It wasn't the end to the day that she'd expected.

The elderly woman who answered the door of the last house on Robin Street was wearing a rather elegant turban with matching dressing-gown, and the expression of someone dragged from a dinner party.

'Yes?'

'Miss Newton?' asked Winnie.

'That is my name.'

'We're just checking every damaged house to make sure there are no undeclared casualties. You live here with your sister?'

'Yes.'

'And neither of you are injured or shocked?'

'No. Is that all you require? Only we have spent the entire evening sweeping up glass and plaster, and I'm rather fatigued, not to mention more than a little surprised that your call has taken place so many hours after the rocket fell.'

'We've been busy, I'm afraid. Is there anyone else staying at the house?'

'Why would there be anyone else staying in our house? What on earth are you implying?'

'I'm not implying anything.' Winnie walked back down the path and paused to chalk 'CDS' on the gate-post.

'Whatever are you doing to my wall?' asked Miss Newton.

'It means I've checked the house and you won't be disturbed again. Council Repairs will be around in the morning.'

'Wash that off immediately!'

Winnie ignored her and turned the corner into Swift Road, thinking of Smiler's usual adage when faced with public recalcitrance – 'Anyone who expects gratitude's a mug' – and then thinking of Smiler, and walking faster.

'I'm going back,' she called to Padmore, a Post 8 warden who was working his way down the houses. 'It's just Walnut Avenue after this. You OK to do it?'

'What about Falcon Road?'

'It's been empty since the last rocket. Declared unsafe.'

Back at the incident, a crane had arrived at the far end of the flooded crater, and was attempting to lift whatever it was that had fractured the water main, while in the house next to the Incident Post, the WVS had set up an inquiry point. A stream of shift workers, returning from their jobs to find their homes empty or flattened, were queuing down the path. A frail-looking chap clutched Winnie's arm as she passed. 'I'm looking for my wife,' he said. 'Number 2 Archer Street. There's no one digging there. Why isn't there anyone digging there?'

'Are you Mr Curry?'

'Yes.'

'Your wife was out shopping. She's safe and she's gone to your daughter's.' He started crying immediately, and apologized, groping for his handkerchief, thanking her with an attempted doff of the hat, managing half a smile as he wiped his eyes.

'I'm glad to do it,' said Winnie.

Constable Orr was standing beside the mobile canteen, eating a Lyons pie. 'It said "plum" on the carton,' he said, his mouth full, 'and "blackcurrant" on the wrapper, and now it turns out it's apple. Here, have you been into the pub just now?'

'Not for an hour.'

'They've heard tapping.'

Winnie arrived there breathless, and could sense immediately the change in atmosphere. The pace was no longer measured but rapid; the squad had formed a chain, passing baskets of rubble out through to the street from a wide-mouthed tunnel in which two men were working; she caught only occasional glimpses of their hands as they passed the baskets upward, their skin covered in a thick paste of grit. She edged around the perimeter until she could see into the hole. It sloped down at a shallow angle, and at the bottom was what looked like part of a solid surface; not floorboards, but something seamless.

'Warden? Could you come over here a moment?'

It was the leader of the brigade, Hubbard, a heavy-set man, his face striped with sweat. Winnie followed him to a smaller excavation on the other side of the pub. 'We thought we heard something earlier,' said Hubbard, 'so we sank a shaft, but the noise stopped. We've just found him – don't know if he's one of yours.'

Winnie crouched beside the hole, and Hubbard shone his torch down and the first thing she saw was a grey hand, and her eyes followed the arm down to the shoulder. The person was lying at an angle, so that the top of his head was still buried, but she could see the lower half of the face, as grey as the hand, the mouth slightly open, a set of false teeth protruding clownishly in the awful indignity of death.

'Oh,' she said, and the back of her neck felt sluiced with ice. 'Oh. It's Basset. Arthur Basset.' Who'd said little, who'd loved his wife, who'd never failed his colleagues. 'Oh, damn it all.' She straightened up. 'Damn it all.' And there was nothing more she could do for him, except determine to tell Min Basset herself; she nodded at Hubbard, and went back across the rubble to the wider dig. Nothing appeared to have changed there, and after a minute or two she left the pub again and returned to the Incident Post, where she added Basset's name to the list of the dead, and the night jerked onward, one decision after another, a running report to write, her hand cramping around the pencil, the mortuary van arriving, a second crane getting stuck at the corner of Longford Row, a missing child, subsequently found asleep under a chair in the rest centre, the sudden realization at 4 a.m. that if she didn't have something to eat, she might keel over, and then there was a streak of grey in the sky and she was summoned again to the Fox and Grapes.

The excavation was as wide as a motor-car, now, and almost as deep, and at the bottom, surrounded by rescue workers, was an object like a long, shallow wooden tent. She stared at it, saw a pump handle sticking out of one side, and realized that she was looking at the bar, knocked horizontal so that underneath it was a potential space: a life-saver. Two jacks had been inserted under one side and were being slowly cranked up.

'Nearly with you,' said one of the Heavy Rescue, crouching so that he could speak under the widening crack, and even from her position several feet above, Winnie could hear a voice in reply, hoarse and blasphemous.

'That's Smiler,' she said, but the first out of the darkness was Alice, the barmaid, her face and shirt soaked with blood from a long head wound. 'I can't see,' she kept saying, as she was lifted up to street-level, 'I can't open my eyes,' and then Addy was eased out into the lamplight, shouting with pain from a broken leg, the knee bending the wrong way, the foot flopping like a piece of wash-leather, the stretcher party handling him with infinite gentleness, and then Smiler, crawling out, talking the whole way: '... didn't hear nothing until the ceiling came down, and then I dived under the bar like a bleeding goalie ... Hi ho, Shorty!' he said, spotting her, clambering up the slope under his own steam, the smell of stale beer and blood and urine preceding him, his eyes feverish with the euphoria she'd seen before, in those who'd miraculously escaped. 'Basset was over by the Gents. Did you find him?'

'Yes.'

He caught her expression. 'Gone, is he? Those bastards. Those bastards flicking a fucking switch somewhere, and never mind who gets it. There was two old chaps in here as well,' he said, looking round towards Hubbard. 'They was sitting at a table by the window.'

'We'll keep looking,' said Hubbard.

Smiler refused to see the first-aid team, or even have a cup of tea, and went stumping off home to his wife and mother-in-law, insisting, too, that he should be the one to tell Mrs Basset ('I was at their bleeding wedding, wasn't I?'), and Winnie went on working until Larwood turned up from Borough Control, and told her that he was taking over and she should hop it. It was nearly eight o'clock, the sky a dirty white and the air full of dust; a bulldozer was beginning to shovel spoil into the bomb crater. On Longford Row, a lorry belonging to the Pioneer Corps had arrived, piled high with tarpaulins for the denuded roofs, and the greengrocer on the corner was arranging a pyramid of cabbages in his glassless shop-window.

Winnie went to Post 9 to lock up, and it wasn't until she noticed the blanketed lump on the camp-bed that she realized that it was hours since she'd last seen Avril.

'Oh,' said her sister, sitting up. 'Is it all over? Sorry, I lasted till around four and then I simply couldn't stay upright any longer. Did they find your wardens?'

'Yes. Yes, they did. Smiler's all right, but Addy's badly injured and Basset was killed – the pale man, with the cheekbones.'

'Oh, Winnie . . .' And the note of sympathy in her sister's voice dislodged something in Winnie, so that she found herself weeping.

'You were marvellous, you know,' said Avril, struggling to her feet from the low bed. 'I almost wish I could write the book again, now that I've actually seen you at work. You really were terrific.'

Genuine praise, untainted with Avril's usual patronage; Winnie turned the words over in her head, like someone examining an unexpectedly valuable present. 'Well, you did all right too,' she said.

'Did I?' Avril looked delighted. 'Well, I tried my best. But I was terribly proud of you. I wanted to tell everyone you were my little sister.'

'That I was your *what*?'

'Oh, don't get cross, Twinnie. It's just the way I think of you.'

'I was born *first* – you really are the limit, Avril.' She blew her nose, hard. 'I'm going home. I'm back on tonight.' She shooed her sister out of the Post and locked the door.

'Bye, darling,' said Avril, heading for the Tube and the Ministry of Information, looking as if she'd slept for twelve hours on satin pillows.

As Winnie walked back to the flat, thinking only of taking off her boots and falling on to the bed, she was stopped by three separate people offering her breakfast, and by a black-and-white cat which ran towards her as she passed the ruins of Falcon Road. She stooped to scratch its head and it butted its hard little nose into her palm. Winnie had seen it before, hanging around the derelict basement flat whose illegal occupant she had never managed to catch up with. Looking along the row, she realized that the shape of the terrace had changed since yesterday – the houses, already roofless from the previous V-2 to hit the sector, had collapsed inward, the lower storeys split by broad cracks. Last night's rocket might have landed a quarter of a mile away, but here it had delivered the *coup de grâce*.

Winnie picked up the cat and walked uncertainly towards the flat she'd previously visited; was it the one with half a gate hanging from a single hinge, or its neighbour with the cream-stuccoed wall, peppered with old shrapnel wounds? The cat answered her question by wriggling from her arms and picking its way towards the latter. The stairs down to the basement entrance still showed evidence of having been cleared by the occupant, but the door itself had burst outward, and as Winnie descended she could see that what had happened at the pub had also happened here, and that the interior was now a dense wedge of ceilings and floorboards from the storeys above.

'Don't,' she said to the cat, who was trying to insert its head between the layers. The whole place felt desperately unsafe, plaster dust trickling through the wreckage. Winnie took out her torch and shone it into some of the gaps in the strata; she glimpsed a section of bannister, a crushed lampshade with a purple silk fringe, a shoe, a row of wrought-iron coat-hooks. She turned the torch off and then, after a moment, turned it back on. She flicked the beam across the piled debris, found the shoe again, and this time leaned closer, her face pushing up against a splintered board. She could see it clearly now: it was a man's shoe, the laces tied in a firm double bow. The sock was rucked around the ankle and above it she could see two or three inches of livid calf, the rest of the leg engulfed in rubble. She moved the torch away, and inserted her hand into the gap. The foot had stiffened and the calf was ice-cold.

'Go home, get some kip,' said Larwood, after she'd retraced her steps to the Incident Post to report the body, but when at last she was sitting, wrapped in a blanket in front of her two-bar fire, the black-and-white cat with its face in a saucer of pilchards (it had followed her the whole way to her front door), an oblong of unexpected sunlight on the wall behind, she no longer felt tired – or rather, she had moved beyond sleepiness into a state in which the events of the day were ineluctably unscrolling in her head, each moment as vivid as the next, her inner eye darting between Basset's face and the circling starlings, the dense khaki of the lentil soup from the WVS van, the shift-worker who'd shouted at her for waking him when she'd knocked on his shattered front door, the raw meat of bodies, a budgerigar pinging its bell in a crumpled cage, the lady who'd sung 'Oh, Mr Porter' from the cupboard under her stairs to guide the diggers towards her, a living child holding the hand of her dead sister, a broken mirror in a hill of rubble, flashing like an Aldis lamp at every touch of a torch-beam.

She was roused from her thoughts by an odd noise from beneath the bed – a series of rustles and snaps – and she leaned over and lifted the counterpane. The cat looked back at her. It was lying on its side, its claws embedded in the wicker of the suitcase in which Winnie kept Emlyn's letters; after a short pause, it resumed its meditative rending of the fibres.

'Get *off*,' said Winnie, pulling the case towards her. Unhurriedly, the cat detached itself and began instead to investigate the fringe of the rug, lifting and carefully examining separate strands, as if working on quality control at the mill.

There was dust on the case. Winnie shoved it back into the narrow gap, and thought immediately of the dark space under the bar of the Fox and Grapes, which had saved three lives today. If she were still sending letters to Emlyn, what platitude would she have written about the last eighteen hours? *'I'm quite tired after a busy time at work, but nothing that a good night's sleep won't cure'? 'There was a bit of damage in our area, but I'm absolutely fine, so no need to worry'?* So much breezy euphemism; if they ever met again, he'd be expecting a twinkling optimist, like Jessie Matthews tap-dancing on a revolving cake while warbling, 'Over my shoulder goes one care.'

Winnie scratched the top of the cat's head, and it abandoned the rug and jumped on to her lap. It was thin but healthy-looking and didn't appear to be pining for its previous minder, whoever he'd been; the dead man's identity would become a police matter now, she supposed.

She leaned back in her chair, closed her eyes and at once saw the mauve-dappled leg in the ruins, and it was no good, she thought, snapping her eyes open again; she wouldn't sleep until she could slough off some of these images, and she transferred the cat on to the bed and poured herself a drop of sloe gin. During the Blitz, when every night had been piled with incident, she had tried keeping a diary, but had found it a chore rather than a release; a trip to the pub with her colleagues had always been far more helpful, the horrors unplugged by caustic language and a stream of macabre jokes.

She sipped the gin. The faintest of noises came from the bed. 'Emlyn,' she said, fixing her eyes on the glass, 'can I tell you about what happened today?'

No one ever telephoned Green Shutters, so when Vee heard the ringing while she was pegging washing the next morning, she assumed it must be coming from the Lumbs' house. There was a stiff wind and the sky was patched with blue, but there was also a line of cloud marching eastward which meant that, chances were, she'd have to take the washing back in again in an hour, and then put it all out for a second time an hour later and that would be the whole morning gone, and she was just retrieving an escaped tea-towel from one of the apple trees when Noel appeared at her elbow.

'Lady Gillett just rang.'

'*Who?*'

'She lives at Greenbanks. The house next to Taormina.'

'At the top of the road?'

'Yes.'

'*Lady* Gillett? But what does she want? Who is she?'

'I think she's the widow of a baronet – you've probably seen her in passing, she looks like Sargent's portrait of Madame X. She says there's a misdelivered letter for you at her house, and what she described as "items for collection".'

'A letter? For me?' Vee's throat was all ice – she hadn't expected another so soon: the blackmailer may have missed one appointment, but he was clearly wasting no time. She pegged the last tea-towel and dried her hands on her apron, wishing that Jepson were home. 'I'd better go and fetch it, I suppose,' she said.

'I think I should warn you that Lady Gillett sounded rather cross. She said, "My front garden is not a goods yard."'

'What does that mean?'

'I have no idea, but she seemed to think it was your fault. Would you like me to come?'

'No, I . . . no, you stay and do your History.'

'It's Geography this morning, the Carpathians. What's the matter?'

'Nothing. I'm just busy, that's all. Have you fed the chickens?'

'You know I have, you saw me from the window when I came back with the eggs.'

'Oh, yes.'

She tried to steady herself, and Noel watched her narrowly, trying to surmise what had rattled her, and there was still that chilly gap between them, plugged with secrets. Vee went in to fetch her coat, and dithered between her beret and her best hat.

'Did she sound very posh?'

'Yes, extremely.'

The hat, then. She wedged it on and caught Noel's eye. 'All right, you can come, in case there's something to carry,' she said. Though mainly in case Lady Gillett tried to start a conversation.

Greenbanks was a three-storey house built of brick the dull purple of uncooked kidneys and set well back from the lane, its long front garden surrounded by high hedges. The area of lawn nearest to the house was a puddled swamp, pock-marked with deep boot-prints.

The door was answered by a maid in a fancy bandeau, who immediately moved aside as a woman a few years older than Vee, with a face like a lurcher and a pair of bottle-green corduroy slacks, came hurtling up the passage.

'It was appallingly inconsiderate,' said Lady Gillett, apparently by way of greeting. '*Eleven at night.* That's the time they arrived, hammering at the door. The maid had gone home and I had to answer it myself, and if you must know, I am still frightfully, frightfully cross about the whole thing. If I hadn't had sharp words, they would have left everything on the *doorstep.* On the *doorstep*! And I have people coming round for luncheon, including a very senior member of the Ways and Means Committee. As it is, they've left the lawn looking like the paddock at Epsom and the entire side-path is blocked. So you'll understand why I am so absolutely furious, and if you don't remove every single item immediately, I shall be forced to ring the authorities. Do you understand?'

'No,' said Noel.

Lady Gillett dragged her gaze from Vee.

'I beg your pardon?'

'We haven't the slightest idea what you mean. Who are the "they" you are talking about?'

'Americans!' she said, as if it were obvious. 'In a jeep! They had already unloaded everything by the time I opened the door, and refused to take it away again, despite the fact they'd delivered it to the wrong person. *Here!*' She took a folded envelope out of her trouser pocket and thrust it at Vee. 'This morning I asked my maid who on earth "Mrs Overs" was, and she told me that you were the woman who runs the boarding-house at the end of the road, and of course those stupid men had confused Greenbanks with Green Shutters.'

'Now, hang on—' began Vee, but Noel had already taken a step forward, his chin raised, his voice as deep as Vee had ever heard it.

'My aunt is not a "woman who runs a boarding-house",' he said, 'but someone who has spent the last four years feeding and accommodating essential war-workers, rather than sitting on her arse being waited on by the only remaining servant in Hampstead. I have heard snobbery defined as the pride of those who are not sure of their position, and your own is clearly balanced on the edge of the abyss. Where are the goods in question?'

Since last she'd spoken, Lady Gillett appeared to have been shot and stuffed, but her eyes flickered to the right, and Noel squelched across the lawn and looked around the corner of the house. 'Bloody hell!' he said, involuntarily, and heard the front door shut sharply.

There were seven crates, each nailed shut, each stamped with 'US ARMY PROPERTY'. He lifted one, and found it extraordinarily heavy.

'Mar!' called Noel. When she didn't reply, he looked round the corner to see her reading the letter.

'It's from Mario,' she said, her voice airy with relief. 'He says he's sorry and he—'

'Sorry about what?'

'For leaving me in the lurch in Brighton. I tried to tell you, but you didn't want to listen. There were no trains and he got arrested and I had to find my own way back and . . .' She scanned the few remaining lines: ' "So, Toots, they've put me in the guardhouse till we leave the country, but the boys are dropping off a few gewgaws from the stores. Thanks a million for looking after Mrs O'Mahoney's Baby Boy. Your pal always, Mario xxxx." '

'So what have they left?' she asked, unwilling to muddy her shoes.

'Unlabelled crates – we won't know till we get them back. I'll have to fetch the wheelbarrow.'

It took forty minutes to transport all the boxes, Noel pushing, Vee steadying, and there was something about the task so reminiscent of their past adventures – the suppressed excitement, the makeshift, furtive speed of the transfer, the unsanctioned nature of the goods – that when Noel saw Lady Gillett peering down at the devastated lawn through an upstairs window, he hissed, 'Peelers!' and Vee jumped about a foot before feinting a smack at his head.

'Anyhow, she should be Digging for Victory on that lawn,' she said, censoriously, as Noel guided the final barrow-load between the gate-posts of Green Shutters and round towards the back garden.

'Or planting rice, given its current state,' he said, and she laughed. He went to fetch the toolbox and, nail by screeching nail, removed the first lid.

'Oh my Lord!' said Vee.

They ate frankfurter sandwiches for lunch, followed by cling-peaches and chopped pineapple, and then opened a can of peanut butter to see what all the fuss was about.

'It's the look of it,' said Vee, declining a taste. 'It reminds me of when we had a cat.'

They'd quickly run out of shelves in the larder and had transferred the bulk of the tins to the lumber room, stacking the Spam, chicken roll, ham-and-eggs, frankfurters and beef stew in a revolving bookcase and the canned fruit and vegetables in the stained-oak linen press. Unclassifiable items ('Cheese? In a *tin*?') were on the windowsill behind a drawn curtain.

Noel ate a second spoonful of peanut butter and washed it down with Florida orange juice. 'Why were you so worried about the letter?' he asked. 'What did you think it was?'

'Oh, I . . .' There was a pause, while she tried to think of a plausible answer.

'The rates,' she said.

'You paid them in December, and they always make you angry, not frightened.' He was looking straight across the table at her, gaze on the level, as tall as she was; grown up, nearly.

'I'm being blackmailed,' she said. 'I got a letter last week from someone who knew I wasn't really your aunt,

I don't know how they found out. I should have told you, it's your business as much as mine – it's just that you've been . . . a bit offish. But I should have told you.'

The room seemed to heave under Noel's feet, like the queasy shrug of an earthquake.

'So you met him,' he said.

'Who? The blackmailer? No, I was supposed to, but he never turned up – I thought the letter would be him, writing again.'

'It's my fault,' said Noel.

'What?'

'It's my fault.'

'How's it your fault?'

He looked away, his features bunched with guilt. In the silence, Vee heard the soft squabble of chickens.

'Tell me,' she said.

He shook his head. 'You'll hate me.'

'I won't.'

'You'll *hate* me.'

'Listen,' she said, sharply. 'I doted on Donald so much I thought he was perfect, and then you came along and all I looked for were faults. Which is why I know there's no badness in you. Not a speck of it. There isn't anything I *could* hate. So tell me.'

And if she hadn't demanded that, if she hadn't made him tell her everything – every last scrap – then what would have happened, four weeks later, when Noel found that item in the *North London Press*, while searching for a suitable article to translate into Latin?

Vee had been making the bed in Miss Appleby's room when she'd looked up and seen him in the doorway, a statue with a newspaper in its marble grip. She'd sat him down on the bed and he'd pointed mutely at the item, a six-line report on a body discovered after a rocket strike, confirmed by a police investigation to be a deserter from the Royal Navy, a Lieutenant Simeon Foster, aged thirty-four, who had absconded while owing 'considerable sums' in gambling debts, and who'd been on the run and living illegally in a ruined building. God forgive her, after the first shock she'd felt a rush of relief as strong as a downed brandy.

Noel had said nothing, and after a moment she'd sat down beside him, and had rested her hand on the back of his head, and they'd stayed like that, not speaking, while a band of pale sunlight had edged slowly down the chest of drawers and across the faded rug, illuminating the stain that a previous lodger called Mr Lomax had insisted wasn't anything to do with him, despite the fact that it exactly matched his hair-dye. And then Noel had stood, rather stiffly, and said that he needed to clean out the chickens, and Vee had said, 'Do you want me to keep that for you?' and he'd nodded and handed her the newspaper. She'd folded it carefully and put it in a shoebox at the bottom of her wardrobe.

And it was then that she'd wondered what would have happened if he'd kept his secret – whether it would have been the start of a slow retreat, with Noel finding less and less to say to her until one day she discovered that everything in his life was a closed door, with her knocking from the other side, a cup of tea in one hand and a clean shirt over her arm – and she went into Mr Reddish's room, which had a window that looked on to the back garden, and she stood and watched as Noel swept out the summerhouse with careful efficiency.

SPRING

1945

It was early May, but so warm that Vee had wedged the back door open, and as she'd done so, a swallow had hurtled in, twisting along the scullery passage before doubling back towards the garden, passing her face so closely that she'd felt the rush of air across her cheek. Her shriek had served instead of a dinner-gong.

'Is that a decoration on the pie?' asked Dr Parry-Jones.

'It's a V,' said Noel, cutting a slice straight through it. 'It was a hasty late addition, after I heard about the German capitulation on the three o'clock news. It should have been "VE", really, of course, but I ran out of pastry scraps.'

'So it's official? The war's over? But there's been nothing from Mr Churchill.'

'Perhaps he's still writing his speech,' said Mr Reddish.

'He must have known the end was coming,' said Vee. 'What's he been doing? Reading a book?' Both Noel and Gerry laughed, but it was true. The last few weeks had been like a bath being drained: almost imperceptible change giving way to a faint stirring, and then suddenly it was all gurgling down the plughole, the Russians pouring into Berlin, Hitler dead at last. What on earth were they waiting for? A bell?

'Well, I'm going down to Trafalgar Square, anyway,'

said Miss Appleby. 'I'll probably be very late, Mrs Overs, but I'll tiptoe in. The end of the war only comes once in a lifetime, doesn't it?'

'Twice,' said Dr Parry-Jones and Mr Reddish simultaneously.

'Oh, yes, I forgot about that one,' said Miss Appleby. Embarrassed, she started to twist her engagement ring and then seemed to remember that it wasn't there any more.

'On the final day of the Great War, I was working in the cashier's office in Aldershot,' said Mr Reddish. 'There was a private sweeping the yard outside. When eleven o'clock struck, he swung the broom round his head in a great circle and let it go, as if it were a hammer, and it went straight through the window of the officers' mess. I have never forgotten it. Today was less memorable. I started a new double-entry book.' He left a brooding pause.

'That's why I'm going into town,' said Miss Appleby. 'If *I'm* ever asked what I was doing on the last day of the war, I don't want to have to say I was typing a memorandum about balsa-wood shortages.'

'Pursuing one's work is nothing to be ashamed of,' said Dr Parry-Jones. 'Noel, for instance, in future years can look back with pride on the fact that today he received ninety-nine per cent in an essay on the oxidation of salts.'

'Why didn't he get a hundred per cent?' demanded Vee. From the corner of her eye she caught Gerry looking amused – *I enjoy it when you unsheathe your sword on Noel's behalf*, as he put it – and she turned away to stop herself smiling.

'Perfection is not within human reach,' said the doctor.

'It may be approached, but not achieved. Somewhat like Zeno's arrow.'

Mr Reddish raised his head like a hound scenting entrails. '"I *shot* an arrow in the air – it fell to earth I know not where. For, so swiftly it flew, the sight, could not follow it in its flight." Beloved, immortal Longfellow. I shall be giving my Hiawatha at a victory concert on Saturday at the Masons' Hall in Kentish Town, should anyone wish for a congenial evening of varied entertainment. The young lady who is organizing it told me that all tickets are in aid of the Hampstead Widows and Orphans Fund.'

Noel and Vee exchanged a brief and inadvertent glance.

'What did you do today, Mr Jepson?' asked Vee, recovering herself. 'Any news for us?'

She still couldn't bring herself to call him by his first name in front of others, though she supposed that at least half the house was aware that they went to the cinema together nearly every Saturday evening. Last week, while leaving the Regal arm in arm, having seen *Blithe Spirit*, they had bumped into Mrs Claxton from the Methodist knitting circle and Vee had felt instantly like the Whore of Babylon, but Mrs Claxton had been perfectly pleasant and had told Mr Jepson that she was a regular reader of the *North London Press* and that the Kwik Krosswords were currently much too difficult. 'I shall pass that on to the relevant department,' Gerry had said, and he probably *had*, since reliability was one of his qualities. He also listened when she spoke, remembered what she said last time, paid for the cinema tickets, and loaned her a clean handkerchief during the sad bits; there was not one single, solitary thing about the situation that Vee was used to. She sometimes felt like a Hottentot walking out with a missionary, except that Jepson was also surprisingly cheerful. When Madame Arcati in *Blithe Spirit* had begun one of her ringing, dramatic pronouncements, he'd whispered, 'Mr Reddish,' and she'd nearly dropped her ice-cream.

'It's been an interesting day,' Jepson was saying. 'I went to interview a soldier who'd been captured at Dunkirk, and who's only just arrived home. He was in a camp in Poland, and just at the point when liberation began to seem likely, all the prisoners were suddenly forced by the guards to evacuate the camp and head towards Germany – they had no warning at all, it was midwinter and some of the men didn't even have proper boots, only rough slippers.'

'Frostbite and worse,' said Dr Parry-Jones. 'There must have been deaths.'

'Yes. A great many. This young man was lucky, in a way. After weeks of the most awful conditions – they had to sleep outdoors, in the fields – he collapsed by the road and was found by someone decent and taken to a German hospital. He was eventually flown back a week ago.'

Lieutenant Emlyn Crowther had looked thin but not moribund, his deprivations more visible in his actions than his appearance – his rounding-up and consuming of every single biscuit crumb on the plate, his use of the coffee mug as a hand-warmer, his stillness, as of someone trying, desperately, to hoard every scrap of energy.

'Did he have a sweetheart waiting?' asked Miss Appleby.

'A wife,' said Jepson. 'A nice woman. She was a full-time warden until last month.'

'No children?'

'No. I think they'd only just married when he went away.' Jepson had stayed with the couple for over an hour, and what had struck him most was how careful, how *polite*, they were with each other – there'd been none of the verbal shorthand of the long relationship, no comfortable slide into mutual memory. It was as if they were on adjacent ships in a convoy, conversing in semaphore.

'Did your letters to each other get through?' Jepson had asked, and had seen the quick glance between them.

'Yes, right up until Christmas,' said Winnie Crowther.

'The trouble is that there's nothing to say about life in camp,' said her husband. 'The monotony is terrible. I was bored rigid for four and a half years while Winnie never stopped working and putting herself in danger. And now that she *has* stopped, I worry that she's probably terribly bored herself.'

'*No*,' she'd said indignantly. 'Of course I'm not.' She'd taken her husband's hand and squeezed the fingers, and her expression had been briefly identical to his – a troubled awareness, perhaps, that the road ahead wasn't the straight track of the fictional reunion, but something branching and unmarked.

Jepson had left shortly afterwards, noticing, on his way out, a small pile of library books on the table – *Modern Interior Decoration, Gardening Today, Home Carpenter.*

'Making plans?' he'd asked, and for the first time, Crowther had almost smiled.

'My wife brought those back for me this morning as a surprise,' he said. 'Which was very kind of her, and very understandable, given that I wrote about little else for four years, but do you know what?' He turned to his wife. 'I've had it up to here with the whole subject, Winnie. I never again want to read about the difference between a shade and a tint. I have no further interest in gazebos or lamp-shades. If we ever get a garden, I'll insist that we also buy goats.'

'Goats?' she'd repeated, sounding amazed. And as the astonishment in her voice had given way to a breathy noise that was very nearly a laugh, it seemed to Jepson that something hopeful had just happened – the flags dispensed with, the ships within hailing distance now. Though he had always been sentimental, had always hoped for happy endings, and not only his own.

'And what did you do today, Noel?' he asked. 'Apart from making this pie, which is very good, I must say.'

'Thank you. I finished reading *The Road to Wigan Pier* and then I went to the library. Oh, and I also saw a female cuckoo in the clump of elders opposite the fishmonger's.'

'"In *May* she sings all *day*,"' said Mr Reddish.

'Yes, except it's the males who give the eponymous call. The females make more of a throaty, chuckling sound. And I researched dessert recipes for tomorrow.'

'A victory sponge?'

'I'm actually thinking of attempting an adapted version of a croquembouche, if we have enough eggs.'

He chose to omit the most memorable moment of the day, which had been the arrival of a letter from Genevieve Lumb, signed with a firmly inscribed kiss and containing the information that she would be spending the whole of the summer – *the whole of the summer!* – with her grandparents, next door. She was also writing a play about Boadicea and Suetonius and needed his help with the Latin. The writing paper had smelled faintly of coal-tar soap and he had held it under his nose for several minutes.

Collecting the eggs the next day – and there were plenty – Noel couldn't quite work out why he felt that something was missing from the morning. A fine rain had wet the grass, but the clouds were lifting and the BBC forecaster had stated with certainty that it would clear in London later, to allow 'a day of sunny celebration'. Churchill (if he'd managed to finish his speech) would address the nation on the wireless mid-morning, and no doubt the King and Queen would appear on the balcony at Buckingham Palace, graciously accepting credit for the victory, but in the meantime it seemed a day like any other, the lodgers at work, Vee hurtling through the housework. Perhaps that's what was odd: a blackcap was singing in the plum tree, and there were no drums, no bells, no fireworks or sirens. War had slid quietly into peace, whereas he'd always somehow assumed that the transition would be vast and seismic, loudspeaker-vans roaring triumph, ululation in the streets.

'Noel!'

He turned to see Vee at the back door, accompanied by a man who was carrying a briefcase and wearing a buttoned mackintosh and a bowler hat. He had exactly the sort of official appearance that would normally send her into a frenzy of nerves, so the fact that she appeared not only calm, but smiling, could mean only one thing.

'This is Mr Barfield from the Ministry of Agriculture,' she said, when Noel approached. 'It's a poultry spot-visit. Here's your records.'

Noel took the yellow notebook that he kept in the kitchen dresser and shook hands with Mr Barfield, who was looking rather disconcerted, obviously far more used to brittle panic at his unannounced arrivals, which were intended to flush out those who were keeping an illegally high number of chickens, or selling on the eggs without a licence, or breaking one of half a dozen other domestic poultry rules as outlined in the Ministry publication *Keeping Chickens, a Householder's Guide*, the contents of which Noel knew off by heart. 'Shall I show you the coop?' he asked, leading the way.

Vee stood by the back door, enjoying the spectacle of a civil servant having his ear bent, and then, after they'd disappeared from view, she filled a bucket from the coal-bunker, keeping one eye on the sky for later, since Gerry had offered to take both her and Noel to a party in the square outside his newspaper office, so she didn't notice the woman coming round the side-path.

'Mrs Overs? Sorry, I didn't mean to startle you.'

She was young, barely thirty, a redhead dressed in a smart blue poplin coat with matching hat, both of which smacked of foreign tailoring, though her accent was English enough.

'Can I help you?' asked Vee, and then, with rising hope, 'Have you come about the card in the newsagent's? There's a very nice room at the front with a view of the lane. Half-board included. Good, plain cooking.'

'No, I haven't come about that.' She must have been five foot nine or more, but had none of the usual apologetic hunch of taller women, and she was good-looking in an unshowy way. No lipstick. She glanced quickly at the garden, and then up at the back of the house, her expression peculiar, guarded. 'Could I talk to you somewhere private?' she asked. 'Perhaps in the summerhouse.'

'It's full of chickens,' said Vee. 'How do you know there's a summerhouse?'

'Because I used to work here when I was a girl. I was Dr Simpkin's char.'

And as she spoke, as the implication of her words broke like a bottle over Vee's head, they both heard Noel's voice from the far end of the garden, the clearly enunciated phrase 'Prevention of Fowl Pox' floating towards them as if borne on a zephyr, and Vee said, 'Conservatory!' and found herself scurrying after the visitor up the scullery passage and through the hall and the drawing room towards the glassed-in lean-to at the back of the house.

It was not a room that Vee sat in very often; it was either, as Noel put it, Bergen or Caracas, depending on the season, and she hadn't noticed till now that the wet spring had sent a densely leafed creeper growing up and over the roof, so that the place had the dim, greenish tint of an undersea grotto.

Neither of them sat down.

'My name is Ida Pearse,' said the woman. She stood with her hands clasped in front of her, as if about to give a formal address.

'I know,' said Vee. 'I know who you are.'

'Did you meet Simeon Foster? Did he give you my name?'

'No, I didn't meet him. Only Noel met him. What do you want?'

'I don't want anything – or, at least, nothing specific.' She had one of those quiet voices that carried, the sort of voice possessed by people who are used to being listened to.

'So why are you here?' Vee's own voice was a defiant squeak, the sound of a surviving mouse who has just discovered that the household has bought a replacement cat. 'I thought you were abroad.'

'I was. I am. I came across with a hospital ship, repatriating serious burns cases, but I'm sailing back tonight. I'm here because I wanted to meet you.'

'*Me?* Not Noel?'

'I don't feel . . .' For the first time, the visitor sounded uncertain. 'I don't feel I have any right to meet Noel.'

'No,' agreed Vee, a little thrown by this unexpected concession. In the momentary silence, they looked at each other, Vee searching the other woman's features for a trace of Noel and seeing it only in the steady self-possession of her gaze.

'You've never come before,' she said.

'I haven't been to England for eleven years.' Ida was standing with her back to the garden, her view comprising the conservatory door, the study beyond it, the tall oak bookcase at the far end, its bottom shelf filled with a set of morocco-bound encyclopaedias; every inch and angle of the rooms were familiar; the only strangeness was

Margery Overs, whose existence she'd known of for less than two months.

'Thank you for your letter,' the reply from Pomeroy and Clarkson had read. 'Unfortunately, we cannot pass your enquiry on to Dr Simpkin, as our client is deceased. Since her death in 1939, her ward has been under the guardianship of Mrs Margery Overs, a widowed cousin of Dr Simpkin.'

She hadn't wanted to write to Dr Simpkin directly; their last encounter had been brusque. Ida, having removed Noel from a children's home, had simply deposited him at Green Shutters, trusting that he would be looked after, and then she had walked away. She had left the house, the city, the country, the whole chill, grey, narrow world she'd grown up in. She had slammed the doors behind her, one after another, and arrived in a place of blinding light and sea on every side, painted houses, bare rock, Africa on one horizon, Europe on another, and it had been easy to begin again, to become a person with a straightforward past and a shining future. And then Simeon had reappeared, and all those doors had burst open, and even when he'd re-embarked – owing money to half of Gibraltar – the draught had remained, whistling from the past, and she hadn't been able to get warm again.

She had written to the solicitor, Mr Pomeroy, hoping that he'd remember her and enquiring in very general terms about Dr Simpkin and the child, and had found that both Pomeroy and his client were dead, and then, just after that, she'd seen the item in the newspaper.

'I might never have come back,' she said, 'but my

aunt – I live with my aunt – has a subscription to a London paper. It arrives very late, of course, but last month I saw a report about a body found after a rocket blast, and—'

'Noel saw that too,' said Vee.

'—and I couldn't stop worrying about . . . about who was looking after the boy. About who was protecting him, now that Dr Simpkin's gone.'

'Bit late for that.'

'Yes. I know.'

'He's perfectly well looked after.'

'I'm sure he is.'

Vee folded her arms tightly, terribly afraid of this calm, poised young woman – she should have chased her away with a broom, not invited her in. In the strained silence, a bird began to sing on the conservatory roof, a parade of trills, and the visitor glanced towards it and said, 'Oh, a blackcap – I've not heard one of those in a long time,' and in that automatic curiosity, in that quick, pleased statement, devoid of boastfulness, Vee saw Noel again.

'Go on, then,' she said, her voice flat. 'What do you want to know?'

Ida's expression softened. The phrase 'a widowed cousin of Dr Simpkin' had conjured up for her someone bosomy, genteel and slow-moving, not this sharp-elbowed gatekeeper from the same world as herself, but beyond that there was something oddly familiar about the woman, something which meant that despite the frosted gaze and terse replies, she felt no deep fears about how Margery Overs might be treating her son.

'Could you . . . could you tell me something about him?' she asked.

'What do you mean? What sort of thing?'

'How is his health? Does he still limp?'

'Only when he's tired.' Vee hesitated, not wanting to make Noel sound like Tiny Tim. 'He's never ill,' she added. 'He's as tall as me and eats three times as much as I do.' And now he sounded like Charles Atlas.

'Is he still at school?'

'No, but he has tutors. He's clever. They say he's going to sail through his matriculation. The lady doctor who teaches him science said that he ought to study medicine, but the last I heard, he wanted to be an architectural historian, whatever that is . . .' Vee could hear herself, clattering away unstoppably, like Mrs Arthur at the knitting circle, going on about her son's accountancy exams, but it seemed as if, once started, she couldn't stop boasting about this paragon that she'd raised, not that she'd ever have said any of this in front of him. '. . . And his Latin tutor says he's a born linguist. *And* he can cook.'

'He can cook?'

'One of the lodgers calls him the Esc— the Escoff— what's the word? A French chef who's very famous.'

'Escoffier,' said Ida, pulling the name out of her past.

'He's making a big pile of eclairs today. For the victory celebrations. And he's always quoting things, poems and Latin, and so on.'

'Dr Simpkin did the same.'

'And he reads all the time. Lives in the library.' There was a pause. 'Anything else?' she enquired, lifting her chin pugnaciously, and Ida all at once knew exactly who this woman reminded her of: her own aunt – a scrappy fighter, fierce, protective and scorchingly proud of her charge.

'No,' she said. 'Except – what's he like?'

The question disconcerted Vee. You could never compare Noel to anything; it was like comparing a banana to a plate of chops.

'He's like . . . he's like himself,' she said, and as she spoke, she heard his voice calling 'Mar?' from somewhere in the house.

Ida looked startled.

'It was his choice to call me that, it wasn't my idea,' said Vee. 'Hang on,' she added, 'I'll put him off.'

She was only out of the room for half a minute, just enough time for Ida to take a couple of steadying breaths; it had taken her three days to summon up the courage to visit the house. She had called on her family but had stayed in the nurses' hostel at St Thomas's, where she'd trained, and both of these circumstances had made her feel junior, shrunken. And London – London itself had been a terrible shock: nothing she'd read or heard about had truly prepared her for its battered, scabbed reality, every view scarred, every street knocked around, the population so used to the destruction that they scarcely noticed it any more, walking straight past, as if ignoring a drunk in a doorway.

'I've told him it's someone from the Methodist knitting circle,' said Vee, reappearing. 'He's going to start on his baking, so I can let you out through the front door.'

'All right,' said Ida. There was a pause. 'I was fifteen,' she said.

'I had a son at seventeen,' said Vee. 'An accident, like yours.'

'What did you do?'

'I brought him up.'

Ida dropped her gaze. The bird was singing on the roof again, like someone whistling in a waiting room. 'I'll go,' she said.

Vee followed her towards the front door, Ida halting involuntarily beside the small framed photograph on one of the drawing-room bookshelves; Noel, the same age as when she'd last seen him, sitting on a bench with Dr Simpkin. It was like a ruled line across her past; she'd had a life before those two, and a life after, and the second was infinitely better.

'Is your boat today?' asked Vee.

'Yes. Ten o'clock this evening.'

'And when do you come back for good?'

Ida shook her head before she spoke. 'I won't. Gibraltar's my home now. I have a little house there with my aunt.' She thought of the balcony, draped in sunlight, the slice of sea that swayed between the houses opposite, the great rock, like a whale breaching above the rooftops.

'You've no family in London?'

'Yes, I have family but . . . they think I've got above myself.' Two days ago, she had visited her parents' flat and had spent all afternoon sitting in the kitchen, her siblings bobbing in and out, two brothers that she'd never met before, her mother visibly older but still pretty, still dispensing affection for only as long as it pleased her, still poised to deride anything she viewed as pretension: advice gained from a book, for instance, or a word she hadn't heard before, or an interest or an ambition that reached beyond her own experience. Ida had been told about bombs and babies and fiancées and celebrations, but no one had asked her any questions, so that anything she'd said about her own life had had to be pushed into the conversation, and had sounded like boasting. By the end of the visit, she'd hated the shrill brightness in her own voice, so different to the way that she usually sounded.

She pulled her eyes from the photograph, and saw behind it the spines of a row of labelled box-files: NOEL, GEOGRAPHY. NOEL, CLASSICS. NOEL, HISTORY. NOEL, RECIPES. NOEL, CHEMISTRY. NOEL, POLISH.

'Thank you,' she said, impulsively. 'Thank you for being a mother to him.'

She held out her hand, and after a surprised second, Vee shook it, and then Ida continued briskly into the hall, and opened the front door with the double tug that it had always needed.

'Wait,' said Vee, but the word stuck in her throat so that Ida couldn't hear it.

'*Wait*,' she said again, just before the door closed. 'Wait there a moment.' There was a pain in Vee's chest, as if she'd been cracked in half, but she turned and walked down the passage towards the kitchen. Noel was weighing ingredients, and he stood and listened to her with a spoon drooping in his hand, a trickle of sugar falling unnoticed on to the table.

'Here?'

'Yes.'

'She's *here*?' His eyes were huge. He made an abrupt movement as if to head to the door, and then swayed back.

'What does she want?'

'Nothing – no, it's not like that, not money or anything. She came to check if I was looking after you properly. To see if I passed muster.'

He looked at the spoon, as if he'd never seen one before. 'Did you?' he asked.

'Cheek. Anyway, it's you she really wants to see.' She jerked her head in the direction of the front hall. 'Go on.'

He dropped the spoon and walked off in a single movement. Slowly, keeping an ear out for voices, Vee dusted the sugar off the table and into a bowl. He was back before she'd finished sweeping the floor.

'We're going for a walk,' he said.

'All right.'

'She's only here until tonight.'

'I know.'

He turned to go and then swung round again, took a step towards her and landed a clumsy kiss next to her ear. 'See you later, Mar,' he said.

Mild anarchy was in the air, the Heath full of aimless, grinning people. Someone had launched a makeshift raft on the mixed bathing pond, and a man with a clarinet was sitting on it cross-legged, playing 'Begin the Beguine', while another man played bongos on the bank. Two nurses were paddling in the shallows and a Dalmatian with a Union Jack tucked into its collar was running in wild circles.

They walked slowly, taking no particular route, talking in spurts, subjects approached randomly, dabbed at, pushed aside, like someone searching through an overstuffed drawer for a lost item.

'Did you see dolphins on the crossing?'

'I didn't, but I saw flying fish, though they don't really fly.'

'No, it's a misnomer, but I suppose "gliding fish" doesn't have the same alliterative ring. Why are you smiling?'

'Because you sound like Dr Simpkin.'

Two Spitfires and a Wellington crossed above them, keeping pace with each other, leaving the sky looking as if it had been scored with a fork.

'What was he like when you first met him?' asked Noel.

'Charming. He made me laugh on an awful day. And he was still charming in Gibraltar. Was he kind to you?'

Noel thought about the answer for a second or two. 'He made me want to see him again.'

'Yes.'

'Do you think he was a bad person?'

'I think . . .' Ida slowed. 'I think he was someone who expected life to be easy, and had no resources when it turned out to be hard. It's as my aunt says: you can't eat charm.'

'And do you think I look like him at all?'

She'd been waiting for the chance to study him properly, rather than snatching sideways glances; he was still an inch or so shorter than her, but with the gangling promise of greater height, and he had her own father's ears and colouring, and her mother's straight nose, and eyes like Dr Simpkin – though that clearly wasn't genetically possible – and he looked likeable and interesting and at this moment rather hopeful.

'A little, yes,' she said. 'And you have the same build – you're definitely going to be tall.'

'And you?' he asked, pleased by this. 'Do I look like you?' He'd been relieved to see that her appearance was less like a drooping pre-Raphaelite and more like an auburn Jeanne d'Arc.

'You have my hands,' said Ida. 'I noticed straight away.'

He looked at his right hand and then held it up, palm towards her, and she fitted her left against it. 'See?' she said. 'Broad palms. Long fingers. Do you play the piano?'

'Not very well. I'm exceptionally fast at peeling carrots, however. What shall I call you? I don't think I could ever . . .'

'No,' she said. 'Don't. Just call me Ida. Miss Ida Pearse, 42 Lynch Lane, Gibraltar, just in case you ever felt like writing.'

'*Pretty lady!*' They turned to see two American sailors approaching along a brambled path. 'We're lost, pretty lady, can you help us?'

'Where do you want to get to?' asked Ida, with the composure of someone who spent most of her professional life sticking needles into servicemen.

'Have you heard of Parliament Hill?'

'I have. Carry on along this path, turn right through the patch of woodland and then bear left up the hill.'

'See, we only know port and starboard. Can you escort us there? Kid, can we escort your sister?'

Noel opened his mouth and then closed it again. 'Sure thing,' he said.

They could hear the noise before they saw its source: a chaotic murmur, cut through with odd whoops, a harmonica razzing above it, a doodling version of 'The Marseillaise' played on a trumpet. The crowd had extended along the whole, broad brow of the hill. Some people were sitting on the grass, some looking at the view, some flirting, some kissing, some dandling babies. Nothing was actually happening; no one was waiting for anything; no one was issuing orders. The sailors spotted a friend and wandered off, and Noel and Ida stood side by side and looked out across the city, and Noel felt as if the laws of gravity had been loosened for the day, and that he might, at any minute, lift just above the grass and swoop like a swallow over London.

Acknowledgements

Two compelling non-fiction books written by air-raid wardens, and actually published during the war, inspired me to tell Winnie's story in *V for Victory*: *Raiders Overhead* by Barbara Nixon, and *Post D* by John Strachey. The *North London Press* – Jepson's paper – was a real weekly newspaper and I spent many hours in the British Library finding inspiration in its 1944 and 1945 editions. Finally, the wartime diaries of Gwladys Cox, a West Hampstead resident, immersed me in the frustrations and terrors of that last, seemingly endless year of conflict. Their volumes are kept at the Imperial War Museum.

ABOUT THE AUTHOR

LISSA EVANS has written several previous novels, including *Crooked Heart* and *Their Finest*, which were both long-listed for the Orange Prize for Fiction (now called the Women's Prize for Fiction), and *Old Baggage*. She lives in London with her family.